He Needed Killing Too

He Needed Killing Too

Book 2
in the
Needed Killing Series

Bill Fitts

He Needed Killing Too

This is a work of fiction. Shelbyville and the people (and pets) who populate it are either products of the author's imagination or used fictitiously. It would be idle to deny, however, that Shelbyville, along with its university, was inspired by my hometown, Tuscaloosa, Ala., and its environs.

ISBN 978-0-9883893-3-5

Cover design: www.EbookLaunch.com

Printed in the United States of America

www.billfittsauthor.com

*For Anne, without whom
this book never would have been written,
and for Janie,
who's probably wondering what took so long*

CONTENTS

All the way home from the Polo Grounds I'd forced myself to be a careful driver. It wasn't that I'd had enough to drink at the bar to impair my driving. It was the excitement running through my body. I was practically vibrating. I had done it. I had figured out that Dr. Sean Thomas had been killed, how he'd been killed, and who had done it, and along the way I'd figured out who killed Albert Worthy. And then I'd handed the double murderer over to the police in front of witnesses.

It was exhilarating—to a degree that I'd never felt before. It was more than satisfying, more than the feeling of a job well done, more than winning a game or . . .

I wondered if this was how people got addicted to danger— climbing mountains, racing cars, extreme sports. Not that I had been in any real danger, I reminded myself. As long as I was considered too stupid to be a threat. That would have been dangerous. I comforted myself with the fact I didn't have a terminal degree as it might have proved to be terminal.

The only blemish to the day was Captain Ward telling Bobby she was a suspect in another murder. At least the police knew this one was a murder straight from the start. Somebody from the university? Odd to think that there was another death so soon after the others.

With a start I realized that I was sitting in my car, in my driveway, in my carport, at my house, with my dog behind the fence barking at me. Tan must be wondering what I was doing sitting here instead of getting out and fixing her supper. As it's her only meal of the day, I could understand her concern.

I came into the kitchen from the carport and came face to face with The Black, tail lashing back and forth. "I'm not that late," I protested and opened the door to the backyard. Tan bounced into the room, tail all a-wag, hoping it was suppertime. Dogs have no sense of time. "It's really not that late." I picked up her food bowl and noticed that the water bowl was almost empty so I picked that up too. "Come on, Tan. Let's see what's for supper." The cat was already in the kitchen.

"Aren't you going to ask how it went?" I walked over and set the water bowl in the sink and the food bowl on the counter. Tan sat in the middle of the kitchen, tongue hanging from her mouth as she panted and waited. The feeding process had started. As long as I didn't get distracted she was ready to wait.

"Just like I planned it! I told you she was a degree snob." I glanced over at the phone and saw the blinking light that meant I had a message. Who would have called the home phone and not tried my cell phone? Telemarketer, I decided. The do-not-call list had, for the most part, worked just as it was supposed to, but some calls still got through.

I felt the cat brush up against my leg. "Right, TB. You're the important one. You'll get your treat."

I got the open can of cat food out of the fridge and bent down to get The Black's treat dish. He only gets a teaspoon or so since I leave his dry food out but he voiced his appreciation as I set it down. If I didn't feed him first, he'd try to eat the dog's food, and while Tan wouldn't like that she'd probably let The Black try. It was just easier to feed the cat a treat.

I added some water to the dog's dry food, stirred it, and then, because we were celebrating, added a couple of tablespoons of canned food on top. Once the food was ready I filled up the water bowl and took them back into the laundry room and set them down. Tan walked up, quickly ate the canned food off the top and then slowly began to work on the dry. I'd learned not to try and hide the canned food in the dry. If Tan could smell the treats but not see them, she would carefully nose the dry food out of her bowl all over the floor to find the treats. In Tan's opinion, treats were to be eaten first. I only did it a couple of times. I'm a quick learner.

With the dog and cat settled I poured myself a drink. The blinking light was beginning to annoy me so I checked to see what kind of message the automated calling machine had left on my automated answering machine.

"Mr. Crawford," the woman's voice was familiar. "This is Victoria Moore calling from the provost's office. Provost George would like for you to call him when you get in. He'll be in his office until about six. If you don't get in until later than that, please call him at home." She gave me both numbers although she knew I'd had them a week ago. Victoria was not one to leave things to chance.

I looked at the phone in my hand. That answered the question as to who had called and why they hadn't called my cell. Rufus didn't like to use them for serious phone calls. But answer one question and create two more. What was so serious and why talk to me about it? I took a sip of scotch and then put the glass down. If the provost thought it was serious, then I'd better think so too. I went downstairs to my office where I'd saved the provost's office and home numbers.

. . .

"James, thank you for calling." His voice held the courtly manners of a true southern gentleman.

"Victoria said to call you at home, sir."

"As I asked her to. I believe Captain Ward of the Shelbyville police mentioned to you that there had been a murder? At the University Press?"

I nodded my head and then caught myself. When vid-phones become ubiquitous, we can take up nodding during phone conversations. I wondered how Rufus would take to face-to-face phone calls. "Well, we were together when he told Ms. Slater that she couldn't go back to work and that she might be a suspect. I deduced that a murder had occurred and the victim was someone at the Press." Talking to Rufus always made me careful to make sure what I said was just the facts—no speculation.

"Philip Douglas, director of the Press, was shot and killed in his office this afternoon. I believe that Captain Ward has been able to dismiss Ms. Slater as a suspect since she has a pretty solid alibi. She was with you and the Captain when Dr. Douglas was killed."

"I see." I said that, but I wasn't sure I did see.

"I knew that would relieve you as I believe that you and Ms. Slater have become close friends of late."

I wondered again how Rufus got his information. "No sparrow shall fall . . ." or some such. If it fell on the university campus, Rufus knew about it. Probably before the sparrow did. "That's true," I agreed. I thought to add, "But I doubt that's why you called" but didn't.

"The police, both university and city, have been in the Press building. Once it was clear that a homicide had occurred Superintendent Forte wisely handed the case over to the city's homicide department. But I can tell you that Dr. Douglas was in his office at the Press when he was shot in the back of the head.

"Melissa," Rufus paused. "Haggle is her last name I believe—yes that's right—was responsible for cleaning the Press building and she discovered the body. As you would expect, if you knew her, she kept her wits and called the University Police immediately. Evidently she even took some pictures of the scene with her phone."

I wasn't familiar with Ms. Haggle, but I wasn't surprised that Rufus was. I do know John Forte, and I'll bet he was thrilled to hand over responsibility to Shelbyville's finest as soon as he could. You didn't get a lot of experience with murders as head of a university police department. Dealing with overprotective parents, petty theft, illegal parking, and drunken students, yes. Murders, not so much. "And the murder took place this afternoon?"

"Exactly so," replied Rufus. "Philip had his hair cut and then returned to the Press sometime after 4:00 p.m."

"And it's safe to assume that if there was a bullet wound at the back of his head, the barber would have noticed it."

Rufus paused for a moment and then gave a small chuckle. "Your detective skills are developing quite nicely. I believe remarks like that are the sign of a true detective, at least in literature. That sounds like something Archie Goodwin might have said."

"Or Spenser," I was trying to get compared to someone who was more current than Rex Stout's detective.

"Hmmm, perhaps."

I decided that Rufus wasn't familiar with Robert B. Parker's novels.

"But that sounded more like Hawk to me than Spenser."

Once again I reminded myself never to underestimate Provost Rufus George. You'd think I'd learn.

"Speaking of detecting skills, we come now to the point of this call. While I understand Chief Forte's decision to remove his department from the investigation, I think the university still needs to have some kind of presence in it. Having murders on campus is not the kind of publicity the trustees look favorably on."

"I understand. Academic awards, research grants, graduation rates, and the occasional national championship are more along the lines of what the trustees want to hear about. And the occasional multimillion-dollar endowment."

"James, as you know, I was impressed that you were able to discover that Albert Worthy was murdered—and Dr. Thomas also—in addition to getting the murderer to make a public confession while the police were present. I was impressed, but I wasn't surprised. Now, could I prevail on you to protect your alma mater's reputation again while assisting the police in bringing a criminal to justice?"

I opened my mouth to speak and suddenly found that I didn't know what to say. At a loss for words, I admitted it. "I don't know what to say."

"Well," Rufus paused again. "I'd like for you to say 'yes' so what can I do to persuade you? I assure you that I'm not asking for anything more than a little sensitivity to the university's reputation. It would be a good deed on your part."

For a moment I regretted leaving the scotch upstairs. I'd have loved a sip right then. "Right. Good deeds done with the best of intentions."

"I believe so."

"Well, that's just it, Rufus. Because for me, doing things with the best of intentions has generally turned around and bitten me in the ass, if you'll pardon the expression. I know your life has been different, Rufus. Just give me a little time to think. I've got some questions to ask myself."

"Of course, James, I don't want you to feel pushed into doing this." Rufus hesitated. "But let me tell you that I believe that this would be good for you and good for the university. Why don't we just leave it that you'll get back to me with your answer in a day or so?"

. . .

I found myself in the kitchen facing Tan and The Black. Tan was wagging her tail with the doglike assurance that whatever I decided would be the right thing to do. TB was looking a little more skeptical. OK, he's a cat, lots more skeptical.

"Look, guys."

I guess not everybody talks to their pets in as much detail as I do judging from the looks I get when I mention that I'd been talking to the dog or the cat when I came up with the idea. Anyway, I always have.

"The fact is that I did a really good job and I like doing really good jobs. There may be some danger. I don't know. You can't really try to find a killer without incurring a little risk. Maybe that's what makes it exciting. Makes me feel alive. Hell," I shrugged at how ludicrous it sounded. "It made me feel younger, sharper, smarter. If that's what comes from investigating murders, I'm for it.

"So I'll sleep on it, but right now my decision is to take Rufus up on his offer. Not because of any good intentions but because I want to!"

Tan seemed fine with the decision and went off to sit on her bed. The Black looked a little quizzical. He cocked his head and looked at me.

"You're not supposed to be on the counter you know."

He looked at me, then at the telephone, and back to me.

"I'm not calling the provost until tomorrow. I told you that."

The cat seemed to shrug and then eased off the counter, onto the floor, and out of the kitchen. I watched him go and wondered what I was missing.

Right, there was somebody who might like to hear she wasn't a suspect. I reached for the phone.

I called the provost's office first thing the next day. Well, not exactly the first thing. I had taken the dog for a walk, showered, shaved, had a cup of coffee and an English muffin before calling. Spenser would have had a doughnut or two but I didn't have any in the house and wasn't going to go out to get some. Maybe I should get an office in a building near a doughnut store so I could pick them up on my way into work?

Victoria answered, said that the Provost had hoped I'd call, and put me on hold.

"James, there's something I want to say before you tell me your decision. At no time did I imagine that you would perform this important work on behalf of the university gratis and I'm afraid I didn't make that clear last night. Please forgive me. The work you did on Dr. Thomas's death was in the nature of 'pro bono' work, as I understand it. Is that not the case?"

For a man who spoke with the slow pace of the South, Rufus George was virtually impossible to interrupt. Maybe that was the trick. He was so polite that I couldn't bring myself to be rude enough to interrupt. I'd have to give that some thought.

"Rufus, that had nothing to do with my hesitation. What with my pension and the insurance proceeds from Eleanor's death, I've no need to dun the university."

"Nevertheless, should you decide to accept this engagement, you will need to come by my office and see Victoria. She has some paperwork for you to fill out."

"I'll be pleased to investigate Philip Douglas's murder for you Rufus but there's no reason to pay me for it. I'm not doing this out of good intentions. I'm doing it because I'll enjoy it. At least I enjoyed the first investigation."

"A man should enjoy his work, James, and I'm glad that your investigative skills give you pleasure, but the university will hire you."

"Rufus, please!"

"I believe that you will find that employment will make your actions more legitimate in many people's eyes."

I don't know how he continued to sound so gentlemanly and gracious while being so adamant. "You may be right. I'll make a point of dropping by to see Victoria. Meanwhile let's get started." I made a mental note to avoid the provost's office. Victoria would hound me unmercifully to fill in the paperwork. I didn't need to be working for the university to do this.

"Excellent! What can I do to help?"

"I'll get in touch with the police so that Captain Ward can fill me in on what they know." I was starting to make this up on the fly. I hadn't really given the next steps any thought.

"Good. I thought you'd like for me to introduce you to the people who work at the Press. I can explain that you're working for the university and ask them to provide you with every assistance."

"That should work." Clearly Rufus had given it some thought. He hadn't waited to see what my answer was going to be. I, on the other hand, had stopped thinking once I'd decided.

"I've asked Victoria to put together a package of information about the Press and the employees for you. My schedule is filled this morning so why don't you meet me at the University Club for lunch? I can bring what Victoria's prepared and we can go on to the Press afterward."

"That sounds like a plan." I was beginning to catch up with Rufus, albeit slowly.

"I'll see you there at noon." There was a slight pause and Rufus added, "Thank you for doing this, James."

"My pleasure," I replied and then hoped it was going to be.

. . .

I sat staring at the notes I'd made before calling Captain Jim Ward of the Homicide Squad. There were painfully few of them but I wasn't going to be as unprepared as I had been calling Rufus. I shook my head. I'd been calling him to say I'd do it and hadn't given any thought as to what the next steps would be. Oh, well, live and learn.

"Ward here."

I was a little surprised not to get his answering machine but I was prepared either way.

"Captain Ward, this is James Crawford and—"

"Of course it's you, Ford. Do you think the police department can't afford caller ID? Or am I supposed to think you got your cat to call me? What's up?"

Jim didn't employ the same phone technique that Rufus did.

"About that murder you mentioned last night, I—"

"The provost has already called the Chief and the Chief has called me. I was wondering when you would get around to calling.

"By the way, I phoned Ms. Slater to assure her that she wasn't a suspect and she said you'd told her that last night. You been seeing a lot of her lately?"

"Uh," was everybody going to be two steps ahead of me today?

"Do I need to get to know her better? Is Bobby a nickname or what?"

"It's short for Barbara. She told me she wasn't going to be a Barbie. I'm guessing she was something of a tomboy growing up." I grinned at the thought. "So she picked Bobby—started off spelling it with an *ie* but changed it to a *y* after Bobby Kennedy was killed."

"Sounds like I'll be getting to know her better. Look, I've got the file, such as it is, here on my desk. Why don't I come out to your place and I'll bring you up to speed on it."

I was trying to rally. "I figured you'd want me to come there. What's up?"

"Yeah, well, normally I would but the coffee machine is on the fritz and I'm suffering from caffeine withdrawal." Jim paused for a moment, "And your coffee is better than most."

I said, "I'll put a fresh pot on," and hung up.

. . .

We were sitting out on the screen porch. It was cool enough with the shade from the old trees and the ceiling fan slowly stirring the air. Fall hadn't reached this far south as yet. Oh the fall semester had started, we'd played a couple of football games, and the trees might be turning in New England, but the air conditioners were still running down here.

Jim reached out and picked up the insulated thermos and refilled his mug. I pushed the carton of half-and-half within his reach. The first cup of coffee had disappeared pretty quickly down his long throat, his Adam's apple bobbing with each swallow.

Over the second one Jim slowed down enough to tell me the timetable that the police had been able to work out.

Since the Press was housed in a university building, there was the omnipresent security system that limited access. Anyone could enter the Press via the main entrance between 8:00 and 4:45, normal working hours. If an employee wanted to use another door they had to swipe their ID card at a magnetic sensor that unlocked the door.

According to logs, Dr. Douglas had come back from getting his hair cut and entered the building via the entrance nearest his office at 4:27 and again at 5:07. Mrs. Haggle was the next person to enter. She came in via the main entrance at 5:30—the earliest access she could get via her ID. The Press director had insisted that cleaning take place after work hours and had, in this and in many other demands, been granted his wish.

I thought about some of my run-ins with campus security and decided that Douglas must have been something else. Security didn't give in to just anybody.

Mrs. Haggle had found the body and called the campus police at 5:32.

"So what's with the two entry times? 4:27 and 5:07?" Jim had paused and I felt compelled to ask something.

"All it means is that the deceased's ID card was used to enter at 4:27 and then 5:07. We don't know who was carrying it."

"And we don't know when the ID card left the building. This guy could have opened the door, remembered something and turned right around and left, right?" As a university employee, I had dealt with ID cards for years.

"Those doors are also fire doors," grumped Captain Ward, "so anybody can leave by them if they want. Can't trap people in a burning building."

"Makes sense," I said. "Wasn't there a night club that caught on fire and a bunch of people died because the fire exits were padlocked shut? They were trying to keep people from sneaking in."

"Yeah, it makes sense, but it doesn't do us any good."

Ward's caffeine level had gotten back to normal and his usual cynical disposition was returning. "But the multimillion-dollar door security system this fine university has installed to protect its staff, faculty, and students is little help in a homicide investigation. All the district attorney could convince a jury of is that person or persons unknown swiped the card at the door at 4:27 and at 5:07. We couldn't prove who did it or even if the unknown person or persons entered the building after unlocking the door."

"Did you find Dr. Douglas's ID? Maybe the killer took it with him."

"It was sitting on top of the deceased's desk, as if he had dropped it there after coming in the door." Ward raised his hand to forestall my question. "No fingerprints we could use."

"So what are you going to do?"

"Same as usual, go with what we can prove and see how that fits in with everything that might be a fact.

"We know the deceased was alive when he left the barber shop. The barber and his next client can testify to that." The policeman shrugged his shoulders and smiled ruefully. "And we know he was dead when Mrs. Haggle walked into his office at 5:32 or thereabouts.

"Judging by the amount of blood, he was killed in his office so we can forget elaborate scenarios that involve him being killed somewhere else. We can be pretty sure that poison wasn't involved—this time. In fact there's no question that he didn't die of "natural causes."'"

I smiled at Jim's reference to my first investigation. At first, we'd thought that Dr. Sean Thomas's death was caused by food poisoning and I thought that it was a pretty petty way for a man so hated to have died. It wasn't until the second death, Albert's suicide that wasn't, that I realized someone had taken the expression "he needed killing" and acted on it.

"No, this one's pretty clear, Ford. Person or persons unknown used a gun to blow off a chunk of the back of a man's head. We recovered the bullet—nothing unusual there—we'll have some ballistics work done once we find a murder weapon."

"One bullet and shot from behind?" For some reason that surprised me.

"Yep," nodded Jim Ward. "One was plenty. He was walking toward his desk when it hit him, knocked him down. Probably dead as he hit the floor."

I cocked my head. "Sounds like he knew his killer, doesn't it?"

"It might," answered Ward. "It might mean that the killer drew his gun after the deceased turned his back on him. I wouldn't have turned my back on a man with a gun."

"Wasn't this guy supposed to be a jerk?"

"Ford, it doesn't matter what kind of a human being he was. He's not supposed to get shot." Ward smiled a half-smile. "I understand that lots of people didn't much care for the man. Just like you and a bunch of other people didn't care for Dr. Thomas. You can check that with Ms. Slater. I've heard that she said and I quote, "He needs killing too."

"Yeah, Bobby's mentioned how much she liked the director to me before, so it's a good thing she was with us." I smiled at the memory. "But if he was that much of a jerk, yeah, I can see him turning his back on somebody holding a gun. Somebody he always treated with contempt? He could have been arrogant enough to do that."

"Well, if he was, the killer certainly showed him otherwise."

"Who do you like for it? The usual suspects?"

Jim Ward shook his head. "Ford, you continue to amaze me. I'd like for it to be straightforward, but this one doesn't feel like it.

"There aren't any obvious suspects. His wife died three years ago, otherwise she'd be suspect number one. No siblings or other relatives that we're aware of. So far it doesn't seem that he had any close friends. Sort of kept to himself after his wife died. Coworkers? If it had been a coworker gone off the tracks he'd have shot more than just the boss. That's usually how it goes, shooting up the workplace. I know," he threw up his hand to cut me off. "But your case was different. Those people were more than just coworkers.

"I hate to admit it and I'll deny it if you tell anybody I said it," Ward went on, "but I'm sort of glad the provost is calling you in on this case. It just isn't looking like the type of case our routine procedure is good at solving. Oh we might get lucky but I've got a bad feeling about it."

"Why do people murder?"

"Eh?" Jim Ward looked a little taken aback at my question. "Murder is personal or absolutely random—in my experience, anyway. The convenience store clerk shot down—a random killing. Husband shot by wife, personal."

"I just asked because my experience—prior to the last week—has been limited to crime shows on TV and murder mysteries."

Ward nodded. "And I've been dealing with them for years. When I said personal I meant the kind motivated by greed, jealousy, fear, or money."

"What about sex, drugs, and rock 'n' roll? Surely we can blame things on that too?"

Ward paused and smiled back. "Sex and drugs certainly are motives. I'm not so sure about rock 'n' roll. I go back and forth."

I changed topics again. My mind was really hopping around this morning. "It sounds like you've gathered a lot of information in a really short time."

Ward snorted. "I haven't found out any of this. I'm the captain of the homicide unit. We, everybody in the unit, take homicides seriously. I'm sitting here while Harry is interviewing the Press employees. We've got patrolmen checking to see if the victim's car is missing, house burgled, bank account empty, anything. The information is just starting to come in."

"The provost is going to take me out to the Press this afternoon—introduce me to the staff."

"Good luck with that. People who find that they are suspects only co-operate enough to implicate other people. They fall all over themselves doing that."

I grinned faintly, just a twitching of my lips, "I was planning on asking them who might have killed Philip Douglas and seeing if anybody includes themselves."

"Good luck with that." Ward stood up from the table. "I've had my caffeine fix. Thanks for the coffee. You'll let me know how your meeting with the Press employees goes? I'll be interested in hearing how it compares to what they told Harry."

I stood up and put out my hand. "It's a deal. Let's get together for lunch tomorrow and compare notes. By the way, who's Harry?"

"Harry Johns, have you met him? He'll be working with me on this case—as the junior member." Jim grinned and winked at me. "That means he gets to do all the stuff I don't want to do—the scut work."

After Jim left I sat and thought for a while about what he'd said and murder in general and I wondered what I was getting into. The Black came out on the porch and decided I should be petting him rather than sitting there doing nothing. After a while my leg fell asleep and I had to push him out of my lap. He walked off with an affronted look as I stamped my foot trying to get the circulation going. "Hey," I said to the retreating cat whose tail was straight up in the air in indignation. "I had to get up to change clothes anyway!"

I walked down the hall to the master bedroom. I had showered and shaved but faded blue jeans and an old T-shirt wouldn't cut it at the University Club. Not for dining with the provost, anyway. OK, I'd go with the classic southern frat boy look. Gray slacks, white button-down dress shirt, red tie, dark blue blazer, and burgundy loafers with tassels. Judging by the mirror, everything fit and the only thing the fashion police would cite me for was lack of originality. Satisfied, I made sure that Tan was outside and The Black wasn't.

. . .

The University Club was located in an antebellum mansion near campus. Members could dine there for lunch and supper, and there were rooms that could be used for various functions. It was off campus and had a liquor license and was not technically owned by the university. I'd never been interested in becoming a member until I met the provost here for lunch—was it only last Sunday? I guess it was.

I walked up the wide stone steps that led to the front doors. The steps were hollowed by the generations of shoes that had walked across them. Idly I wondered if they didn't present a safety threat to the older members who weren't as steady on their feet. If the university's lawyers had their way I was sure they'd have addressed that potential liability. Of course, I smiled to myself, it would be the older members who would complain about the steps being replaced. "Perfectly serviceable," I could hear them say. "Why replace them just because they're old?"

After pushing the massive door open I stepped into the mansion's entryway, the ceiling easily thirty feet over my head. A staircase wide enough for antebellum beauties in hoop skirts to easily pass by each other going up and down was on my right. To my left was the entrance to a sitting room where members could wait on their guests or vice versa. And in front of me the only reason the thought of joining had ever crossed my mind. She was as beautiful as I remembered. I mean hostesses were rarely unattractive but she was special.

"Why, Mr. Crawford, how nice to see you again."

"The pleasure is mine, Stephanie." I found myself almost bowing. I'm not sure if it was the antebellum setting or just appreciation of her beauty. Probably a combination of both. "I assume that our mutual friend the provost told you I'd be here. If I thought that you remembered me from my only other visit to the Club, I would become insufferably proud."

"Uncle Rufus," the smile on her lips matched the twinkle in her eyes, "did happen to mention you'd be joining him for lunch today. But I do try to remember all our guests. If you'll follow me?"

I figure she's been dealing with awestruck boys and men for most of her life. She handles it well. I followed with a smile on my face as I tried to decide if her hair was a very pale shade of red or blonde with red highlights. With a start, I realized that she wasn't leading me to the private room Rufus and I had dined in last time, but a large common room filled with tablecloth-covered tables for two, four, and six. Most of them were filled. I glanced around and noticed a few familiar faces, mostly people I knew of not those I really knew. A different level of professional staff and academe than I usually traveled in. In the middle of the room at a table for four sat Provost Rufus George reading from a file folder.

I decided that Rufus didn't think today's conversation would warrant a private room.

As we approached, Rufus glanced up, carefully closed the file, and stood. A smile stretched across his broad face and he hugged Stephanie as soon as she got in range. "James," he reached out to shake my hand. "Good to see you again, regardless of the circumstances. Thanks for coming."

I figured the smile was mostly for his goddaughter who, as is appropriate in the South, referred to him as "uncle," an honorary title that used to be more prevalent. I blame my generation for the demise of many of the social conventions that I now regret our losing.

"Good to see you too, Rufus."

"I hope you gentlemen have a pleasant lunch." Stephanie had a smile for both of us and if the smile I got was only that wide because I was dining with Rufus, I didn't care. "Thank you, Stephanie."

I pulled my chair out and we sat.

"I hope you don't mind us dining with the public, as it were." Rufus picked up his cloth napkin and unfolded it.

I followed suit noting that the napkin had been so heavily starched that I doubted it could absorb water. "No problem. I suspect you had your reasons."

"Yes. I did." Rufus looked over the room nodding at people all across the room as their eyes met.

It surprised me to see how often Rufus was nodding then I looked past him at the people who were seated behind him and saw the surreptitious glances that were being directed our way.

"The murder of Philip Douglas coming so quickly after the revelation that Dr. Thomas had been murdered has made senior staff and faculty concerned for their own safety. I thought it worthwhile to be seen dining with the man who uncovered Dr. Thomas's murder and the murderer." He smiled gently. "It will comfort some that I am seen taking steps instead of issuing statements."

I looked down at the table and saw that the menu of the day had been put at each place setting. "I'm a step?"

"Don't underestimate yourself, James. Modesty is a good trait, but, personally, I find false modesty annoying."

I lifted my eyes to meet his gray ones and wondered what he saw in my washed-out hazel ones.

"Might have been luck," I ventured.

We stared at each other.

"Indeed," responded Rufus. "I suggest we order. I have a meeting later this afternoon after I've introduced you to the Press."

. . .

I ordered the seafood gumbo, which came in a large bowl with a ball of white rice in the middle surrounded by a sea of shrimp, sausage, okra, fish, celery, onion, crayfish, and various other delectable and unidentifiable objects. It was a good thing that all I had to do was listen because my mouth was too busy enjoying the flavor sensations to do anything as mundane as speak. Rufus might have been just as excited by his roast beef, mashed potatoes and gravy, green beans, side salad, and spoonbread but he was able to talk between bites.

His food looked pretty good but I was hooked on the gumbo. In the back of my mind I was wondering how big a pot of gumbo you had to make to be able to fit all these goodies into it. This was definitely not a dish you made to serve one or two people—unless that was all they were going to eat for a week or two. Meanwhile the front of my mind was listening.

"Poor Douglas's wife died of cancer about three years ago. She'd been sick for one or two years before that."

Rufus paused to chew his food. I made a murmuring noise of sympathy around the gumbo.

"While the death of his wife did not seem to be a crushing blow to Douglas at the time . . ." He paused again.

So you didn't think his wife meant that much to him, huh? I made a mental note.

"In hindsight I can see that her death freed him to turn all of his attention to the Press."

Gumbo is surprisingly filling. I slowed down. The reason I had ordered just soup and a sandwich was because heavy lunches tend to make me sluggish an hour or so afterward—exactly the time I needed to be at my sharpest today.

"How much do you know about the Press?" asked Rufus.

"I know it publishes books, most of which are academic in nature." I shrugged my shoulders. "I've been to their annual tent sale where they try to get rid of books that aren't selling. Judging by some of the titles trees died unnecessarily."

"The purpose of a university press is not to entertain the masses. Their goal is to encourage scholarship, to publish books that need to be published, books that are seminal in their fields. They may not sell more than a few hundred copies, and those only to libraries."

I nodded, "I've heard Bobby—uh, Ms. Slater say something similar about books she's worked on at the Press."

"Indeed," Rufus wiped his lips with his napkin. "Philip's predecessor was the founding director of the Press. In fact, the building that houses the Press is named after him, M. W. Stefenson.

"M.W., as he was called, was a pioneer here at the university. He attracted promising writers and developed a stable of authors whose works were regularly published by the Press. In fact, he delighted in finding literary talent at other universities before their presses did. Authors can be very loyal to the Press that gives them their first start, as it were.

"Strong-willed, arrogant, demanding, a perfectionist, he was all that and a genius too. His skill at selecting writers and their works was astonishing. He acquired manuscripts, he edited, he designed, he marketed. He was what they call nowadays a Renaissance man. When he died it took a while before we realized how his greatness had stunted the development of the staff and the board of directors. He had hand-picked them all and with him gone, they had no idea how to function.

"And that's what Philip inherited when he accepted the position. To be fair, it is very difficult to follow a paragon and Philip had a hard time of it. Oh, he was able to recruit staff but in large part that was due to the reputation of the Press. And the authors Stefenson had recruited and developed were loyal to the Press, at least at first."

Rufus paused and I ventured a guess. "Then his wife died and he dedicated his life to the Press?"

He nodded. "To the detriment of the Press, unfortunately. He's alienated authors, editors, staff, printers, graphic designers, and a large part of the University support staff. The number of our faculty members who have elected to submit their manuscripts to other university presses has become a source of some concern on the part of the board of directors and university administration."

University administration? That would be you, I thought to myself. "And the board of directors? What were they doing while this was going on?"

"Remember," Rufus held up an admonishing forefinger, "that under M.W. the board didn't need to do anything except rubber-stamp what he'd decided. He didn't want a strong board and, as he selected the members, he didn't have one."

"And now?"

Rufus drummed his fingers on the table. "The fiscal realities of university presses have changed since M.W.'s time. Once, it was common for universities to subsidize their affiliated presses. That is no longer the case."

During my career at the university I had noticed that among many other things, the fiscal orientation had changed as well. Ernie Casey, my old boss, had blamed it on the proliferation of MBAs in the land of academe. I agreed. Trying to determine the "return on investment" of a degree in Latin was too difficult for me to even begin to calculate. But the difficulty hadn't scared others. "And then came the era of 'value added' and 'profit centers.' Like education was the same as investing in the stock market." I was surprised to hear how much contempt was in my voice. Judging from Rufus's expression, he was surprised too.

"Why is it that you aren't a trustee?" asked Rufus.

I wondered for a second if he was serious.

"Why Provost George! How nice to see you! Don't get up."

I looked up to see a slender, well-dressed man in his mid-forties, standing by our table. I stood up a nanosecond later than Rufus wondering as I got to my feet, how anybody that knew Rufus would think he wouldn't stand?

"Just a quick word with you, Provost. You really didn't have to stand. I just wanted you to know," he took Rufus's offered hand and shook it, "that if there's anything I can do to help out at the Press during this unfortunate period, I will be happy to oblige. If we need to extend my term on the board there's no problem. Why, if you need someone to serve as an interim director? Whatever, all you have to do is say the word."

While Rufus was trying to get a word in edgewise, I took the opportunity to judge a book by its cover, recognizing that I'd already been unimpressed by his telling Rufus not to stand. In a word from a different era this guy was a "dandy." From head to toe there wasn't a hair out of place. He was starched, creased, pressed, and color-coordinated.

"Thank you Steven," Rufus took advantage of the man stopping to catch his breath to respond. "It is nice to see you too.

"James," he turned his head to face me, "I'd like to introduce you to Steven Stefenson. Steven is on the board of the Press." He turned back to Steven. "Steven, this is James Crawford."

Interesting, I thought, Rufus introduced me to him. Rufus thinks I'm either more important or older than this guy—I went with older. I put my hand out, "Nice to meet you."

We shook and I realized that while his nails might be manicured his grip was anything but feeble.

"So nice to meet you, Dr.," his voice rose in a question, "Crawford."

"No," this guy was beginning to annoy me. "The first name is James."

"Oh." Steven turned back to Rufus. "Please remember my offer, Rufus."

"I will, Steven, and thank you for offering. It's still early to be making plans but I'll keep what you said in mind.

"Mister Crawford is the man who solved the mystery of Dr. Sean Thomas's untimely death and the suicide that wasn't a suicide. He's agreed to investigate Philip's death as well—at my urging."

"Indeed?" Steven turned back to face me. "Then I must give you my card in case I can be of any assistance to you as it appears the provost doesn't want my help." He pulled a long wallet out of the pocket inside his jacket and took out a stiff, cream-colored card and held it out to me.

I took the card from him and tucked it in my side pocket. I thought about emailing him my electronic business card but it didn't seem right. As far as I could tell he didn't even have a cell phone with him. Besides I hadn't yet created one for the detecting business. "I seem to have left mine at home."

Steven Stefenson nodded at both of us, "Gentlemen, I'll let you get back to your lunches. Good day."

Rufus sat, picked up his napkin, and put it back in his lap. I stood for a moment longer watching Stefenson as he left the room, then sat down, looked at Rufus, and raised an eyebrow (the left one if it matters).

"Dr. Stefenson is something of a degree snob."

"So I noticed," I replied.

"Really, James, it's one of his least offensive traits."

"And his last name, is that a coincidence?"

"That we were just talking about M.W.?" Rufus shook his head. "Steven is his nephew. M.W. put him on the board to give him something to do, I think. He's been on it ever since. In many ways he does know more about the Press than anyone else alive. He might be a good source of information for you if you can put up with him."

"Huh." I doubted it. The gumbo was now almost cool. It was probably for the best but I resented it anyway. Another reason to dislike Steven Stefenson.

"But that brings us back to what I was saying before he came up. The Press has to become self-sufficient. The university won't be able to subsidize it as it has in the past. The trustees have made that decision.

"The board needs to be more involved and hands-on than it has been so I'm forcing longtime members like Steven to resign so they can be replaced. It will mean the loss of institutional memory and I feel somewhat sorry about that. Still, maybe freeing themselves from how things have always been done will help to prepare for the future."

"You said this guy was M.W. Stefenson's nephew?"

"Yes, his mother was M.W.'s sister, Brinda Stefenson Sharpe. She was a local beauty, a Maid of Cotton finalist when she was young. Married an older man, a man of means who died a few years after Steven's birth. After his mother died Steven took the name Stefenson since M.W. was the last of that line. Of course, it was the end of the Sharpe line as well, but that is Steven for you."

Rufus looked thoughtful. "That was Brinda with an *i*. Unusual spelling. You normally hear it spelled with an *e*, Brenda."

As I couldn't hear the difference between Brinda and Brenda, I just nodded.

CHAPTER 4
THURSDAY AFTERNOON

I followed Rufus's car to the Press. He had another meeting he had to go to after introducing me to the staff of the Press hence the two cars. We passed the front of the building and I slowed down to take a look at it. The architecture was nothing remarkable by university standards. It was made of brick, there were four columns in front, two to each side of the entrance. A small sign proclaimed it to be the "M.W. Stefenson Building, deliveries in the rear." Since there was no parking in front of the building I thought the "delivery" part was redundant.

Still following Rufus, I turned into the driveway and circled around to the back where the parking lot was. Along the front row of parking places I could see a series of signs marking the different spots. Some of the signs held titles, Director, Senior Acquisitions Editor, Managing Editor, and a few others said Visitor. Rufus pulled into one of the visitor spots. I passed him and pulled into an unmarked place in the third row.

As I walked across the lot to where Rufus was standing, I could see that the building was composed of a center building with two wings attached. It looked to me like the center predated the wings. There were several picnic tables off to the right as well as an old loading dock. That must be the business side: deliveries, shipments, and the like. The landscaping on the left wing hinted at more refined pursuits. The director's office, I decided, must be on the left. The lack of air conditioning units in the windows argued that the building had been extensively remodeled. "Extensive" was the university's catchphrase for remodeling projects that included upgrading the HVAC systems.

"In all the years I worked for the university, I've never been here," I told Rufus as I walked up.

"Not surprising." He handed me a bulky campus mail envelope. "You were too high tech for the Press, or the Press too low tech for you."

I lifted the flap of the envelope, peered in, and looked back at Rufus.

"It's that packet of information I promised you." He pointed at the Press building. "Victoria put it together. I think it has staff names, positions, maybe a short biography, organizational chart, floor plans—that sort of thing."

"Ah," I tucked it under my arm. "Thank you and Victoria. I'm sure it will prove valuable."

We walked down the sidewalk and up the four steps it took to reach the doorway. I pushed the door open, held it for Rufus, took a deep breath, and followed Provost Rufus George into the Press building. Once inside I felt like we had entered a museum or exhibition hall. A short entryway with floor-to-ceiling displays on either side led into a central square. That square was surrounded by offices opening into it while there were archways leading to the left and right wings. The center was dotted with small displays, some enclosed in glass some open. There was always at least one book involved in what I could see but along with the books were busts, portraits, artifacts, maps, sculpture, and the like. Some of the displays had the look of trade show exhibits reused as interior decorations. At the back of the central area was a group of people. Since we'd come in the back, I guess they were around the front entrance.

We walked toward them and Rufus gestured at the displays, "They used to sell books here, in the old days. This used to be filled with books and bookcases—but that's not how university

presses work any more. Oh, they've got some stock on hand."
He gestured to the right. "Over there. But they're phasing that
out I understand. Computers and UPS have made local inventory
obsolete. Or so I'm told."

It all made modern-day sense. Minimize your onsite inventory, take advantage of companies that specialize in warehousing,
shipping, and handling. You see it everywhere. Nobody has anything in stock but they can always get it tomorrow or the next
day. Whenever the delivery service makes its normal run. It
made me sad. I liked to wander through old-fashioned hardware
stores and bookstores and actually touch the stock. It just wasn't
quite the same feel as doing an online search.

A heavyset woman dressed in a business-like blue suit separated from the group and walked straight toward Rufus with her
hand extended. "Provost George, Ms. Moore called and told me
that you were coming to see us and I took the liberty of assem-
bling the professional staff and the rest of the Press family."

It took me a second to remember that Victoria's last name
was Moore. I should have expected it, I thought to myself. Rufus
might leave it to chance but Victoria wouldn't.

"Thank you, Hazel." Rufus took her hand and shook it but
his gesture had the feel of a southern gentleman bowing over a
lady's hand. "You did exactly as you should. Thank you."

"Well, I am the senior acquisitions editor and the member of
the professional staff who has been here the longest and it
seemed . . ."

"Yes, I have often suspected that the university was in viola-
tion of the child labor laws during earlier administrations.
There's no other way people so young could have worked here
for so long."

I could see her struggle to resist Rufus's charm and then succumb to it.

"Now let me do what I came here to do." Rufus turned to face me. "Dr. Murphy, I'd like for you to meet James Crawford." She nodded her head at me in a slightly puzzled manner and I reached out to shake her hand trying to project confident competence. As if I knew what I was doing. If I'd had a real business card I'd have given her one. It might have helped me project confident competence or competent confidence— whatever. I'd have to think about it.

"James has agreed to help the university and the Press out during this difficult time."

Hazel Murphy looked somewhat uncertain of my ability to even tie my shoes. I was glad I had picked out loafers.

We reached the open area where the rest of the people had gathered. I'm sure it was the site of all the office parties. There was the office coffee machine and its attendant paraphernalia. People were standing in the doorways of some glass-fronted offices, sitting in chairs, in clusters and small groups all looking at us. Technically they were looking in our direction but I had the feeling that everybody was actually looking at me what with Hazel and the provost being known entities.

I stopped and let Rufus and Hazel take a few more steps. Hazel cleared her voice and began to speak when Rufus stopped her. "I believe I can take it from here. Thank you, Dr. Murphy." Rufus glanced around the room. "My name is Rufus George and I'm the provost of this university. That is," he smiled and corrected himself, "the university this organization is the press of."

I could feel the tension level in the room drop with that small joke. Well, to be honest Rufus himself was enough to make most people feel better, knowing he's in charge I mean. As he contin-

ued with his unprepared remarks I eyed the crowd. There had to
be between fifteen to twenty in the group with a broad span of
ages. Hazel appeared to be the oldest. The youngest, well he
looked the youngest, you never know with a baby face like that,
might have just finished college.

Bobby was clearly the most striking person there with her
curly, silver hair contrasting with her black outfit. I dismissed
the thought that I was biased. With one or two exceptions, Press
employees all seemed to dress better than would an equivalent
bunch of geeks, pardon me, information technologists.

Rufus was going on about how the campus police were co-
ordinating with the town police, something about increased security. I went back to people-watching—detecting, I corrected myself. So I counted how many people were here, seventeen as it
turned out. One man was leaning against the doorjamb of somebody's office. Every so often he would exhale through his mustache making the hairs puff out. The mustache and ponytail
marked him as the free spirit of the group—late forties at a
guess. He kept on leaning over to murmur to the man seated next
to him. The other man looked about the same age. He was bald,
wearing round gold-rimmed glasses, clean shaven. His eyesight
must be pretty poor; the glasses magnified his eyes, giving him
an owlish look.

On top of one of the taller bookcases sat a cat. Looked like a
Russian blue from where I stood. Beautiful cats, silver-blue fur
that looked like felt or velvet and vivid green eyes. I had never
lived with one but had admired them. The cat stood up and
stared straight at me. I nodded. He yawned then eased off the
bookcase, flowing down to the floor.

I'd been half-listening to Rufus so I heard him begin my in-
troduction.

"While we were able to avoid undue publicity, I'm sure you are all aware of the recent unpleasantness that resulted in the death of two members of our academic community at the hand of a third. The man who single-handedly solved the murder, James Crawford, has agreed to help us resolve this unfortunate occurrence."

I stepped forward and as I did you could hear someone say in a stage whisper. "Isn't that Bobby Slater's new main squeeze? Guess she timed that right." It was the man with the mustache.

"What was that you said, Mr. Manning?"

If you had asked me to guess if the provost would know any names of Press employees much less what they looked like, I'd have figured two or three. Ones that had been at the university for years like Hazel. I'm sure Mr. Manning had no idea Rufus could call him by name.

Rufus's eyes were fixed on the man. "I didn't quite hear you. It is Manning, isn't it? Frank Manning?"

Mr. Manning's face by that time had turned beet red. The class clown hadn't expected the substitute teacher to slap him down. I had forgotten that Rufus had taught before moving into administration. Still did teach an undergraduate seminar now that I thought about it.

"Just a comment about how Ms. Slater had already met Mr. Crawford, sir. Or so I had heard." He blew a little air through his mustache and swallowed.

"Indeed." The ice in Rufus's voice dropped the temperature in the room by a good five degrees, maybe ten. "And I have been assured by the Shelbyville police that she has an ironclad alibi for the time Dr. Douglas was murdered.

"Was your comment meant to suggest that I would have put Mr. Crawford into a situation where his impartiality was in question? And that he would have accepted?"

Yep, easily ten degrees. I was glad I was wearing the sports coat.

"No sir." Frank Manning folded up like damp cardboard and sat down.

Rufus looked around the room. "Are there any other questions? Comments?" The room was perfectly silent. "I'll remind you that Mr. Crawford is here as my representative. I expect you to assist him just as you would me.

"Now if you will excuse me, I have other pressing matters I have to deal with." The provost turned to me, shook my hand, and said, "James?"

"Thank you Provost George. I'll take it from here." I stepped forward into the group near a table in the middle. I stopped, put the envelope the provost had brought me down on the table, then halfway sat on the corner of the table, one leg dangling, and crossed my arms—a picture of confident competence, I hoped.

"I know that most if not all of you spent the morning talking to the police." I grinned. "Well, I'm not going to put you through that again. In fact, they probably talked to you individually. I want all of you to be part of this together.

"I think the police will spend the next couple of days convincing themselves that none of you are really viable suspects before looking further afield. I've got a different approach." I glanced around at my audience. Everyone seemed to be paying attention. "It's simple. Philip Douglas was not killed by anyone in this room. Individually none of you know who the murderer is. But, together, collectively, you know who did it. You just don't know you know."

That confused them, every one of them, even Bobby, at least at first. "Each one of you may just hold a piece of a puzzle that can give us a clue or a hint and if we bring them together we can solve this case.

"Now I want you to think back over the last days, weeks, months here at the Press. Does anything strike you as strange or a little out of the ordinary? Something an author, would-be-author, agent, printer, graphic artist, freelancer, anybody said or did that struck you as odd. Now does it make you wonder? Or did you wonder at the time and then dismiss it? Shucks, does this remind you of a scene out of a book you've read?" They looked like they had gotten the idea. I reassured myself that Bobby had started nodding her head earlier than most, if not all.

"I want you to think about it and talk among yourselves. See what comes up. I'll be around. Don't hesitate to speak up, no matter how trivial it seems."

"You mean something like the trash can at the picnic table catching on fire?" Hazel Murphy had half raised her hand before speaking, as if wanting to be called on in class.

"Exactly," I smiled encouragingly. "When did that happen? Anybody know what caused it?"

"That was this morning," Frank said dismissively, "while we were waiting for the police to let us in the building. All that happened was that Kent didn't put his cigarette out before throwing it in the trash."

"There was a whoosh and then flames. I consider that noteworthy." Hazel could put a lot of frost in her voice when she wanted to.

I stepped in before things deteriorated into an office spat. "That is precisely the kind of thing I want to hear about—even if it seems insignificant to others.

"Dr. Murphy, what I'd like to do is to set up a brainstorming session so that everybody can bring up items like the trash can catching on fire."

"I'm well aware of brainstorming, Mr. Crawford. It's a technique we use in academe. I've used it here at the Press as well as in other venues."

Hazel Murphy still didn't seem to think I could tie my own shoes despite the provost's kind words.

"Excellent! As senior member of the professional staff would you be so kind as to act as moderator? Just see if you, as a group or as individuals, can think of any recent events that were odd or otherwise noteworthy. That would be very helpful. Perhaps you could have somebody serve as secretary?"

"Moderate a brainstorming session—here, now?"

"Exactly! I know you all have things to do, but I would hope you could manage a short session now. The provost will be so pleased when I tell him."

"Well," she looked like she couldn't decide if my idea was too stupid to put up with or—if by asking her to run it—the session had metamorphosed into a wonderful suggestion. "I do have some experience in that area, but wouldn't you like to—"

"No, no." I held up my hand. "I'm sure my presence would inhibit comments. If necessary we can have another session later.

"Now, while you're brainstorming, I'd like for someone to show me around the Press. No doubt the crime scene is off-limits, but I would like to see as much of the rest of the building as possible. Two is probably better than one." I looked around and realized that I only knew three of their names. "Ms. Slater? Mr. Manning? Would you be so kind?" My victims both looked startled but nodded their heads in agreement.

I picked up the envelope and stood up. "All right. Dr. Murphy, I'll leave you and the rest to talk among yourselves. Once I'm through with the tour I'll be back to hear what you've got to say."

. . .

I watched Dr. Murphy begin to organize the group into what looked like the most structured brainstorming session ever conducted and I wondered if I'd just asked the murderer to collect evidence against herself.

Bobby walked up to where I was standing and I whispered "So, how did I do?" when she got close enough that we wouldn't be overheard.

Bobby's voice was little more than a whisper. "Pretty well. I was impressed but I might be prejudiced. The provost doesn't leave any doubt as to who's in charge, does he?"

Frank had stopped to speak to the owl-eyed man who'd been sitting next to him. The man held a pack of cigarettes in one hand and was patting his pockets with the other.

"Who's the guy talking to Frank? The smoker?"

"Kent," answered Bobby without even looking around. "If you're talking about tobacco. I really can't testify as to the other."

Frank took a lighter out of his pants pocket, handed it to Kent, made some comment, and then walked up to where we were standing.

"Poor, Kent." Frank pointed a thumb at the man who was headed out the back door to the parking lot. "Hazel rounded us up before he had his after lunch smoke and he's been suffering through our little meeting."

He stuck his hand out. "Sorry about that jerky comment, James. Sometimes my mouth operates with a mind of its own. And thanks for getting us out of that meeting with Hazel."

I shook his hand. "I was wondering about my choice as moderator. As far as jerky comments, I've been there; done that, Frank. Is it Frank? People usually call me Crawford."

"Frank is fine with me." He puffed his mustache and grinned. "You save James for close personal friends?"

"I call him Ford."

I'm not sure Bobby was as willing to forgive and forget Frank's comment about her "main squeeze" as I was. I changed the subject.

"That's Kent going out the door?"

"Yeah, Kent Fulmer." Frank pointed at the envelope I was holding. "Guess you haven't had time to read all about us yet."

I looked down at it and back at him. "Is it that obvious?"

"How long you been at this detecting game? It's a campus mail envelope. Hell, I think it's university property. You were carrying it when you walked in with the provost. He must have given it to you when you met in the parking lot since you came in separate cars." Frank threw up his hands. "What else could it be but a dossier on Press employees?"

"Wow." I was impressed.

"Ford," Bobby's tone was dry. "He was looking out the window and saw Rufus hand the envelope to you and point at the building."

"Watson," Frank puffed air through his mustache again. "You know my methods too well."

"So, I take it that you two are friends?"

Both Bobby and Frank were grinning widely.

Frank nodded. "You do detecting pretty well, stranger."
"So show me the building."

. . .

We started off walking toward the archway that led to the left
wing. Left from the back, I reminded myself. As we walked out
of the center part of the building we found ourselves in a hall
flanked by offices and meeting rooms to the right and left. I noted that there was wainscoting and bookcases, breaking up the
wall space, but no paintings or pictures—just books. Makes
sense, they publish books. Bound to have a lot of them around.

Frank and Bobby were making comments about whose office was whose, where the photocopiers were, and what the conference rooms were used for while I tried to remember everything they were saying. Say what you will about killers, I was
operating on the belief that this one knew the layout of
his murder scene.

We must have walked about two-thirds of the way down the
wing, when we walked out of the hallway into a large room that
clearly was a waiting room outside the director's office. The far
wall was paneled in a dark wood. To the side were some big
leather chairs and a matching sofa carefully arranged on an Oriental rug with a low glass and chrome coffee table between
them. The table was covered in, not surprisingly, coffee table
books. All published by the Press, I assumed.

An ornate wooden desk sat in the middle of the wall in front
of a door that led to the room beyond—the director's office.

"This is primarily a waiting room," continued Frank. "Sometimes Philip would meet with people out here, but generally he

made them wait here until he condescended to see them in his office. There, through that doorway behind the desk."

"That doorway" was in the center of the room; to the left of it I could see a narrow hallway that meant the director's office wasn't as wide as this room although it might be deeper.

"Over there is the hall that leads to the fire exit. I'm sure Philip would have preferred to have his office take up the entire end of this wing, but the fire marshal must have prevailed."

I stopped in the center of the room and looked around. It was decorated pretty much like the rest of the building except for one thing or rather things. While there was an occasional bookcase here and there, the walls were arrayed with rifles horizontally mounted on what looked like individual gun racks.

"Guns?" I looked around the room.

"Rifles." Bobby and Frank replied in unison and then burst into laughter.

"Philip was quite emphatic about calling them rifles." Bobby added. "I quote, 'Educated people know better than to call them guns.'"

"It's part of his private collection—the overflow part." Frank pointed toward the door. "The rest of it is in his office."

"How the hell did he get away with a collection of—rifles displayed on university property? This is crazy. Even in the museum they'd be displayed under glass."

"You forget," Frank turned to face me, "Or maybe you don't know. The Press is a quasi-independent entity. It has its own board and, while the building is university property, the contents aren't. It makes things very complicated." He waved his arms at the walls. "The prior director—the original director—was specifically allowed to display his own private collection in the building as part of his employment contract. Philip's contract contains the same language."

"Right." Bobby stepped up to form a conversational triangle. "The fact is that M. W. Stefenson's collection happened to be composed of rare books. which makes a lot more sense in a press building. He was worried that the university might object to some of his volumes."

Frank grinned. "Yeah, well the university's lawyers didn't think to modify the employment contract wording to exclude weapons when they hired Philip. Besides, we should believe that books can be just as dangerous as rifles, shouldn't we?"

I decided that I'd better check with Rufus about rifle collections and employment contracts.

While we were talking, we had walked over to the doorway into Philip's office—the one behind his secretary's desk. It had a strips of yellow Caution—Crime Scene—Do Not Cross tape hanging across it, but stood open. I peered into the room.

"He just collected rifles," said Bobby. "He wouldn't stoop to collecting handguns. He considered pistols to be so plebeian."

"How many does he have in his collection? There must be thirty or forty of them just in his office." I was still astonished. Why hadn't Jim Ward mentioned them? How could you describe a place and not mention the guns?

"Hundreds!" Frank laughed at the expression on my face. "No, not really. I know it looks like a lot but if you stop and count them it's really around sixty of them." Frank scratched his head. "I don't remember the exact number."

I tried to stop thinking about rifles and pay attention to what the murder scene looked like—at least from the doorway. The office was massive—larger than Rufus's I think. The walls weren't covered in books, but rifles instead. Directly across from this entrance was Philip's desk. From here it looked like a small aircraft carrier. An immense stretch of flat surface broken by a pen-and-pencil set and a modern telephone. Not that modern, I corrected myself. Today's modern phone would have been cordless. The desk looked strangely barren and then I realized there wasn't a computer monitor and keyboard on it.

There was something behind the desk other than the high-backed executive chair that I couldn't quite make out. Maybe a bookcase? On the left-hand wall there was another doorway with its own yellow warning tape. That must lead to the exit he used as his private entrance and egress that Jim had mentioned. The flooring was carpeted like the rest of the building but on top of it there was an Oriental rug centered under the desk. The rug had to be enormous since the desk didn't make it look small. And there, on the rug beside the desk I could just make out the man-datory chalk outline of the body.

According to Jim, Philip had fallen face-first with no detect-ible attempt to break his fall, which led them to believe he was dead before he hit the floor. That and the extent of the head wound. If his heart had still been beating the pool of blood would have been larger.

"What's behind the desk?"

"I think it was just Philip's way of saying 'bigger is better.'" Bobby smiled. "He liked to hide behind it."

"No, I meant what's actually, physically behind it." I point-ed. "I can see the top of something."

Bobby shook her head. "I'm too short to see it from here. Probably the safe? Can't think of anything else."

I noticed again the way her curls bounced and then fell back in place. "Safe?"

"Yep, it's the safe. You can see it better from over here."
Frank waved from the doorway on the left. I hadn't noticed that
he'd left us.

"That's where he kept the ammunition," explained Bobby.
We turned around, went by the empty secretary's desk, and into
the hallway. Frank was standing about two-thirds of the way
down the hall. Light came in from the windows facing the parking lot. Decorating with guns, rifles, I mentally corrected myself,
carried on even into the hallway. At the end of the hall was the
traditional gray metal exit door seen in every university building.
Emergency crash bar to open the door that overrode the electro-
magnetic lock. Lighted exit sign above the door, fire alarm to the
side, and a sign that said Emergency Exit Only in the middle of
it. An interior decorator's nightmare. It was reassuring to see
that Philip had lost a few battles with the university's
fire marshals.

"Ammunition?" I realized I was speaking in one-word sentences.

"Guns don't kill people." Frank dropped his voice in what
had to be his imitation of Philip Douglas. "Bullets kill people."
He shrugged his shoulders. "Philip was an 'ammo' control advocate. Said people should be able to buy all the guns they wanted,
we just needed to control access to the ammunition."

I looked over Frank's shoulder into the director's office.
From here you had a much better view of the chalk outline and
you could see the size of the bloodstain. I wondered how much
larger it would have been if his heart had been pumping.

"Ammo in safe?" There. I'd strung together three whole
words. Frank moved out of the way and I could see part of the
safe—standalone, maybe bolted to the floor, big combination
dial on the door. Maybe an antique? Do styles change in safes?

"By keeping the ammunition locked up he justified his claim that it was safe to display the rifles—at least to himself."

"Safe? You mean the rifles work? I could just take one down and shoot somebody with it?" I was shocked into multiword sentences. "I assumed they were display pieces!"

"Oh, you're not allowed to touch them. Even the cleaning people were told to keep their hands off of the rifles—not even to dust. Only Philip could touch them. Maybe that was another way he kept them safe. Everybody assumed the firing pin had been removed or something. But they all work."

Bobby chimed in. "You didn't know Philip. He wouldn't have it any other way. He said that the rifles 'had been made safe' but all he meant was they weren't loaded."

"Yeah, it was a big joke to Philip." Frank picked back up the story. "He'd put one over on all the 'real' gun experts. He used to laugh and brag about it, how all the hook and bullet authors assumed the guns were 'bowdlerized' as he called it. It didn't make any sense to me."

"Reminded me of those pet owners who refuse to have their animals neutered. Stupid." Bobby shook her head again and I was momentarily distracted.

"Philip treated those rifles better than he did the staff." Frank was leaning against the wall between a rifle and the window. Ever so often he'd stroke his mustache, smoothing it down. "One of his more annoying habits was to work on a rifle while he was having a scheduled one-on-one with you. He'd clean one of those damned rifles and grunt ever so often. You'd never know if he was paying attention or not while you were supposed to be discussing your career goals or whether the Press should publish a certain book."

I pointed across the room to the opposite wall. "Is that another door over there?"

"Yep, it's another pocket door. It matches this one," said Frank. "When the doors are closed they almost blend into the paneling. That's the executive bathroom." Frank put a little emphasis on the word "executive."

I hadn't noticed that this entrance was through a pocket door. I pulled it a little way out, watched the caution tape sag, and slid it back in.

"Careful, it automatically locks from this side when you close it."

"Is it usually open?"

"Oh, no." Frank was quick to respond. "Couldn't leave it open or PTG might get in. Same with his front door. Our 'chief executive' had his own bathroom, his own entrance and exit, and an executive secretary to keep everybody else at bay—in theory. He couldn't keep a secretary. Still, lots of privacy for a twenty-person office."

I had noticed that some of the staff were in cubicles and wondered if that was part of Frank's attitude about Philip's office or if it was just that his attitude about Philip extended to his office. "Pee-Tea-Gee?" Just like that there I was back to one-word sentences.

Bobby took pity on me. "Peter the Gray. That's the office cat. Have you seen him? We call him PTG for short. He's a magnificent Russian blue."

"I saw him. He was in the room when Rufus was talking."

"Really?" said Bobby.

"Yes. He was on top of a bookcase at the beginning. Then he jumped down and left."

"Hmmm. I thought he didn't like crowds."

Frank laughed. "I don't know about crowds, but he sure didn't like Philip and Philip felt the same way about the cat."

I was beginning to agree with the cat. I had yet to hear anything close to positive about the man. "There's no computer monitor in there? In his office, I mean. Unless . . ." I find it almost impossible to believe that anybody doesn't have a computer in their office. So impossible that I make up ways for it to be there. "Is it inset in the desk?"

"Neo-Luddite." It seemed that Bobby had caught whatever it was that caused my one-word sentences.

"I beg pardon?"

"There are tales on campus of a physics professor who claimed that there was nothing you could do with a personal computer that he couldn't do with an IBM Selectric. Biology has a professor who refuses to read emails. The departmental secretary has to print them out and put them in his mailbox."

Frank looked at me and I nodded. I'd heard the tales too. People swore they were true.

"They had nothing on Philip."

"So, no to the monitor." I figured that answered my question but Frank was just getting started.

"Those people just held themselves back. They're the ones who suffered because of their attitudes. OK, maybe Biology had to hire another secretary but that didn't keep the whole department in the dark ages!

"But this guy." Frank pointed at the desk. "This guy held back the entire Press with his stupid, bone-headed, backward attitude to computers in the workplace.

"Oh, fine, he refused to have a computer in his office. Made his secretary print out his emails, schedule appointments, maintain his calendar, remind him of appointments. Hell, that's why

he couldn't keep a secretary. But why did he have to keep us in
the days of lead type and red ink! Just think what his attitude has
cost the Press in time, money, and lost opportunities."

I cut my eyes over to see how Bobby was reacting to Frank's
tirade. She was nodding her head in agreement.

"And where were you when Philip was shot?" I smiled when
I said it, but Frank clearly had a motive.

"I." Frank paused. "Taking a walk. Kent and I take a walk
every day around 4:20. Ask him why don't you."

Smiling, I shook my head. I knew the police already had. I
could read the transcripts or just get the CliffsNotes from Jim
Ward. "Where is his secretary? Out celebrating?"

Frank seemed to be regretting his outburst and refused to
speak.

"He hasn't had one for a couple of months now. Human Resources must have given up on him. That or they don't have anybody they are trying to make quit. The Press hired a retired librarian to come in every workday morning to print out his email,
enter his appointments, and give him the day's agenda." Bobby
smiled. "Librarians must be able to put up with anybody for
short periods of time."

. . .

Before I left the Press I stopped by Hazel Murphy's office and
picked up the results of the brainstorming session. She had
sealed it in an envelope but I could tell by the feel of it there was
a single sheet of paper in it. Unless it was her confession I had a
bad feeling about how productive the session had been. Hazel
was dismissive—she didn't have time to talk—so much time had

been wasted. She picked up her phone and waved me out of her office.

I tore open the envelope and looked at the list. I was reminded of the priest who routinely listened to confession at a nunnery. When asked what it was like he replied, "Like being peppered with popcorn." With the exception of the fire in the trash can all I had was popcorn—and it was stale and unsalted.

I headed back down the hall to where I'd left Bobby and Frank. Between the two of them I knew they could do better than what I had—better than popcorn.

. . .

I got back to the house before Mary finished cleaning. Last week I'd forgotten that it was her day to come and had almost missed her. She was wiping down the kitchen counters when I caught up with her.

"Mary, I can always tell when you've been here. The house just seems so much fresher."

"Humph. If you'd use some furniture polish—or mop a floor or two you could make it smell like this too."

I laughed and went to get my checkbook. Mary no longer cleaned the whole house on the days she came. The extra bedrooms and baths didn't get used enough to need it so she would cycle through the rooms other than my bedroom, the kitchen, den, and laundry. My office was my affair—had been since she'd started—too many wires, computers, expensive gadgets, and my own filing system for her to be comfortable doing more than sweeping. However the house felt so good after she'd cleaned that I usually wiped the office down after she left. It worked for us and the house was generally presentable—if there was anyone to present it to.

I walked back into the kitchen and stepped around the pile of sweepings—mostly cat and dog hair. "How's the rheumatism, Mary?"

"You know it's the cold that makes it worse, Mr. Crawford. You notice it getting cold around here lately?"

"Glad to hear that it hasn't gotten worse." I put her check next to her purse. "How's Levi doing?"

"Same as ever."

There was something about her voice that made me turn and face her. She'd picked up the broom and was drumming her fingers on the handle. Her other hand was on her hip, elbow out from her side. "He's not the one whose life has changed. He's not solving crimes and having women spend the night, is he?"

So much for my being the great detective—I had no idea how Mary knew about Bobby, but I never even thought about keeping it secret.

"I suspect I can put a name to who she is. Hear good things about her. Isn't that enough change for you? What's this about solving murders?"

I had the floor plans that Victoria had included in her Press dossier spread out on the dining room table and was trying to make sense out of what I'd been told yesterday and what the documentation said. The Black was helping. Victoria had included a list of employees with their titles and job descriptions in the packet. Having dealt with human resources and their attitudes toward job descriptions and titles I was surprised to find how useful they were. I'd have to check with Bobby to see how accurate they were.

Victoria had also sent a list of the people who were on the board. It turned out that Rufus was the chairman since he's provost. There was another university person on the list—a dean but he was a poet of some renown so I wasn't sure in which capacity he was on the board, poet or dean. Maybe it was both. The only other name on the list I was familiar with was Steven Stefenson. But the floor plans were by far the most helpful thing I'd been given.

"So here's where the body was." I pointed to a spot on the floor plan where I'd penciled in a rough approximation of the body outline, desk, and safe. I say rough because I'm not much of an artist. Looking at it from above, if you will, made it pretty clear that the killer had stood close to if not in the doorway from the hall. I'd check with Ward at lunch to see if that fit with what the police thought. Frank had said the pocket door locked automatically. I grabbed my iPad and added that to the notes I'd typed last night.

I had copied over the pictures I'd taken with my phone when I was at the Press and had made notes on most of them last night.

I didn't really have a picture of the door since it had been in its pocket. For a moment I wondered how Sherlock Holmes had kept all he had detected in his mind. I don't remember any detective actually writing out notes. Since the detectives I was thinking about were all fictional I decided not to worry about it. I was pretty sure at least Doyle had made notes!

TB had decided that the mechanical pencil had the potential to be a great toy and batted it again trying to get it to roll across the table. He wasn't having a lot of success.

I had called Jim Ward earlier but the message I got back was that unless I'd figured out who the murderer was, it could wait until lunch. So be it.

"So it's almost like one of those British drawing room mysteries. Right?" I picked up the pencil before The Black pushed it off the table. "It's similar to a 'locked room' mystery even though the doors into the room were unlocked." I stopped talking. Had the doors been locked? What about the one in the hall? Frank said it locked automatically. Did the killer close it when he left or leave it open? And did it matter?

I stared at the cat for a minute. "What we need is a butler. In the British mysteries the butler is always hiding something. Maybe we should see if anybody named Butler is involved?"

The Black yawned and flicked his tail.

"That reminds me. Did I tell you that the Press has a cat?" The tail continued to twitch. "Looks like a Russian blue with great big green eyes, like you. His name is Peter the Gray and he'd be a prime suspect except we can't figure out how he'd fire a rifle. He hated Philip and Philip hated him. He kept the doors to his office closed." To TB that would be the greatest sin a human could commit. He hated closed doors.

I started to fold the plans back up to take with me and TB hopped off the table and left the room, tail held high. I don't think he liked talking about another cat even as a murder suspect. I put the floor plans with the iPad and both of them under my car keys. That should prevent me from forgetting them.

I went down the hall to change clothes. I had an appointment with Victoria and then lunch with Ward.

. . .

"Well, Jim Rockford always said his standard rate was 'two hundred dollars a day plus expenses.'"

Victoria shook her head. "Mr. Crawford, the *Rockford Files* were set during the 1970s. You can't expect me to agree to that."

"Too much, huh?" I crossed my legs and smiled back at her. "What do you normally pay private investigators?" We were meeting in her office, which was just outside of Rufus's. And I was right. Philip's office is, or was—what tense do you use when comparing a dead man's office to anything? I gave up and recast the sentence. The Press director's office is larger than the provost's.

"We've never hired anyone to investigate a murder before."

"No precedent, huh? Guess that makes it harder." I wasn't really trying to be difficult. Just the thought of getting paid to find out who had killed a man seemed, I don't know, surreal? I was having trouble taking it seriously.

"We handle things without precedent all the time."

"I'm sorry, Ms. Moore. It's just I've never been hired to investigate a murder. I don't have a precedent for this either." I didn't want to irritate her. Rufus had told her to take care of this and she took that seriously. That's why she was so good at what she did.

"All you have to do is give me a reasonable figure for an hourly or daily rate. It's a simple professional services agreement between you and the university. We've already agreed on the 'description of services.' You're to assist the police in their investigation into Philip Douglas's murder while protecting the reputation of the university to the best of your abilities. You're comfortable with that, right?"

"Yes, yes I am. What about lawyers? I wouldn't think I should get paid more than a lawyer."

Victoria sighed. "The university has lawyers on staff, Mr. Crawford."

"It's Crawford. Please call me Crawford."

"If you'll call me Victoria."

"It's a deal." I thought for a second. "Daily, I think. I'm not used to keeping track of my time. Expenses, yeah, I can track that, meals and stuff."

"Mileage?"

"Oh, I wouldn't think I'd need to do that, do you?"

"Crawford, who does your taxes? You do realize that you're going to have to report this income and pay taxes on it, don't you?"

Actually, no, I hadn't given it any thought. "I should talk to my accountant?"

"I think that would be wise." She smiled. "Why don't you do that? Perhaps he can help you set a daily rate."

"Good idea! I'll give her a call after lunch and get back to you. Thanks, Victoria."

"Not at all." She clasped her hands together and set them on her desk. "Is there anything else I can help you with?"

I stood up and glanced at my phone to see what time it was. It was later than I thought. I needed to get going or I was going to be late for lunch. "There is one thing."

Victoria cocked her head and looked questioningly at me.

"Do you think I should get business cards made up? Something to make it seem like I know what I'm doing?"

"Would you put your rates on it? Go to lunch, Crawford."

"Right."

. . .

I met Jim at the door to the restaurant, Will's Sports Bar, so I wasn't late. It was a sports bar located downtown, which meant it wasn't busy for lunch. I don't know if it wasn't busy for lunch because it was a sports bar or because it was downtown.

Jim had started complaining about his day from the moment I walked up and he kept on until we were seated. I picked up the menu and realized I'd gotten the beer menu. I usually don't drink at lunch unless I'm planning on taking a nap afterward. I was wondering just what it was I was going to do in the afternoon and whether a nap was possible when Jim interrupted.

"Sorry, I just had to get that off my chest. So what did you call about?"

What had I called about? Oh, yeah. "You didn't tell me that Philip Douglas had a rifle collection and it covered the walls."

"I didn't?" He shrugged his shoulders and picked up the food menu. His hands are so large that the menu looked small in them. "Sorry. What of it?"

"Have you been able to eliminate all of them from being possible murder weapons?"

"So what are you going to—huh?" He took his eyes off the menu and looked straight at me. "They're display pieces."

I shook my head no.

"What are you trying to tell me? That they're not display pieces?"

I pursed my lips. "Yep. Both Bobby and Frank Manning say they all work just fine. That Douglas used to tell people they were safe just because they weren't loaded."

He just sat there for a couple of heartbeats staring at me. "I will be dipped in—"

He pulled his phone out of his coat pocket. He used the speed dial so whoever it was he called pretty regularly. I put the beer menu down and picked up the food one.

"Harry."

Jim had mentioned that Harry was working with him on this case. I was pretty sure I hadn't met him yet.

"Did you check out those rifles on the wall? The ones at the murder scene?" Jim's face didn't show any emotion. When we play poker I consider that a bad sign. "Right. Somebody would have to be crazy to display rifles like that if they hadn't been disabled. So you didn't check?" He nodded once. "Right. I didn't check either. Go. Check. Now."

I hoped Harry knew Jim well enough to know that he was mad at himself not at Harry.

"So, Harry doesn't get to eat lunch?"

"I didn't tell him not to eat. What did you say was good here?" We'd been here a couple of times together. I ignored the fact that he'd suggested the place. "Burgers are good. The chips are homemade. You like the onion rings."

The waitress walked up to the table. "Can I get you gentlemen something to drink?"

I was hesitating about ordering the beer when Jim spoke. "I'm headed to the Press after this. Want to come?"

"Sweet tea and a glass of water too, thanks."

"I'll have unsweet tea." He glanced at the waitress and back at me. "You know what you want? I'm in a hurry now."

"Go ahead." I waved him on and started skimming the menu. "The turkey wrap, slaw instead of chips."

"And I'll have the French dip and chips."

"I'll put those orders in and be right back with your drinks." She flashed her dimples at us and walked away.

I sat back. "Nice dimples."

"Huh?"

"Yeah, and you didn't notice that her T-shirt was too tight and low-cut either."

Jim's lips twitched with the beginnings of a smile. "I'm a trained investigator. I'm supposed to notice these things."

"But you didn't stop to check and see if they were genuine or just display pieces, did you?"

That got him. He laughed outright. "OK. Point taken. But here we are looking for a murder weapon and there must be a hundred rifles hanging on the walls."

"Nayh, more like sixty says Frank. And we don't know if the murder weapon is one of them."

This time both Jim and I noticed the waitress as she approached the table with our drinks.

"I told the kitchen you were in a hurry. Your food should be right out." She really did have excellent dimples. "Thanks," I said. "I'm going to try and get my friend to calm down and not bolt his food." She just smiled and walked away.

"What else did you learn at the Press?" Jim seemed to have relaxed. "Are you going to tell me who killed him?"

"Nope, but I can tell you if the killer used one of those rifles he brought his own ammunition with him—or her. I don't guess you know anything to limit it to men, right?"

"Ammunition?"

"Our deceased kept all the different ammo for those guns locked up in his safe. It's behind his desk." I took a sip of tea. "He believed that 'guns don't kill people, bullets kill people.' Sort of an ammo control advocate, I guess."

Jim snorted. "I guess he never saw anybody whose head was bashed in by a rifle butt, huh? Did you check to make sure the safe is locked?"

"Whoa!" I held my hands up. "I didn't cross the crime scene tape. We just looked in. I wouldn't have gone past the police line in front of witnesses. The safe looked closed."

"Not with witnesses?"

I tried to look innocent but all that got me was another snort of disbelief.

"Well, it doesn't look like any of the staff are good suspects." Jim drummed his fingers on the table. "The police might ignore sixty or so potential murder weapons but we're pretty good about checking alibis. Some of them had been at a review meeting, others at a training seminar, one had been with a captain of police, they all had solid alibis. The three with the weakest alibis were Murphy, Manning, and Fulmer. Manning and Fulmer claim to have taken a walk outside and were pretty vague about the details. I don't think Harry likes the Murphy woman."

"What was her alibi?"

"She told Harry it was none of his damn business where she'd been and none of his damn business what she'd been doing. She would tell his boss, but she wasn't about to tell him."

"Sounds to me like Hazel didn't like Harry. She didn't much care for me either." I wondered at the shortness of the list I'd gotten from her brainstorming session. Could I have picked the killer to be the moderator?

"Yeah, well in your case I can understand it, but she really got under Harry's skin. You should have heard him when he called me to see if he could arrest her. He was so mad he was stuttering."

The waitress arrived with our food and Jim's phone rang at the same time. He glanced at the caller ID and answered it. "Yeah?" She held up the turkey wrap and I pointed to Jim. She put it down in front of him and then the French dip in front of me. They both looked good. I smiled and gave her a thumbs up while Jim was listening to whoever it was on the phone.

"Don't beat yourself up. I didn't check them either."

Must be Harry, I thought.

"Close off the area, make sure it's secure, and then go and get some lunch. I'll meet you there this afternoon. Did you get the fingerprinting kit? Yeah, OK, good work. Now go eat." He shoved the phone back into his pocket.

"That Harry?" I asked.

Jim picked up half the wrap. "Yeah. The rifles will fire. He's sure."

"Well, I think I can at least explain Frank and Kent's reluctance to give you any details about their walk."

"Huh?"

"They take a walk about 4:20 every day. You do know about 420 don't you? I forget you were never on the narc squad."

"You're telling me that those two go out and smoke a joint every day at 4:20?" Jim stabbed at the coleslaw with his fork.

"Frank said he and Kent take a walk every day at 4:20." I shrugged my shoulders. "He certainly looks like a pothead. Ponytail, mustache, faded jeans, carries a cigarette lighter but doesn't smoke tobacco. Yeah, I'd say that's what he and Kent are doing every day. You going to bust them?"

"That's probably why they wouldn't agree to a paraffin test. Afraid we'd detect marijuana particles." He looked disgusted.

"Wouldn't you?" I was mildly interested.

"Paraffin tests? We don't use them anymore—useless in court. Doesn't keep us from asking suspects if they'd be willing to submit to one.

"Damn fool nonsense, that's what it is. So they are scared to tell us why they went for the walk and are hesitant to prove their own innocence because smoking marijuana is illegal."

I dipped the edge of my sandwich into the broth and took another bite. We'd had this discussion before.

"We've just got too many laws to enforce and the politicians keep adding to them. Then they turn around and cut staffing and add paperwork."

"Don't forget the mandatory sentencing laws and then refusing to fund prison expansion." What the heck, I decided to jump in. "And what's happening to teachers. They've got way more to do than just teach and that gets added to every year."

Jim glared at me. "I'm talking about the policemen here."

"I thought misery loved company? How about if I talk to the two? I'll just confirm that they went out for a smoke. Do you want me to convince them to say yes to the paraffin test?"

Jim thought for a moment. "Yeah, everybody else has got more than one person who can vouch for their whereabouts. Those guys just alibi each other. You handle that and I'll take care of Ms. Murphy."

"You might want to call her Dr. Murphy—just a hunch." I wiped my mouth with my napkin. "I'll take care of it this afternoon." I waved, caught the waitress's eye, and mouthed "check please."

"Now, changing the subject, what do you think about me getting business cards?"

I caught up with Jim Ward in the press director's office. I'd a couple of things that needed doing. I wanted to talk to my tax person as Victoria had suggested, but she wasn't in, of course. I left a voicemail asking her to call.

There was a guy standing next to Jim whom I didn't recognize. Since they were looking at a rifle, I thought I could put a name to him anyway. He was a big guy, not as tall as Jim, but few were, heavy-set but not soft, jet-black hair and a broad uncomplicated face. Jim turned away and started talking on his phone.

I walked up and stuck my hand out. "Harry? I'm Crawford. Nice to meet you."

Harry was a little slow doing it but he took my hand. "So you're the one who tipped us off to these rifles. Thanks, I guess. Don't know if I'll ever live it down."

"Dumb luck. The people I was talking to just happened to mention it. I guess they didn't think it was that strange."

Harry shrugged his shoulders. "From what I hear our deceased was one twirling son-of-a-bitch."

"So they tell me."

"Well, he may have been a bastard, but he sure knew his rifles. Amazing collection, if you ask me."

"Is it?" I was startled to hear somebody say anything that could be construed as positive about Philip Douglas. "I don't know enough about them to be impressed except by the number of them."

Harry nodded vigorously. "That's part of it for sure—the pure number of them. I've got guns but damn. Not only in his office but outside it too!"

"Yeah, and into the hall over there." I pointed in the direction of the exit door.

"And as far as I can tell he was going to wear them out cleaning them. What a dip-wad."

I wasn't too sure what a dip-wad was but I could tell I was back in familiar territory. Harry didn't think much of Philip Douglas and he'd never met the man.

"How's that?"

"Been asking the witnesses about the collection. They've all got some tale of him calling them in to talk about something important and then he'd start cleaning one of the rifles. Not just wiping them down, now, but wire-brush and solvent cleaning and they hadn't even been fired! Hell I'm surprised there's any bluing left on some of them."

I was pretty much at sea. I'd learned to clean rifles in the military and they'd been pretty compulsive about it—particularly in boot camp. Something about the residue corroding the chamber and barrel.

"Preventive maintenance they said he called it."

I didn't need to ask, Harry was going to explain it to me.

"What'd he think? Once the gun is clean, it's clean. Oh, keep them oiled of course. Don't want them to rust, but he was wearing them out. Hell, screw the bluing; it's a wonder there's any rifling left."

Jim had gotten off the phone and walked up to hear the end of Harry's diatribe.

"I see you've met." He glanced at Harry and then nodded in my direction. "Don't worry, Harry, he's not nearly as stupid as he looks." Jim then turned to me. "What'd you learn?"

"It's amazing what you can get away with as long as you are following precedence."

"How so?"

"I told you that Philip's employment contract gave him the right to 'house and display his private collection' just like his predecessor, right? According to the lawyers, he also accepted 'all liability arising from and/or derived from the collection's presence on or off University property.' Fact is the lawyers aren't sure if the Press building really belongs to the university. This, of course, is what they said after I told them about it being a gun, excuse me, rifle collection. Nobody had ever mentioned it to them before."

"We're talking over a hundred thousand dollars worth of guns here, Crawford."

"More than that, I'd say, Jim," added Harry.

"The university self-insures its property except for things in special collections, rare books, specimens, stuff like that. Generally they decide what to do when they are donated, or the university buys whatever it is. Risk Management had no idea the guns were here. And they weren't real pleased to learn about it. RM can't decide if the university has an insurable interest in them or not. At least that's what I think they were arguing about when I left."

"Well I don't feel so stupid," said Harry. "Hell, I could tell they were here. I just didn't think they were potential murder weapons." He looked at Jim and they both chuckled.

"All of them?" I'd wondered about that.

"Every damn one of them. It's a fact." Harry shook his head. "And every damn one of them cleaned and wiped to death. Not a fingerprint on a one of them."

"That surprising?" I asked.

"Nayh, that's what you'd do after cleaning a piece. Fingerprints mar the surfaces and can cause rust. Wipe them off the metal and the wood."

"Any of them loaded?" Jim was looking around the office at the different rifles. "And did we put them back in the same spot?"

A light dawned. "You thinking the murderer pulled a switch and had his own gun here? Or maybe moved one so he could put the rifle he wanted where he needed it?"

Harry stared at me. "Crap." He shook his head. "What do you think I did, Captain Ward? Pile 'em in the middle of the floor and then sort through them? I took them off the wall one at a time, dowel through the barrel so I didn't have to touch 'em. Dusted 'em, finding nothing, and put 'em back. Oh, I wiped the dust off before we put them back, of course."

I was intrigued with the idea of the murderer being able to hide his murder weapon in the midst of Philip's collection. Or moving the weapon he wanted to use from one side of the room to the other.

"And even if I had gotten confused, the brass plaques would have told us what went where."

Poof. Another imaginative idea run aground on the shoals of reality. I hadn't noticed the plaques. I went back to the ammunition. "They tell me that the deceased kept the ammunition for all the rifles in his safe. Did anybody check to see if it was locked?"

Harry's face got red. "Did anybody—what's with you, peck-erwood? You figure I didn't check the guns so maybe I didn't check anything!"

Jim held up his hand. "Easy, Sergeant Johns. Mr. Crawford is here as a representative of the university. He can't help it if he gets excited and annoys people—evidently."

I shut my mouth. Jim and Harry were now Captain Ward and Sergeant Johns—and I was Mr. Crawford. If we got any more formal I might have to submit requests in writing.

"He doesn't know that the green sticky note on the safe means that you fingerprinted it and found it clean or whatever fingerprints were found weren't usable or they were the de-ceased's. He probably thinks it is the combination written out so anybody can open it."

The extent of my ignorance had now been established and I was starting to get a little annoyed. "I also wonder if you've giv-en any thought to opening the safe? The contents, I think, might be informative."

"Yeah, we think so too." Jim sounded more like himself. "Since it's supposed to be full of ammunition we've been reluc-tant just to blow it open."

Harry, on the other hand, still seemed to have an attitude. I thought for a moment. Philip Douglas didn't use computers. He didn't use passwords. He for sure didn't know anything about what was considered secure and what wasn't. It was worth a try.

I walked over to the safe and squatted down beside it, gave one tug on the handle—it was locked—and said, "Anybody know his birthdate? Or his wedding anniversary?" I spun the combination dial and it twirled easily.

Harry and Jim hesitated. "It's probably in the file."

I stood up and grabbed the pen and pencil set. I had noticed it the other day. Flipped it over and there, taped to the bottom was a slip of paper with three two digit numbers separated by hyphens. I moved the set over to the safe where I could see the combination. I had to try it twice but it worked.

Standing up I looked at Jim and Harry. "I'm guessing that the green sticky note doesn't cover the contents?"

Jim turned around and looked at Harry. "Great job on the rifles, Harry; get a bunch of evidence bags. We need to inventory and tag the contents of the safe."

Harry continued to look at me. "You know I was hoping that was going to turn out to be the combination to his bicycle lock."

I grinned at him. "Wouldn't that have been something? Boy I'd have had egg on my face."

"Yeah," replied Harry unhappily. It didn't sound like he would have minded seeing me with egg on my face.

"Can you tell me about the collection?" Maybe I could cheer him up without making a fool of myself.

"Most of them were made between WWI and WWII, as far as I can tell." He glanced around the room. "Three or four antiques—Civil War stuff."

"A World War I rifle isn't an antique?"

"Nope, they are classified as curio and relic guns. They have to have been produced prior to 1899 to be called antiques. Gun collecting is more complicated than it looks."

Collecting anything is more complicated for the collector than it looks to anybody else. I let it go and glanced over at the safe. Harry had started carefully unloading the safe's contents. From here it looked like lots of boxes of ammunition, some legal documents, letters, and a journal. The journal might be interesting. I'd have to remember to ask about it.

"Harry, I'm sorry, Detective Johns. When you get a chance would you mind writing out the names of a few of these rifles for me?"

Harry eyed me suspiciously. "Why?"

I shrugged. "I thought I'd do a little research on what he collected. Might give me a better feel for what the deceased was like. Might not. Besides, it interests me—rifles and gun collecting, that is."

"The names will be on the evidence list." Harry nodded toward where Jim Ward stood talking on his phone. "He says give it to you and you've got it."

"Thanks." So much for trying to get on Harry Johns's good side. I walked over to where Jim was talking and then past him to the doorway into the hall. I checked my cell phone to see what time it was. The police had roped off this wing of the Press building and denied access to all the civilians—except me—as I was neither fish nor fowl. I was tempted to see if Bobby was in her office—sorely tempted.

Stepping out into the hallway, I found myself facing Peter the Gray. He was sitting in the middle of the hall, feet neatly hidden by his tail wrapped around them. His green eyes met mine and he stood, stretching. I squatted down and held my hand out to let him sniff it.

The cat stepped a little closer and I was bold enough to scratch behind his ears. He seemed to like it so I tried again. This time, of course, he moved just out of reach. "So who do you think killed him?" Peter the Gray turned around and cocked his head at me. "I bet you know but just don't care. The world's a better place with one less cat-hater in it, isn't it?"

I could hear a gentle rumble and I wondered if he was purring. "The only good cat-hater is a dead one? Is that your opin-

ion?" Yep, he was purring. "There's a cat at my house that
would probably feel the same way if he'd ever met one." My
knees started reminding me that I wasn't used to squatting so I
stood up. The cat immediately walked up and started rubbing
against my trousers. The Black was going to have something to
say to me when I got home.

. . .

I took a step forward and nearly stumbled trying to avoid the cat.
I put my hand out to steady myself and stubbed a finger on one
of the countless gun racks that lined the walls. I'd have to watch
myself. If I left fingerprints on one of the weapons I was sure
Harry would consider me a prime suspect. The rifle in the rack
looked pretty ordinary to me. I looked at the small brass plaque
that was screwed on to the rack. "Remington Model 700 30-06."
I read the first line out loud. There was smaller lettering beneath
it, but I couldn't make it out. "So what do you think?" I looked
down at Peter the Gray and watched as he ambled down the hall.
"Nice meeting you."

"So now you talk to any cat?"

I started at Ward's voice. I hadn't realized anyone else was
in the hall. "Only the intelligent ones." I turned to face him and
saw that he was alone. I glanced around. "I believe Sergeant
Johns has something of an attitude."

Jim shrugged. "He sees you as a civilian sticking his nose into police business."

I pulled my phone out of my pocket and took a picture of the
Model 700 rifle.

"That one get your vote for murder weapon?"

"No, I'd just forgotten to take pictures. You figure the killer used one of the guns from the collection? He didn't bring his own?"

"I got no idea. Seems ridiculous to depend on a weapon you don't know to kill somebody, but it also seems stupid to bring a weapon here. Coals to Newcastle?"

"Any chance he took advantage of the situation? Maybe found the safe open and Douglas out of the room? Spur-of-the-moment kind of thing? Our killer just grabbed some ammo, loaded the rifle, and waited for Philip to come back from getting his hair cut?"

"And after this spur-of-the-moment murder, our killer unloaded the rifle, cleaned it, wiped it free of fingerprints, put it back, put the extra ammo back—if he had extra ammo—locked the safe, walked out of the building holding Philip's ID card, reentered the building, put the ID card on the desk, and then left."

I scratched my chin. "Hmmm. Doesn't sound real spontaneous does it?"

"Since there don't appear to be anybody's fingerprints on the inside of the safe other than the deceased's, it doesn't seem very likely at all." Jim's voice was as dry as paper. "I'm leaning toward the killer bringing his own gun, pistol or revolver—something easily concealed. A weapon he's familiar with and one fully loaded. Otherwise we've got as cold-blooded a killer as I've ever heard of."

I nodded my head. "Harry says that information on all the rifles will be on the evidence list."

He nodded his head. "Yeah."

"Any chance I could get a copy of that list?"

"Sure. I'll do you that favor if you'll do me one."

I hesitated. "What's the favor?"

"I've got a little puzzle. You love puzzles, right?" Jim scratched his ear. "There was a book, a what-do-you-call-it? Ledger. Found in the safe."

"I thought I saw one being marked for evidence. What about it?"

Jim held out a manila folder. "We used the Press copier to make photocopies of the pages. Take a look."

I opened up the folder and looked at the first couple of pages. It looked like some kind of elaborate code. At the top of each page was some combination of upper and lower case letters, numbers interspersed. I flipped through some more pages. Dollar amounts, if that's what the dollar sign stood for, were under the code. It looked like dates and numbers. Maybe times? I couldn't make heads nor tails out of it. "What the hell is this?"

He shrugged. "Something important enough that the deceased kept it in his safe. Handwriting looks like the handwriting that signed his will and wrote a few other things. This is the kind of thing that we were talking about earlier. Breaking this code or whatever it is doesn't fall under normal police procedures." He smiled. "And neither do you. This is more up your alley. Oh I'll help, we'll help. If you can think of any way regular police procedures can help you figure out what it means."

I looked down at the folder. There must have been sixty to seventy pages all covered with chicken scratches. I looked back at Jim. He nodded encouragingly.

"I'll get you the list of rifles first thing tomorrow. No, wait, tomorrow is Saturday. I'll get you that list on Monday."

When I got home, I could still tell that Mary had cleaned the day before. I'm not sure what I'm going to do when she decides to retire from this job. Aside from the cleaning, guess I'll have to find somebody else to keep me from getting "too full of myself." I had thought that The Black was pretty good at keeping me in my place but there were a few areas that he missed and Mary took care of them. Thank God I'd had enough sense to mention to her that I was going to retire before I did. Now that I think about it, I guess I'd gotten her approval.

I let Tan in the house, checked on the water dish, cleaned out the litter, and glanced at the mail—going through it while standing at the trash can since most of it was junk. Having finished the chores I headed down to my office where I found TB asleep in my chair. I picked him up, sat, and put him in my lap. Most of the time when I wake him he leaves, this time he went back to sleep. That was OK, I could work with him there.

First I connected my cell phone to the iMac, then I started dragging the pictures across, making a collection of the different rooms and weapons with whatever comments I could come up with. I could produce a pretty good virtual tour of the building now—with emphasis on the director's end of the building. His wing, I guess it was. I'd taken some pics of Peter the Gray and put them near what I had taken to calling his rifle. I was toying with making a pdf of the floor plan Victoria had provided me and linking the images I had to it. I stopped because while it was a perfectly feasible project I had no idea whether it would help.

After that, I pulled out the folder of photocopies that Jim had given me. I wasn't sure how to decrypt what might be code or Douglas's shorthand. I couldn't for the life of me figure out what would be so secret that he'd want to record it in some kind of code. On the other hand, here were sixty some odd pages of something that neither Jim nor I could make sense of. Maybe I was working at it from the wrong end? What if I came up with some way to decipher the pages and then see how it fit into the deceased's life? Thinking that far out of the box made my head hurt.

I gave up on that idea and started making a list of the alpha-numeric strings of characters that were at the top of the pages. Mentally I called them titles just to have something to call them other than strings-of-numbers-and-letters-in-no-particular-order. It didn't take more than two or three of them before I realized that they were also of random length. My headache came back.

I stared at the pages a little longer. There's a saying, "If you only have a hammer, you tend to see every problem as nail." Maybe I had too many tools. It didn't look like anything. So I picked a tool and started a database. If it was a code then I should be able to find some patterns.

After entering all the titles I discovered that there were du-plicates. Damn. There was one field, or possible field, that looked to be common to all—1Y, 2Y, 3Y, or 4Y. But if that was common then the Ys were wasted space.

I stared at the screen for a little while longer and decided that it was time to call it a day. I'd just let the puzzle of the titles cook in the morass that was my subconscious. Who knows? It might come to me in the shower tomorrow morning.

. . .

It was dusk turning into evening and we were all out on the screen porch. By all, I mean Tan, The Black, and I were lounging around. I had my feet propped up, TB was in my lap, and Tan was asleep on her bed. I had poured myself a scotch and was telling them about the day's events while watching the fireflies flicker in the backyard.

We'd gone over the fact that Harry Johns didn't think I was nearly as funny as I thought I was and how I was now Mr. Crawford dealing with Sergeant Johns and Captain Ward. The animals seemed shocked.

I ruffled the fur between TB's ears. "Harry was putting me in my place, you see. That's why he used the mister. He's not ready to be friends just yet." I picked up my drink and took a small sip. Working with the police was going to mean more than just working with Jim Ward, and be trickier too.

The Black had started to purr so I changed the subject and went back to describing the day. I had just gotten to the point where Peter the Gray had nearly tripped me and I'd come face-to-barrel with the 30-06 that was hanging on the wall when The Black stopped purring, sat up, and yawned. "What? You can't even put up with me mentioning another cat? I know it's not canned cat food, TB, but it is interesting. Sixty plus rifles mounted on the walls any one of them capable of being used to kill that man. I'm glad Ward is the one who has to figure a way to eliminate all sixty rifles from being used as the murder weapon. It's more up his alley than mine."

The cat moved onto the table and proceeded to lick its ears. I hesitated to reprimand him since we were both more comfortable with him there, me because he wasn't digging into my flesh to maintain his balance and him because he wasn't losing his balance. Still, this was a table that I ate at, not a cat perch.

"My guess is that they'll—that's the police." I poked TB in the side. "Get down. They'll take the bullet and work backward from there. What rifles could have fired a bullet of that caliber or whatever they call it. Then they'll do a ballistics test and see if the rifling matches. If it doesn't then we're still looking for the murder weapon. If it does match, then we've found the murder weapon." The Black stood up and walked to the center of the table, sat back down and resumed his grooming. So much for taking hints.

I frowned. "If it is one of the rifles, I don't know how much good that will do us. Seems like using one of those rifles makes this murder even more complicated. Sure the murderer didn't have to get a weapon to kill Philip, but you've got to be a little arrogant to think you could kill somebody with an old gun you'd never fired before.

"Oh, Harry did say that some of the rifles had been cleaned recently while others didn't appear to have been cleaned in months." I leaned forward to see if I could prod TB to get off the table without me having to get up—no such luck. With a sigh, I stood up and TB immediately jumped down from the table.

"Thanks." Now that I was on my feet Tan woke up and lifted her head from the pillow wondering if I was going to do something interesting enough to justify her getting up too. I glanced at the time. It was a little early compared to our normal routine, but the pets wouldn't mind. "Supper?"

It met with universal approval.

. . .

TB and Tan were eating away. Their meals were always the easy ones to fix—a benefit of eating the same thing day after day. OK, the dog got the same dry food. The cat's food changed from can to can. I couldn't keep up with all the different varieties and I doubted if he could either.

I stared at the refrigerator and considered my own supper. There was no need to open it and stare at the contents. I knew what was in there. In fact, how up to date is my food app? The one that generates menus? I thought about it for a minute and decided that if I couldn't remember when was the last time I updated it, then it had to be out of date. I fired it off anyway. Baked shrimp, leeks, and asparagus in a butter and dill sauce over angel hair pasta—good recipe except I didn't have any of the ingredients except the butter and pasta. I closed the app and walked over to the pantry where I kept the basics. There was a chicken and rice recipe on the back of one of the boxes that had sounded good in the supermarket.

I found the box and the recipe still sounded good—maybe better. Pulled a frozen boneless, skinless, chicken breast out of the freezer and put it in a skillet with a couple of teaspoons of olive oil, turned the burner on low, and began to wait for the chicken to thaw.

I had over half a bottle of chardonnay left over from some other supper. If I had read the ingredients off the back of the box correctly, the wine should go well with the finished dish. Meanwhile it would go well with the chef.

Bobby and I had agreed to meet tomorrow at a bar I didn't often frequent. A group she liked was playing there and since the football game was in South Carolina this weekend we might be able to get in without too much trouble. I wondered if I should have asked her out tonight as well. It seemed a little needy to make plans like that but maybe that's what I was—needy. Or maybe it was more than that. My mind shied away from that train of thought. So what to do on a Friday night? I flipped the breast over to thaw the other side. Perry Mason re-runs? A BBC adaptation of one of the British mysteries? Did I have the software to design a business card?

It was Friday night—Friday night lights. That meant high school football, at least around here it did. I went over to the stereo and switched over to the tuner. It was still set on the station I'd listened to the game on a week ago.

Tommy Oh's distinctive voice came out of the speakers. He was wrapping up a commercial about a tire sale where the owner would "do right by you." I had to smile. Tommy's advertisers were all said to "do right by their customers." Saved him the trouble of memorizing new advertising slogans.

I went back to the stove, turned off the heat, and moved the breast over to a cutting board. Once I'd cubed it, exposing the raw centers, I returned it to the pan and turned the heat back on and added a little more oil. I wonder if that freshman, no he was a sophomore quarterback can pull out another one? What was his name? Oh, yeah, Jason. I enjoy football, after all it's part of the culture, but I try to do so in moderation.

I had spent the morning and most of the afternoon doing chores around the house and yard. The answer to what those pages from Philip's journal meant hadn't come to me when I woke up, but I had them in the back of my mind as I went around performing routine tasks. Nothing came of it except I got some things done.

When I retired I decided to spread the chores out during the workweek instead of having to do them all on the weekend. It had worked pretty well until I got involved in detecting. When you're trying to investigate a murder or prove to yourself that there had been a murder, you had to talk to people when they were there. Face it, the world isn't retired and you have to adjust your schedule to fit.

I paused around lunch time and had some leftovers that heated up nicely. A friend had recently introduced me to a mixture of iced tea and lemonade called half-and-half or an Arnold Palmer. I had no idea why a retired professional golfer from Latrobe, Pennsylvania, would have such a mixture named after himself. For that matter, the only other thing I knew that came from Latrobe was Rolling Rock beer. So why not a mixture of beer and lemonade? Iced tea was a southern phenomenon. At any rate, I'd become addicted to the stuff and continued to drink it during the afternoon.

The satisfaction of a chore well done was beginning to pale and the thought of being with Bobby occupying more and more of my mind, so I decided that it was time to shower and get ready to meet her.

Even in the shower nothing came to me to answer the riddle of those damn pages. So much for my subconscious coming up with the answer. I had a sneaking suspicion that my subconscious had been more interested in thinking about Bobby than clues to a murder. I couldn't blame it.

The band was playing at the Train Station, an old building downtown that used to be a train station. There were no signs of the old Louisville and Nashville tracks that used to run beside it and cut the city in half.

Parking downtown was always a problem so we'd agreed that it made more sense for us to take one car. I stopped by her house on the way to the bar to pick her up. Having been raised right I parked my car and walked up to her door and politely rang the front doorbell. I could hear her footsteps as she walked across the hardwood floor. She opened the door and there she was dressed in black from her black boots, black jeans, and black silk blouse with a scooped neckline and wide sleeves. Peasant blouse was the description that popped into my head. There were points of color, a silver belt buckle, silver bracelets and earrings, bright green eyes and her silver white hair. I felt my heart hammer at my chest.

"Wow, you look like why they decided to have a party." I wasn't sure exactly what that meant, but as I was rewarded by one of her megawatt smiles it didn't really matter.

"Let me get my purse." She turned and went back into the house. I glanced around and noticed an overnight bag by the door.

I had slung the bag over my shoulder by the time she returned.

. . .

The old building had been converted into a number of different venues over the years since the railway had shut down. But it always seemed to come back to a bar/restaurant. In it's current incarnation it had an outdoor stage separate from the restaurant that was covered against the elements. In other words the band was protected. In front of the stage was an uncovered, open area where people could sit, stand, dance, and listen to the music. To one side of the open area was a stockade fence that kept the non-paying public out. The other side was the old train platform elevated above the ground where there were tall pub tables and chairs scattered under the overhang. It was a great place to sit, listen to music, and watch the crowd. I had never experienced this particular configuration and fell in love with it. It seemed perfect.

"What's the name of the group we're going to hear?" Members of the band were wandering across the stage checking on instruments, microphones, and other things. They looked like they knew what they were doing.

"I'm not sure," Bobby replied. "That guy in the cowboy hat is Mike Henderson. I've been a fan of his for a long time and this is his new group."

I sat back in my chair and picked up my beer. Bobby had wanted a wine cooler to start and I'd opted for a draft beer. It was football season, but it still wasn't fall. We were having warm weather drinks. Actually, I was having a year-round drink for me. Bobby had more seasonality in what she drank.

She took her eyes off of the Henderson guy long enough to look at me. "Don't get too comfortable. I told Frank we were coming to hear Mike and he said he'll see us here. We talked about it and he's got a list for you."

For old times' sake, I had tried to order Rolling Rock on tap
but they didn't have it. So then I had asked what their non-light
beers on tap were. Poor guy who was waiting on us couldn't
leave them off. I knew the feeling. I couldn't tell anybody the
last four digits of my social security number without mentally
running through the first five. Anyway after wading through all
the varieties of light, low-carb, high-fiber, and whatever else
people keep on doing to beer to make it tasteless, I was able to
get a basic lager, Yuengling, from America's oldest brewery.

I took a sip. So I wasn't going to take the rest of the day off
after all.

"Suspects? The result of your brainstorming?" Well, duh, I
thought. What else?

Bobby nodded her head and I noticed again how her curls
would fall back into place. "Yes. Frank's much better at getting
people to brainstorm than Hazel is. Hazel doesn't really like ideas that aren't hers. Frank went over the list they'd come up with
and I had to agree that Philip had gone out of his way to make
each of them angry."

"Angry enough to kill?"

She shrugged her shoulders. "I don't know about that. I've
never gotten that angry."

She even looked good shrugging her shoulders. I had to face
it. I was smitten. "I'll make it a point not to be around when you
get that angry."

"See to it that you're not the one that makes me that angry!"

We laughed and agreed that would the best solution.

The guy in the cowboy hat announced that the band would
start their first set in fifteen minutes and then they cleared the
stage. I saw Frank emerge from the crowd that was in the desig-
nated smoking area. No roof over their heads but some part of

the outdoors was for smokers and the other part for nonsmokers. I really hadn't given it any thought before but the antismoking crusade must be making life difficult for non-tobacco smokers. Those individuals that wanted to slip a little illegal drug use unnoticed in the tobacco smoke were losing their cover as the anti-tobacco campaign drove smokers into hiding. I guess both now waited until dark before lighting up. In the era I grew up in, good music and the smell of marijuana were inevitably intertwined. I don't suppose I should miss the tobacco smell.

I stood when Frank approached the table. He was carrying a plastic cup of beer and I could see that whatever brand it was it wasn't one of the light ones. It was way too dark for that. While I don't automatically dislike anybody that drinks beer that has a misspelling in its name, the fact that he didn't was a plus.

He blew through his mustache making it flair—a habit he probably wasn't even aware of. "Bobby." He nodded in her direction then turned to me. "Crawford."

"Frank." I replied.

We shook hands.

"Bobby just told me that you were going to be here too." I pointed at the plastic cup. "Can I buy you another?"

He glanced at his cup. "Sure. Might as well let the man pay for it. You are on an expense account, aren't you, Mister Detective Man?"

There was an Arlo Guthrie-ish sound to mister-detective-man, which took some of the hostility out of it. "Actually, mister detective man thought he was out on a date and hadn't even thought about expense accounts." I looked around trying to spot the waiter.

Frank walked over to Bobby and gave her a hug. "So, out on a date, huh? Is mister-detective-man going to get lucky?" Bobby punched him in the arm. I blinked. It looked like a pretty solid hit.

She laughed. "He's got a hell-of-a-lot better chance than you ever would."

Frank rubbed his arm. "Are we all ready for another round?"

"We would be if I could find our waiter."

"Ready for another round?" The guy appeared at my elbow and I jumped.

"Yeah, and add a Sam Adams in a go cup to it," said Frank.

Bobby decided to drop the cooler part and just go with a glass of wine. I sent the waiter off with the drink orders and a request for two menus.

"So I hear you've got a list and you've checked it twice. Well, that you've checked it with Bobby, anyway."

"I asked around like you suggested." He reached into the back pocket of his jeans and brought out several folded sheets of paper. He tapped them on the tabletop. "Thanks for the information on paraffin tests. That's good to know."

"Thought there might be some miscommunication between Captain Ward and yourself. He doesn't care what you and Kent do on your walks."

He handed me the pieces of paper and I unfolded them. There were three pages. I glanced at the top of each page and noted the names at the top, centered, and in bold type, Joyce Fines, Calvin Beck, and Bernard Charles. I looked at Frank and then at Bobby. "So is the only thing they have in common their hatred of Philip Douglas?"

"Do you mean would they have teamed up to kill him?" Frank shrugged. "I doubt they even know each other. The Press has published some of their works over the years. None of them were unknowns as far as the Press is concerned."

The waiter showed up with our drinks and two menus. He took away Bobby's and my empty glasses. Frank still had a half inch of beer in his.

"You want to tell me about these people?" I took a sip of my beer.

Frank shook his head. "Not particularly. I never cared for snitches and don't see where this is much different. I don't know all the facts, but I know that Philip made these people very mad, extremely mad in fact, during the last three or four weeks. It's like Philip was working overtime or something. Usually he kept it down to one or two outraged individuals a month." He drained the rest of his cup in one swallow. "I'd rather tell you than tell the police, that's all. Read what you've got. Then if you've got questions you can call me, or Bobby for that matter. She knows most of them or knows their story."

I stared at him for a minute and he stared back. I nodded, folded up the pages and slipped them into my back pocket. "So what do you know about this group?" I nodded toward the stage as the musicians started to return.

Frank accepted my attempt to change the subject with a nod. "Out of Nashville right now. Don't know where each one comes from. Each of them has been playing long enough that none of them can be overnight sensations. They just got together a year ago, I think. They've paid their dues. It's original stuff." He smiled. "And it isn't easy-listening for sure." He stood up. "If we're through here for tonight, I'd like to get more than a contact high before they start to play." He nodded to Bobby, "I'll see you Monday." Then he walked back into the crowd, which had grown significantly while we talked.

I drummed my fingers on the table and then turned to face Bobby. She looked at me questioningly. "I'm not sure I can ex-

press this but I believe we're at the beginning of our relationship—just the start." I paused and was relieved to see her nod in
agreement. "And investigating a murder isn't a great way—
well," I corrected myself. "Certainly not a typical way to get to
know each other better, anyway."

She flashed her megawatt smile at me and chuckled deep
within her throat. "So you don't want to use investigating me as
a potential murderer as a way to get to know me better?"

"Not so much," I admitted. We smiled at each other for a
moment. "Since you've got an alibi."

"I was with you!"

"Right, there is that. So you're not much of a suspect as far
as murder goes. But if that's my only chance to get to know you
better—the only way it's going to happen? I'll take it."

Bobby looked at me, cocking her head to the side as if she
was getting a better look at what was sitting across from her. "I
think there are other ways for us to get to know each other better
and I bet you do too." This time it was a small smile on her lips.
"So what do you have in mind, Ford? What next?"

After I'd taken Bobby back to her house I ended up wandering around aimlessly in my house and yard, unable to concentrate on anything. I finally put Tan in the car and we drove out to the cemetery where Eleanor is buried. The Black had never known her, so it didn't make sense to bring him, besides he hates riding in the car. Tan, on the other hand, loves to go for rides. Tan and I had been out here before, a number of times. If you'd asked, I couldn't have told you why we had come, not for certain.

I parked near the entrance and we made our way past the rows of headstones as we walked along the curved roadway. I had Tan's lead in my hand in case we needed to pay attention to the leash law, but we had the place pretty much to our selves. Tan was enjoying all the different smells, nose to the ground as she wandered around me as I walked down the road. Idly I looked at the family names with no real thought involved. The day held the hint of fall in the way the light fell, but there was no nip to the air—a lack of heat was all that fall could promise.

I stopped at the Crawford plot where my parents and Eleanor were buried and walked across the grass to look at the individual grave markers that were set flush to the ground. There's a song about how what's important is the little dash between the dates. What you did with the time in between, not when you started or stopped.

I nodded my head and snapped my fingers at Tan. She looked up, ears cocked, tail wagging. "Let's go girl." If I'd come out here looking for answers, I didn't think I found any. But I felt better and it was time to move on.

After the automobile accident that took Eleanor's life, my life was a blur for a while. When I came to I realized that the Casserole Brigade, as other widowers have dubbed them, had moved in without my noticing. Women of varying ages and marital status were suddenly deciding that I needed the equivalent of a "home-cooked meal."

Don't misunderstand me. There's nothing so southern as the desire to bring food to people suffering sorrow. I'm not sure why we do it, but we do. But amid the old friends and family bringing comfort there are those whose motives are more complicated and complex. The married ones generally had somebody they wanted me to meet, supporting the general consensus that "the way to a man's heart is through his stomach" and its corollary "men can't cook." However, I do cook—better than some of the ladies who were bringing food over. Some got the idea after I suggested that their recipe needed a touch more tarragon, oregano, garlic, or real butter instead of margarine. And some I suggested needed more than just a touch.

Some were better cooks and more persistent. One was particularly inventive in that she tried to use her children, who might have been perceived as a detriment when chasing a childless widower, as a means to draw us closer. Something good did come out of it, as often happens in life. In this case it was The Black.

The woman I am referring to, who shall remain nameless, had a daughter who volunteered at the local no-kill animal shelter. She was old enough to be a volunteer, but not old enough to drive. So I was asked to do a little favor or two by picking up the girl at the shelter and taking her to wherever she needed to be. Mom was trying to get me involved in her life. The daughter was aware of what was going on and was embarrassed, but she did need a ride. I liked the girl but her mother was a bit too much for me. It was a relief when she shifted her sights to a recently widowed doctor and dropped me cold.

Anyway, while I was still a target, one day I arrived at the shelter before the end of the girl's shift and we had to wait for her relief. It was just a small two-bedroom house that had been donated to the animal rescue league, which had converted it into a home for homeless cats.

I thought at the time that the neighbors would have been happier if the league had sold the house and used the proceeds in their work but maybe they consoled themselves with the knowledge that at least it wasn't a real cat house.

Anyway, we were standing in what had been the kitchen of this house when the girl, Jaclyn I think her name was, offered to show me some of her favorite residents. I agreed with the smug assurance that there were no dogs in the house. I considered myself a dog person at the time with no need for a cat.

The house had been split into three or four zones, as I recall. The kitchen was for cats with special dietary needs. The living room/dining room area was for normal cats who all got along with one another. One bedroom was for submissive cats that would have been bullied by the other cats, as it was explained to me, and the second bedroom for kittens. The doors into the bedrooms had been replaced with glass storm doors so you could see what was on the other side. Looking back, I bet that was so the staff would have a chance of keeping cats from darting out of or in to rooms they weren't supposed to be in.

That's obviously what had happened in the kitten room. There was a sign on the door saying that the kittens were in quarantine because of an outbreak of conjunctivitis or pinkeye signed by a local veterinarian. The public was barred from entering for at least another week. And there, in the midst of kittens of all colors, shapes, and sizes, was a full-grown cat, jet-black fur, with bright green eyes. He was staring up at me. I stared back. "What's with the adult cat?" I pointed at the door. "The black?"

Jaclyn, who by this time had one cat draped over her shoulders and another in her arms, glanced at the door. "Johnny? That's his name, well, that's what we call him while he's here. It might not be his forever name that he gets when he's adopted into his forever home. He likes to play with the kittens. That's why he's in there. He was playing with them when the vet said they had to be quarantined."

I watched as the cat flipped the end of his tail from side to side as some kittens tried to pounce on it. He was still staring at me so I hunkered down until I was almost eye-level with the cat and met his gaze. As soon as I squatted down, cats in the room I was in closed in on me. They'd been rubbing up against my legs but now one jumped on my back and another tried to climb into what passed for my lap.

"Johnny has been here since he was a kitten himself, almost two years now." Jaclyn's face fell. "I don't know if he'll ever find his forever home. He's waited so long."

Jaclyn's shift relief came in at that point and we were able to leave.

A week later Johnny was out of quarantine. He had his name changed to one that we agreed was more fitting and came to live with Tan and me.

. . .

We pulled into the driveway. I got out and opened the back car door for Tan. Together we entered the house to meet The Black sitting on the counter by the door. He met my gaze and, seemingly satisfied, dropped soundlessly to the floor, rubbed up against my pants legs, and then turned and strolled away. Tan went straight to the water bowl and then to her bed.

It was time to get to work.

I'd been trying to figure out the timeline of the murder, how the timing worked. How did the murderer know when Philip would be in his office available to be killed? I was trying to think like a murderer, I guess. How frustrating would it be to work yourself up to being able to murder him, getting into the building in order to kill him and then not finding him there to murder? I could almost see the killer shooting someone else—or running away in relief, never to try again.

At first I'd wondered if Philip had a standing appointment with his barber so that he was always getting a haircut on a certain Wednesday of every month. Habits like that would help a killer, but that got shot down. Frank said he hadn't noticed any pattern to Philip's haircut appointments saying that they showed up on the calendar the day of or maybe the day before the appointment.

I snapped my fingers. A calendar, from the way Frank had described it, it was a universally accessible, user-friendly group calendar. That's right. And he had said that Philip's secretary had to keep his entries up to date for him—or had Bobby made that comment? Never mind, it didn't matter. Web-based? He hadn't said, but at a guess it would have to be—my guess anyway. And if it was on the web, how secure was it? I knew enough about computer security to cringe at that thought. It was a simple equation. The more accessible and the more user-friendly you made a site, the less secure it was. It was just a fact of nature—human nature anyway.

I sat down at my computer, opened up a terminal emulator, and used secure shell to connect to the university's main academic computer. I needed to be sure I was querying the university's domain name server when I ran nslookup. It's a simple program that you run from the command line. I started trying different names trying to see how clever they had been in naming the website. Since the university was hosting it, it had to be on the university's domain so that would be the end of the URL, but what was the start? Sometimes you protect a site by not publishing its URL. It's called "security through obscurity." Which works OK unless somebody knows it exists and is willing to spend some time finding it. I tried combinations of Press, university, and calendar and got a response after about three or four variations—calpress. Sweet, the webmaster must be an old Unix guy—holding to the "eight-dot-three" naming convention. It had the same IP address as the university's main web server so it was a virtual address.

I opened up a browser on my computer and typed the name in the address bar and got nothing—just the page not found error. "Not found?" I murmured to my self. I copy-and-pasted the name field from the nslookup response in case I'd mistyped the name, then the IP address itself. Got the same response.

"So they did put some security on it." As I wasn't being prompted for a name and password, the webmaster had decided to limit access to the university's domain. Easy enough to do if you could modify the Apache httpd config file.

I shut down the browser and connected to the university's network via a VPN, a virtual private network, reopened the browser, repasted the URL, and bingo—there it was—the common appointment calendar for the Press. I could see who was taking leave and when, what meetings were scheduled for today, tomorrow, next week—and who had been invited and had accepted. It was so simple it made me want to cry. This was not going to help narrow the field of suspects. Just to be sure I checked last Wednesday. Philip's appointment to get his haircut was there. So if somebody was interested they could find out when Philip would be out of the office and where the rest of the staff was too. All they had to have was access to the Internet—and authorization to connect via a VPN.

I wondered if it would do any good to try and get access to the log files on the server. Might be worth looking into if the administrator had set up logs for individual virtual addresses. I emailed the head of the area who was responsible for administering those servers asking for the logs to be saved if they still existed and I made sure to copy Captain Ward and the provost.

Jim Ward was sitting on my screen porch and drinking my coffee while he looked at the pages Frank had given me.

"Tell me again why we're meeting here?"

"Because your coffee is better."

I nodded. He was right. My coffee was better but his office equipment was much better than mine. I'd gone out to the drugstore to make photocopies so that we both would have a copy to look at.

"Yeah, but you've got photocopiers and all that other office equipment at the police station."

Jim looked at me. "So buy a photocopier. What are you spending all of the university's money on if not equipment?"

"Well, it looked like I was going to be spending it on coffee beans and half-and-half."

Jim sat back in his chair holding his coffee cup in both hands. "You need to take this serious, Crawford. If you want to do it.

"Have you settled on a daily rate with Victoria? Have you even checked on how you get a license to be a private detective in this state?"

"I've been thinking about getting business cards."

Ward snorted and shook his head. "Business cards. That's funny. You remember that what you are doing can be dangerous, don't you? People who start resorting to murder as a solution to their problems have a tendency to keep on using that as a solution to other problems—like somebody trying to convict them of murder."

"Now, Jim." I tried to protest.

"Don't 'now Jim' me, Crawford. Hunting people is a dangerous business and I'll be damned if you'll act like it isn't. Hell, enforcing traffic laws can get a cop killed! How much more dangerous is a known murderer?"

I stopped myself from pointing out that this was an unknown murderer—that being the problem. He was right. Heck, part of the reason I was doing this was the feeling of excitement I'd gotten when I'd closed in on the truth about Sean Thomas's death—murder, that is.

"There is no private investigator licensing for the state of Alabama although a state business license is required to operate any business. Certain cities like Mobile and Birmingham have their own licensing requirements." I hoped it sounded like I was quoting.

"Certain cities including Shelbyville." Jim stared at me. "Get your damn license and then you can meet me at the police station. Until then I'm drinking your damn coffee and you can pay for your own stupid photocopies. OK?"

"Right."

After a pause we went back to the three suspects that Frank had identified—Joyce Fines, Calvin Beck, and Bernard Charles.

I had read the descriptions over the weekend, but Jim was going over them for the first time. I followed along in my copy while Jim read his.

According to the brief biography Frank had included, Joyce Fines was a wildlife ecologist here at the university—a professor emerita. The Press had published her first popular book—meaning the first one she'd written for the general public—twenty-five years ago. It had sold slowly but steadily ever since then and was considered to be one of the Press's successes. Joyce had contacted the Press about updating and releasing a

new version. After some back and forth, Philip had flatly rejected the project and had gone so far as to drop the original book
from the catalog. Frank noted that it had been the prior Press director that had published the book. Philip didn't like being reminded of what his predecessor had done. He told Fines that he
didn't like the book and didn't think much of her as an author.
She had lost her temper with Philip and suggested that it was
people like him who gave snakes a bad reputation. She told him
that he was toxic waste and didn't deserve to be breathing.

"Toxic waste?" Ward raised his eyebrows questioningly.

"Bobby says that pond scum has a place in nature, in the en-
vironment, but not toxic waste."

"Hmmm." Ward didn't look convinced. "You figure being
told you're a lousy writer is grounds to kill a man?"

"Beats me. I've never written a book."

Ward scratched his chin. He seemed to be having a little
trouble buying Joyce's motivation. Finally he shrugged. "People
get killed for some damn strange reasons. I guess that's one of
the strangest I've heard of. What about the next guy?"

The next guy was Calvin Beck—a published nonfiction writer and an aspiring novelist. He had published a number of articles and short stories of the "hook and bullet" genre and was
now trying to graduate to full-length novels. He'd submitted his
novel directly to Philip. Philip then proceeded to slash the manuscript to pieces and demand extensive changes. Calvin had done
all that Philip asked and resubmitted the novel. At that point
Philip refused the novel because the author had made all the
changes he had suggested.

"Huh?" said Ward. He looked up from the page. "After the
author had done what he told him to do?"

"Yeah, Bobby said the guy needed killing."

Frank had gone on to explain that Philip had decided that authors who accept all the changes editors suggest lack the necessary "backbone" to defend their work—a lack of passion. He felt that if Calvin had gone out on a book tour to promote his own book he'd have ended up apologizing for it. Calvin had shown plenty of "passion" at that point. He'd cussed Philip out "down-one-side-and-up-the-other" and, before storming out of the building, had promised to "see Philip in hell even if he had to go there himself."

"Got to say I'd have been mighty angry at that line of reasoning." Jim tapped the page with his forefinger.

"It might interest you to know that 'hook and bullet' means that he writes about fishing and hunting." I'd had to ask Bobby but didn't see any reason to mention that to Jim. "And Bobby said he was more bullet than hook. Didn't write that much about fishing."

"Might not mean much, but I guess knowing which end of a rifle is which is evidence of a sort." He picked up the third sheet of paper. "Did you save the best for last?"

Actually I hadn't even thought to do that. They were still in the order that Frank had given them to me. "See what you think."

For his third suspect, Frank had picked Bernard Charles, the son of Adele Morgan Charles. She was deceased but she had been a famous chronicler of the civil rights movement particularly in Alabama and on this campus. She had written a series of books about her and her colleagues' experiences—none of which were particularly flattering to the state or its institutions of higher education. No one had ever challenged the veracity of what she had written but lots of people hadn't appreciated being written about. Philip's predecessor had decided to publish her works and had upset a number of people in the state.

"You ever read anything she wrote?" Jim stopped to look across the table at me—his finger holding his place on the page.

I shook my head. "Don't think so. Did you?"

"If you had, you'd remember it. People in the black community say she got it right—dead solid right. Pretty impressive for a white woman from Detroit." He dropped his eyes back to the page.

Bernard wanted the Press to reissue those books and publish them as a collection, along with her last book, which she had started but he had finished after her death. A book in which she traced what had happened in the movement in the following decades.

"Bet some people would be happy if that book never saw the light of day." Jim was so quiet it almost seemed like he was talking to himself.

Philip had no intention of publishing anything that was potentially controversial, not to mention reissuing books that had been controversial. The Press held the copyrights and he swore that "as long as he was director" those books would never be reprinted.

Frank went on to note that Bernard had kept his temper and had refrained from saying anything more than, "At least now I know what to do. My mother's books will be reissued. I'll see to that."

"Frank appears to have interpreted that as a death threat."

"So would the district attorney." Jim was staring at the sheets of paper. "And this guy was like this with everybody? Almost seems a shame to try to find out who the murderer was.

"Any more coffee?"

I pushed the thermos over to him.

"I don't know, Crawford. Like I say, murder is either personal or random and this one doesn't feel like there's any randomness to it at all.

"Still we've eliminated most of the Press employees. With the exception of Fulmer and Manning they all have multiple witnesses that clear them. Those two have just got each other to vouch for their whereabouts."

I started to speak and he waved me off. "Oh, I know you are sure they were both blowing smoke at the time, but it doesn't take that long to smoke a joint. They could have come back."

"You seriously believe that they got stoned on marijuana, came back to the Press, shot their boss, and then went home? Is the police department using *Reefer Madness* as a training film? Hell, the worst thing that probably happened was they got the munchies."

Jim grinned sheepishly and shrugged his shoulders. "OK. So it's weak."

"What about Hazel Murphy? Did she tell you what she refused to tell Harry?"

"I haven't had a chance to interrogate her. She's coming in this afternoon."

"So what do we do next? You want to call these three in? Or wait until you've eliminated all the employees."

Jim sat back in his chair, his coffee cup cradled in his huge hands. "I'm thinking that's just what your provost doesn't want the police doing. He's thinking you'd do it quieter, lower profile, kid gloves, that kind of thing.

"Oh, don't get me wrong. I'll start the routine background checks on all three. We'll find out if any one of them has a history of anger management issues."

"Yeah," I had to agree but it seemed like a strange way to progress. Still, what did I know? This was only my second murder investigation.

"No looking at video in this case, Crawford. This is one where you need to go out and ask questions. Get some answers. See if you can spot the lies because, I'm telling you, everybody lies to the police and they'll lie to you too."

"I was thinking," I started to speak.

"No harm in that."

"I'd like to run these names by somebody else. See if another party would agree with Frank's assessment."

"I thought you said Bobby agreed with Frank? That he'd asked other people at the Press?"

I nodded my head in agreement.

"Then who are you going ask? Provost George?"

"I might, but I was thinking about somebody else—a member of the Press's board of directors. Rufus said that Steven Stefenson had been on the board for so long that he was the institutional memory."

"Stefenson? That's the name of the building the Press is in, right?"

"Yes, his uncle—the uncle of the guy I'm thinking about talking to—was the founder of the Press. He—the uncle—was Philip's predecessor."

Jim frowned. "Can he keep a secret? We don't want to have a list of our suspects floating around."

I pointed at the sheets of paper. "We already do, Jim. I doubt that Frank can keep his mouth shut. Besides I asked the Press employees to discuss among themselves who might have done it. But I'll ask him to be discreet."

. . .

I went looking for Steven's card and found it in my coat pocket. Not quite sure why I was stalling, I entered his information in my address book. Hmmm, he didn't include his email address. I made a note to be sure and include mine on my card when I got around to designing it. I picked up the phone and dialed his number. On the fourth ring he answered.

"Yes?" His voice was cold and distant.

"Dr. Stefenson?"

"Yes."

"This is James Crawford, Provost George introduced us at the University Club?"

"Yes."

Damn. The jerk was certainly making this difficult. "At the time you told me that I should call you if you could be of any assistance."

"I remember."

"Well, I was wondering if that offer still stood."

"I'm not the kind of man that makes an offer like that and then forgets it."

Great, I thought to myself, this is like pulling hen's teeth.

"Mr. Crawford, if you would bypass these pleasantries and ask your question we could continue with our lives. I, for one, have other things to do today."

"I asked the Press staff to think about who might have wanted to kill Philip Douglas."

"Indeed."

If anything his voice got even colder. "Frank Manning was able to give me the names of three authors who had loud arguments with the director over the last month or so."

Total silence on the other end. "And the provost told me that you knew quite a lot about the history of the Press. That I would do well to consult you." That wasn't exactly what Rufus had said, of course.

"How kind of the provost—and accurate, I confess. So you want me to confirm Mr. Manning's opinion?"

He seemed to be thawing slightly—either from my naturally charming nature or my buttering him up. "Yes, sir."

"I rather think that Mr. Manning has done an adequate job, but I am willing to comment on it. What names did he give you?"

One by one I told him the three names that were on Frank's list and he confirmed that he knew them and that, indeed, they had all had recent disagreements with poor Philip. That it had seemed as if Philip had almost gone out of his way to anger them.

Steven even warmed up enough to say that they were likely suspects—at least from his limited experience regarding murders. He preferred nonfiction over the popular potboilers referred to as murder mysteries.

I thanked him for his assistance and he encouraged me to call him again if I had any need of further assistance.

I hung up the phone feeling like I'd been patted on the head and told to go out and play. TB was sitting on the other end of my desk. "Yeah, now I understand the 'pat' part of patronizing. But, heck, I guess I can take a little condescension now and again. After all, I'm not a cat."

The Black didn't appear impressed with my logic and hopped down and left the room.

Armed with Frank's list and Steven's confirmation, I picked up the phone to call the provost's office—to call Victoria more accurately. Somebody was going to have to help me get in touch with these people and I couldn't think of anybody better at it.

Victoria was able to set up an interview with Professor Emerita Fines that very afternoon. She had agreed to meet with me at her home, which was located in an old subdivision east of town. It was an interesting design for a subdivision. I could understand why it hadn't caught on.

The road through the subdivision was one-way. So no matter if your destination was the next to last house, you still had to start at the beginning of the subdivision and drive all the way through it. On the way, you'd wind your way up and down the hills through the heavily wooded areas being careful not to take the wrong forks that would lead you off of the main road through some twists and turns and back farther along. Like I said, it was an old subdivision. Nowadays they would have packed three or four times as many houses in it and there would be two or three more entrances—and fewer trees.

I found the driveway only because Victoria had given me very detailed directions. I eased off the main road onto a gravel drive that was scattered with pine straw and fallen oak leaves. The drive dropped quickly and turned to the left, then back to the right as the driveway zigzagged down the hillside. I really couldn't see more than ten or fifteen feet ahead as densely wooded as it was.

I was considering what I would do if while I was coming in I met somebody coming out when I noticed the turnouts. So there was a way, but neither one of us was going to do it at any speed. The driveway leveled out and I drove into a clearing where an old battered pickup was parked next to a new Prius. About what I would expect an ecologist to drive. Victoria had told me to park here and walk to the house. Doing what I was told, I pulled up next to the hybrid, got out and was immediately spellbound.

It took a second to bring it into focus but now I could see where the pine trees and dogwoods left off and the house started. Frank Lloyd Wright would have been pleased. Hell, he'd have been proud to have designed it. I started down the path that led to the front door when I realized the path included a footbridge. There was a small stream running between me and the house. I had heard the gentle gurgling but hadn't really taken notice of what was causing it. I wondered what a naturalist would call it— a rivulet? It looked crystal clear. Acting on a hunch, I squatted down and put my hand in the water—it was almost ice cold— spring fed. I stood up and dried my hand on my handkerchief.

When I reached the middle of the bridge I just stopped and stood there, turning around and absorbing the serenity. I was maybe four, five miles from campus? It was amazing.

I turned back around and there was a woman standing outside the front door smiling broadly at me. She must have come out while I had my back to the door. She was tall, slender, with curly gray hair framing her face. She was wearing khakis and a blue chambray shirt, open at the neck.

"I'm glad you like it." Her voice was deeper than I expected and a little husky.

"Like it? It's wonderful! How far are we from the center of town?"

"Oh four and half, five miles from the courthouse."

"And light years from the strip malls and asphalt." I walked up to her and held out my hand. "I'm James Crawford, and it's a pleasure to meet you."

Her grip was firm and dry. "I like people who can appreciate what I've got out here. It's taken a little work."

"I can see that. It took a lot of work to make it look this natural."

Chuckling she looked around, "Some work and lots of time. I didn't plant these trees yesterday. Come with me, Mr. Crawford. Let's find some chairs and discuss whatever it is that made you want to come out here and talk to an old woman."

I followed her through the screen door and into the house wondering how Victoria had justified our meeting. I was beginning to wonder if I was here under false pretenses. As I wondered how to proceed, I glanced around. There were screens on the open windows and the house was filled with the smells of pine and fresh air. The house itself appeared to be built around a center courtyard that was a mixture of flagstone and ground cover.

We were in what must be the living room. There were bookcases built into the walls on either side of the empty fireplace and several chairs and small tables scattered around the room. There was no sign of a television, which really wasn't that much of a surprise. A portrait of a young woman hung above the mantle and the mantle itself was covered in what looked like trophies and awards.

She pointed at an old rocker and said, "That should hold your weight." She smiled again. "Some of my furniture has been in the family longer than I have so I have to protect my old friends."

The deep smile lines that marked her face were clear signs of years spent enjoying life. I stood in front of the rocker and waited until she sat before doing the same. The rocker creaked, but not alarmingly so. Her armchair had a high back that framed her head and shoulders so it looked almost like a throne.

"So what have I done to have Rufus George send one of the university's computer gurus out to visit me?

"That is the Crawford you are isn't it? You helped some colleagues of mine set up motion-triggered cameras for a field study. They were impressed with you and I was impressed with their findings."

I frantically searched my memory. I'd worked with a bunch of faculty members and their graduate students but motion-triggered cameras out in the field didn't immediately ring any bells. "That sounds like something I should have done, but . . ."

"Oh it wasn't here in Alabama. You couldn't put expensive equipment like that out in the woods around here and expect to find it when you got back. This was over on the Savannah River Site near Augusta, Georgia. You advised them on what technology to use."

"I never had any problem spending other people's money." I still didn't remember her colleagues, but it was certainly something I used to do. I decided I'd better clear up any misunderstanding before we went any further.

"But that's not why I'm here. I suppose you've heard about Philip Douglas, the director of the University Press?"

She lifted her chin, looked me dead in the eye, and stopped being friendly. Her pale blue eyes glinted with frost. "I would appreciate it if you'd not mention that name again in my presence."

There was plenty of steel underneath Joyce Fines's charming exterior. "You do know that he's dead, don't you? Murdered almost a week ago. The funeral is going to be tomorrow afternoon."

She sniffed and looked down her nose at me. "Don't expect me to mourn for that one. Burying him is a waste of land."

I plowed on. "And making comments like that is how you become 'a person of interest' in a police investigation."

"Aren't you the man who retired from the university so you wouldn't have to work for a man you hated? And then came out of retirement to prove he'd been murdered?"

The change of subject startled me. So much for feeling guilty about meeting her under false pretenses.

She continued. "After the provost's assistant called, I wondered why I was being asked to meet with a high-tech computer type, which is how you'd been described to me years ago—by my friends. I decided to do some checking. I'm out of touch with what's going on at the university now but I still know people who aren't. What made you suspect poison? And what made you care?"

"The murderer—she didn't stop with the man I hated. Curiosity? I'm not really sure." I found myself answering her questions in reverse order. "Trying to come up with a theory supported by facts?"

The corner of her mouth gave a small twitch. "Sounds almost scientific. Academic curiosity?"

I held out my hands, palms up. "Whatever you want to call it, I believe I should have explained the purpose of my visit from the beginning—or had Victoria do so."

Dr. Fines cocked her head at me. "Maybe—maybe not. I don't remember telling the fauna and flora I researched about my credentials or the purpose of the study. There can be reasons why subjects are misled about the purpose of experiments—quite sound reasons in the fields of psychology and criminology. Are you a student of criminal behavior? I admit my knowledge is limited to murder mysteries."

"Until recently that was the extent of my knowledge. Perry Mason, Jim Rockford, Spenser, and the like."

"Rex Stout? Dorothy Sayers? Dick Francis?"

"Yep, them too." I agreed.

"Well, then." She sat back in her chair. "Then I'm in capable hands. I should have trusted Rufus George more.

"I despised the man, but I didn't kill him and can prove it. One," she held up her index finger. "The man was shot dead. I am a terrible marksman and would never have depended on my shooting ability had I decided to kill him. And, if I had decided to kill him he would be dead.

Two," she held up her middle finger. "I was in Birmingham last Wednesday afternoon attending a party for a fellow ecologist who is retiring from the university there. You can ask anyone in the department. They all saw me."

"So if you had done it you would have done it another way and, besides, you were someplace else?"

"Yes," she agreed regally. "I have an ironclad alibi."

. . .

"Nope, I'd say she doesn't have a pet—neither a cat or a dog." Tan was watching me intently. I was in the kitchen slicing cheese, which explained her interest. Tan was certain that I was going to drop some kind of food even though it rarely happened. Hope springs eternal in the heart of a dog.

The Black wasn't paying any attention. He didn't like the idea of a cat being a pet—that was for other, inferior animals. He had found his old orange mouse that had been lost for some time. At this point the only reason to call it a mouse was the fact that it had started out as a small, stuffed toy mouse. It was still orange and small but there were no clues as to what it had been. The whiskers hadn't lasted a week to the best of my memory. The tail had hung around for some time. TB had liked carrying it by the tail as he stalked through the house—the big cat and his prey.

I put the cheese on a plate and added crackers. Ward was going to stop by to talk about my interview with Joyce Fines and have a beer. I got out a can of salted peanuts and poured the last of them into a wooden bowl. I'd been trying to lose a little weight by eating less. It was a novel idea, but held some real promise. It had worked before. Anyway, I was hungry and wanted to make sure I had some protein in my stomach when the beer hit it.

Tan raced to the door and started barking. This was a pretty good sign that she knew who was coming up to the door. Strangers didn't get barked at until they actually rang the doorbell. Of course with Tan barking her fool head off my friends never needed to ring the doorbell. I tried to remember if she'd started barking at Bobby yet, but couldn't remember. Probably not, I got excited enough—the dog didn't need to.

I opened the door and Ward walked into the room, handed me a paper sack, and knelt down to pat Tan. "That's a good girl. Glad to see me?" Tan was about to fall all over herself with delight.

In the bag was a six-pack of beer. I put it on the counter and pulled out a bottle. "Red Stripe! What's the occasion?" He didn't always bring the beer and we generally didn't pay for the more expensive brands.

Jim stood up and walked over to the sink to wash his hands and face. Tan liked to lick her favorites. "Best reason in the world to buy really good beer—it was on sale."

"You're right about that. And the best reason in the world to drink really good beer is that it's really good."

There were a couple of lager glasses in the freezer so I got them out. I try to keep some cold since it's hard to spontaneously pull out chilled glasses if you're not prepared.

Jim had already scooped a handful of peanuts out of the bowl and was popping them into his mouth one at a time.

I put the glasses down, took another beer out of the bag and set it next to one of the glasses. "The opener is in the drawer next to the sink." I took the time to put the beer in the refrigerator, taking them out of the cardboard carrier they came in. I know lots of people leave the glass bottles in the carrier but I'm too cheap to chill cardboard.

"Did you break her down and get a written confession? Is she waiting at the police station for me to come and arrest her? Did you think to use a rubber hose when you went to beat the truth out of her?"

"What's with you?" Ward wasn't usually so enthusiastic, particularly at the end of the day.

"How often do you find Red Stripe marked down 75 percent?"

"Where?"

"Doesn't matter. I bought all they had." He smiled. "Since this six-pack was cold, I thought I'd share."

I used the opener on the other bottle. I couldn't remember if the brewer had upgraded to the twist-top or not and didn't really care. There was something a little more civilized in using an opener.

"You have a kind and generous heart. As to today's suspect, she certainly didn't confess to anything—except she loathed Philip Douglas." I picked up the cheese board and nodded at the bowl of peanuts. "Grab that and let's go sit on the porch. I'll tell you what I learned and you can tell me why Hazel Murphy won't tell anybody but you where she was when Philip Douglas was killed."

Jim went expressionless, beyond the deadpan look he used in poker games. "Oh, that. Forget her, she's not a suspect."

If I'd been Harry, I'd have dropped it—but I'm not, and I didn't. "How so? She show you her special 'get-out-of-jail" card? If smoking dope isn't an alibi, what's hers?"

If I'd been Harry, I think Jim would have bitten my head off—as it was he had to count to ten and then nodded. "Fair enough. She was meeting with her oncologist. They were discussing treatment options—such as they are. The oncologist confirmed her alibi—and the prognosis."

"Ouch," was all I could think to say.

"Nobody at the Press knows—hell, she didn't really know until that meeting. Anyway, she apologized for being so rude to Harry—said she 'wasn't handling things as well as she might have hoped.'"

"Shit." I was stuck on four-letter words.

"Yeah. Sometimes this investigating can be a lot of fun." Jim shook himself and then took a long swallow of beer.

"So, Fines admitted she loathed the deceased?" Jim's hand swallowed up the bowl and he followed me out onto the screen porch. "She didn't deny her motive? Or did she claim that 'she didn't really mean it' when she wished him dead?"

"She said that burying him was a waste of space, but don't get excited. She's got an alibi."

I pulled some paper napkins out of the holder that was on the table, gave Jim one, and took one for myself. Jim helped himself to the cheese and crackers and put several on his napkin.

"What kind of alibi?" He took a bite of cheese and cracker.

"Ironclad, according to her. She was at a retirement party in Birmingham."

Jim snorted. "Birmingham's not that far away—that's a cocktail party alibi."

I raised one eyebrow questioningly. My mouth was full of peanuts.

"Anybody ever ask you if you'd seen somebody at a cocktail party? Sometimes you can't remember if they were there or not, other times you remember them being there, but you've got no idea what time it was. Was it before the speech or afterward?

"I wouldn't write her off as a suspect until I have the Birmingham police check it out."

"She did say she was a lousy shot and if she'd been planning on killing him she would have used another weapon."

"That is an interesting way to prove your innocence." Jim looked off into the distance. "I'm not sure I've heard that one before. She wouldn't have used a gun since she couldn't be sure of killing him with one? Is that what she said?"

I took another swallow of beer and set the glass back down in the water ring the condensation had formed. I'd had various sets of coasters over the years but I'd given up on them. They never dried out properly and, because of all the humidity, they all got covered in mold sooner or later. "She said that there were two reasons she could prove she hadn't killed 'that man' as she called him. Oh, I forgot, she also told me to never mention his name to her. I don't think you'll be seeing her at the funeral."

"You should go to that, you know." Jim glanced at his empty glass and back to me.

"What? Why me?" I pointed at his glass. "You got time for another?"

"Because it would be good for you. See if you can spot some suspects we don't know about." He pushed his glass toward me. "Sure, I've got time for one more."

I stood up. "How about a light beer? Somebody brought their own and left it here."

He glared at me. "Funny man."

"Right—Red Stripe. I don't know how I'm going to get rid of the light beer."

"Pour it out."

I went into the kitchen, got two more beers out of the fridge, opened them, and walked back onto the porch.

I put one bottle down in front of Jim and then took a sip out of mine before pouring it into the glass. "You serious about going to the funeral?"

"Yes. Check out the mourners. You might learn about somebody we're not aware of who should be a suspect. Anyway, who knows? Maybe murderers are like arsonists?"

"Arsonists really hang around the fires they set?"

"That's what they tell me. I'm in homicide not arson."

I thought about the idea of a murderer attending his victim's funeral. Maybe so, maybe not. "Do you remember when it is?"

"The funeral? Nope. Check the paper." Jim scooped up the last piece of cheese.

"What about the murder weapon?"

"What about it?"

"Have you found it yet?"

"And where should we be looking?" Ward reached for some peanuts and came up empty. "This all the food you got?"

"You'll spoil your supper. I figured you'd run ballistic tests on all the rifles that could have fired the bullet."

"Oh you did, did you? And why would we do that? We normally like the murder weapon to help us find out who the murderer is. How's it going to help if we find out that one of the rifles on the wall was used to kill him? They've all been wiped clean of fingerprints."

I was floored. "But—the murder weapon . . ."

"It costs time and money to run ballistic tests and you might find this hard to believe, but both of those things are in short supply around here."

I tried to remember how other detectives approached finding the murder weapon but couldn't come up with anything. I must have looked stricken.

"Tell you what. You come up with a way to narrow down the field to two or three guns and I'll have the lab take a look at them."

"Could you tell me which ones could have fired the bullet? That might make it easier."

"Sure, I'll get you a list of the rifles and have Harry mark the ones he thinks are contenders. You can scratch off the muzzle loaders, anyway."

Ward stood up. "As you mentioned supper, I think I'd best be going. I told you that there weren't any fingerprints in the safe but Douglas's, right? Nothing in there out of the ordinary except that journal."

"I've been looking at it. Haven't gotten anywhere but I've started putting it into a database." I stood up and started cleaning off the table.

Ward made a face. "Is that going to help?" He picked up his empty bottle and glass and followed me into the kitchen.

"So far the only thing I've found is that each page has got a 1Y, 2Y, 3Y, or 4Y on it. What the heck that stands for I don't know—yet."

Ward scratched his head. "Once a year, twice a year? It might make more sense if we knew what he was keeping records on."

"Why use the letter then if everything was yearly? Poor database design. Go home."

Last night, after Ward had left, I called Bobby, ostensibly to ask if she was going to Philip Douglas's funeral but really just to hear her voice. It turned out she was going and even seemed a little surprised that I had had to ask.

The plan was for the Press to shut down at noon since all the office staff were going to the funeral at two o'clock. It was just going to be a graveside service as he had no family and hadn't been much of a churchgoer. I interpreted "not much of a church-goer" as being somewhere between agnostic and totally uninterested. It wasn't until I had hung up after talking to Bobby that I thought to wonder who had organized the service. I'd have to find out, it might be important.

Afterward, before I'd given up and gone to bed, I'd poked around with the ledger for a little while and hadn't gotten anywhere. I decided to ask Bobby to look at it as it might have something to do with the Press—some kind of method of keeping track of things? Maybe it wasn't a code after all? Anyway, I needed help and she'd offered—if there was anything she could do.

Since we were going "funeraling" as it were, it was easy enough to decide what to wear—the funeral/wedding/interview suit—dark with only a faint pattern, if any at all. With it the traditional white shirt, somber wine-colored tie, and black dress shoes. I wondered what single men did in other sections of the country. How did you know what to wear if you didn't know the traditions and didn't have a significant other to ask?

Before I left, I checked to make sure there was plenty of water in the water bowls inside and out. Satisfied on that count, I put Tan in the yard, filled up The Black's dry food dish, and headed for the car. I'd put the set of photocopies Ward had given me in the car already, so I wouldn't forget them. They were in a folder sitting on the passenger seat so I was sure Bobby would see them.

As I drove to the Press, I began to wonder just what I was going to detect at the funeral and how I was going to go about detecting. I didn't think taking pictures of people I didn't recognize was something one "did" at graveside services. If there was a guestbook maybe I could get a copy of it from the funeral home before they gave it to—to whom? He had no wife or children. After Eleanor's funeral they—the funeral home people—had given me the guest book and a box of thank-you notes. It had taken a while, but I'd worked my way through it even though it seemed that Eleanor had known a heck a lot more people than I did—or than *we* did for that matter. I shook my head and decided I'd have to play it by ear. Bobby would know who was from the Press. Maybe between us we could spot a potential suspect or suspects.

I pulled into the Press's parking lot. We were going out to lunch before the service. Bobby had wanted to go to a place called OC's—a new restaurant in town and the first one advertising that it offered "California cuisine"—whatever that might be. I parked in one of the visitor spots, got out of the car, and headed toward the door. Before I could get there, Bobby walked out and headed my way. I stopped and watched as she approached. She usually wore slacks or jeans but today she was dressed in what I guess was the female equivalent of my funeral suit—a sedate black dress, square neckline, no obvious jewelry, small black handbag, and some black low heeled pumps. I say pumps but I really don't know what pumps are. Eleanor used to say pumps and I used to nod as if I understood.

Anyway, Bobby had more sense than to wear high heels to a graveside service. I had smiled at the first sight of her and the closer she got the broader my smile got.

She looked wonderful.

"Ford, you clean up pretty well!"

"Thanks, lady. You look pretty fine yourself."

I turned and walked beside her as we made our way to my car. It was a nice day, warm in the direct sunlight, but pleasant in the shade. It would be hot at the graveyard but there didn't seem to be any chance of rain. I offered my opinion. "Not a bad day for a funeral."

"Not a bad day for lunch. I'm hungry."

I laughed, opened the car door, and held it while she got in. "First things first. Direct and to the point. That's one of the things I love about you." I was shocked to hear myself say that. It was the first time either one of us had said anything about love.

Bobby picked up the folder of photocopies before she sat down then put it in her lap and smoothed her dress. I started to close the door as she reached for the seat belt. "One thing you love?" She was looking down at the envelope.

"Out of lots and lots of things." So we'd gotten past my use of the word. She'd used it too. I went back around the car to the driver's side, opened the door, and slid in under the steering wheel.

"Well, I've got a question."

"And it is?" I started the car but turned to look at her before putting it in gear.

She tapped her index finger on the folder she was holding. "What is this that I didn't sit on?"

"Oh, I forgot. Something I thought you could look at during lunch. It's a puzzle and I need some help."

"OK." She put her purse on top of it. "But I didn't realize I was going to work for my lunch when I said I'd come."

I put the car in reverse and eased out of the parking space. The Press was located far enough away from the student parking lots that there wasn't much pedestrian traffic. There were some spots on campus where there were so many pedestrians that a driver was hard put not to run somebody down. The fact that, as far as I knew, nobody had been run over speaks well for the drivers—because the students are asking for it—at least that's the way it looks.

It was a short drive to the restaurant. Since we were headed away from campus we got there quickly. As I pulled up I wondered for a moment what it had been before it had turned into OC's. In a college town, well, this college town anyway, the turnover in the restaurant business is pretty amazing. Once a building gets used as an eating place it sort of stays one. I remembered now. This had been an upscale steak house six months ago. Forty-five dollar steak entrees put a pretty big dent in a student's wallet. I think they had done all right at the beginning of the semester when everybody was flush, but business had dropped off pretty quickly.

I was able to find a parking space—generally a bad sign, but we were early enough that it wasn't conclusive. By the time I had gotten around to Bobby's side of the car she'd opened the door but hadn't gotten out. I held the door and looked in the car. Bobby smiled back at me. "I'm sort of out of practice at having doors opened for me."

"It's that younger crowd that you hang around with."

Once we entered OC's we had to stand and let our eyes adjust. Was it Californian to have the lights so dim? Before us was a counter with three cash register stations each manned by an attractive young lady, smiling and ready to take our orders.

"The menu is over there on the wall. We just tell them what we want, pay for it, and then go sit down. They'll give us a number to put on a little stand so the servers will know how to find us."

"I thought you hadn't been here."

Bobby was carefully scrutinizing the wall. "They were talking about it at work. I think the soups change every day."

The menu was mostly sandwiches and salads, some being variations of the others—a grilled chicken salad or sandwich, that kind of thing. I wasn't sure what made this "Californian" except there seemed to be a lot of sun-dried tomatoes, avocados, and pine nuts advertised as showing up in dishes. Maybe that's what did it. I glanced at the sandwiches that were listed and found one named after the restaurant. I figure that in the food business you don't put your name on something unless you think it's pretty good. Generally I'm right.

"You know what you want?" Bobby nodded and we stepped up to the first register. Bobby ordered a salad and water to drink while I ordered the OC sandwich and iced tea. Money changed hands and then we were given a plastic square with a number on it and empty plastic cups. It turns out that we were responsible for getting our drinks, but the food would be delivered. As this meant I could create my own mixture of lemonade and iced tea without having to explain it to an uncomprehending and uninterested server, I was pleased. Still, I'm not convinced that making the customers serve themselves is the way to go. I kind of like the idea of being waited on. What else am I paying for? But maybe this was the California touch?

As we left the drink station and started looking for a table, I noticed that the place was beginning to fill up. I glanced around trying to figure the traffic pattern. I hate sitting right in front of the door into the kitchen. There is always a constant stream of servers coming back and forth. Equally, I don't like to be too close to the entrance. I'd rather sit in a backwater where the foot traffic is lighter. I spotted a table for two near a corner and pointed to it. "How about over there?"

She nodded agreement and we eased our way across the floor between the tables that were carefully arranged to be too close together. Maybe that's what they meant by Californian? I decided that if retirement didn't pan out and I didn't make it as a detective that I wasn't going to apply to wait on tables here. You'd have to be rail thin to squeeze between the diners and I'm not.

I started to pull the chair out for Bobby and nearly hurt my back. Damn thing had to weigh fifty pounds. "Uumpth," I said.

"What's that?" Bobby sat down in the chair and looked up at me.

"The chair. It must weigh a ton."

She tried to shift it and her eyes widened. "Who wants a chair this heavy?"

I was able to help her push the chair closer to the table and then dragged my own chair out far enough for me to get into it. "Maybe they don't want the patrons to be able to use the chairs if a fight breaks out? Lord knows nobody's going to swing one of those things over their head."

I put the plastic square into a loop on top of a metal stand and made sure the number was facing the general direction of the kitchen. Seemed to me that the owners had made this place hard enough to work in, I didn't want to add to it. I had my back to a wall—Bobby and the rest of the restaurant could absorb my full attention.

"Do you think the clientele is likely to get into fights?"

I looked around paying more attention to what the crowd looked like and realized that it was predominately female. Not only that, the females tended to be young and attractive—or so it seemed to a casual observer. I straightened up and glanced around the room and wondered where the men were. There were tables of two, four, six, or eight and only occasionally would there be a man seated at one of them. Oh, there were a few tables where men were sitting, but they tended to be a decade or so older than the women.

"I don't get it. Why aren't there a bunch of college-age guys here?"

Bobby smiled. "Frank said that he really liked the way the restaurant was decorated. He called it eye candy."

I decided that it wasn't the right time to ask Bobby if she could explain to me why I kept on seeing parties of girls at nice restaurants and rarely any guys with them. I made a mental note to remember to ask the question when it seemed appropriate.

Bobby held up the folder. "Want to show me the puzzle? Or should we wait until after we eat?"

"It won't take long to point out the puzzle, it's the solution that's taking up all the time. Go ahead, take a look." I had high-lighted the puzzling titles with a yellow marker.

She slipped the pages out of the folder and glanced at the first couple of pages. I could see a double line form between her eyebrows as she glanced from page to page.

"They are photocopies of pages in a ledger that Philip Douglas had in his safe."

The lines between her eyes disappeared. "So what do I get for solving the mystery?"

"Dinner at any restaurant in town—your choice—the sky's the limit." I couldn't lose. It was a great excuse to take her out.

"Including wine and dessert?"

"And preprandial drinks." Maybe I should check on the expense account issue?

"It's the rifles."

Like clockwork the waiter arrived with our food before I could find out what she meant. After we got it straight that the salad was hers, the sandwich was mine, and the waiter could leave, I repeated what she had said. "The rifles?"

The salad was in a bowl so large that it partially blocked my view of Bobby. The first visual negative I'd found in the place. "What do you mean the rifles?" She was serenely using her fork to poke at the salad uncovering the goodies that had been included with the bleu cheese and blackened steak slices—sun-dried tomatoes and avocados, no doubt.

She looked up from her salad, saw the total confusion writ large on my face, and took pity on me—she put down her fork. "These strings of letters and numbers are on those brass plaques Philip had mounted next to the rifles—little tiny font in the bottom right corner of the plaque? You might not have noticed them, I didn't at first. I'm not sure when I did notice them but when I did I wondered about them.

"So I asked Philip about them and what they stood for." She shook her head from side to side and picked up her fork. "All he said was that it was a code he'd come up with to identify the pieces in his collection. What a jerk." With that she stabbed the bowl and pulled out a fork full of lettuce and popped it in her mouth.

I sagged in my chair. "A secret code to identify the rifles? What ailed the man? Why not just write out something like 'Remington Model A, circa 1900, 48 caliber, muzzle loader?'"

Bobby stopped chewing and swallowed. "I don't think a Remington is a muzzle loader."

"And I think you paid way more attention to his collection than it deserved." I looked down at my sandwich. It was a hoagie roll made out of real bread, nice golden crust, and hand sliced. There was a sun-dried tomato, and a couple of pine nuts along with something that looked like feta that had escaped the roll along with a little sauce.

"Oh he was always so secretive about the rifles and where he'd gotten them and who might have owned them before. You couldn't help wondering."

"I could have." Fortunately they'd cut the sandwich in half. I picked up one half and could feel that instability in a sandwich that had more filling than the integrity of the bread could contain. Quickly I brought my other hand up to add stability and stuck a corner of the sandwich in my mouth. I took a large bite.

My theory about dishes that are named after the establishment proved true, once again. It was delicious.

"Philip was so proud of the rifles and so secretive about how he got them that I once accused him of having the gun that John Wilkes Booth used to kill Lincoln."

I was still chewing so I just looked at her questioningly.

"He just pointed out to me that Booth had used a Derringer—a handgun he wouldn't consider worthy of collecting—but there was a 30-06 of Hemingway's that he'd be proud to hang on the wall.

Bobby looked at me as if to see whether I understood. "Ernest Hemingway? He mentions a 30-06 in some of his stories. Philip said that no one knew what had become of Hemingway's rifle."

I swallowed and decided not to expose the extent of my ignorance of the works of Ernest "Papa" Hemingway at this moment. "Well, the shotgun he killed himself with is still probably police evidence." Having proved I knew something about Hemingway's death if not his literature, I returned to the puzzle.

"So all I have to do is to match up the," I pointed at the sheets of paper that Bobby had left on the table, "the titles—is what I was calling them—with the rifles at the Press?"

"That's right. We can do that after lunch—no, after the funeral. Oh, that's right the Press is closed for the day."

"Tomorrow is plenty soon enough." I settled in to enjoy the sandwich and what I could swear were home-made potato chips. Part of a puzzle solved, good food, and a good looking companion, the day was turning out pretty well.

. . .

The minister at the graveside had never met Philip Douglas or so he said. I'm not sure if it was Christian charity or an arrogance that Christ would have disapproved of that had made him willing to preside over the funeral, but I will admit he did his best. It can't be easy to find the words to bury Caesar when most of the people in the audience were—all-in-all—better off with him dead—at least happier anyway. And there was the chance that one of the people here had actually usurped the divine prerogative and had taken the man's life. Like I said, it was a challenge that not every minister would have accepted.

It was a sparse crowd, more like the graveside service for an elderly person—one of those who had been living in the eddies and backwaters of society. The staff members of the Press were all there, I thought. I made a mental note to check with Bobby if anybody was missing. A funeral didn't seem the right place to take roll. She'd pointed out the board members who'd come, whispering their names to me. I'd recognized Stefenson, of course, and the dean who was a published poet, but had no reason to recognize the rest and hadn't.

Oh, if Rufus had been here I'd have recognized him. And if he'd sent Victoria in his place I'd have spotted her too. There was a vice provost type who showed up who didn't look like she really knew why she was there. I guessed that Rufus had sent her in his stead. I was sort of surprised that Rufus hadn't come himself but I didn't question it.

If Ward thought I'd see a new suspect at the funeral he was sadly mistaken. There wasn't anyone skulking around. No ominous strangers that could be potential murderers. Just a bunch of university types who were uncomfortably attending the funeral of somebody they didn't really care for or know that well.

No breath-taking blond in widow's weeds, black veil, and fish-net stockings. Philip Marlowe would have been disappointed. For that matter, so was I.

The minister sprinkled some dirt on the casket, we bowed our heads in a final prayer, and the funeral was over. Bobby and I headed for my car.

"I thought the minister did a good job, didn't you? Particularly under the circumstances."

"Absolutely. I wonder why he agreed to officiate, if that's the expression."

"I think Hazel had to practically force him to do it. Told him it would have been unchristian to refuse."

"Hazel?"

"Hazel Murphy from the Press. You remember. She was the one who greeted you and Rufus when you first came to the Press."

"Right. She got the minister?"

I followed her to the passenger side of the car and opened the door.

"She organized the whole thing. She said there wasn't anybody else to do it and she'd had practice, having buried her parents."

"Practice? I guess I never thought of it that way." I closed her door and walked around to the driver's side.

"Where to?"

"You'd better take me back to the Press so I can get my car. I've got some errands to run this afternoon. Nothing like a funeral to make you stop procrastinating."

. . .

I got home and changed back into hanging-around-the-house clothes—an old pair of cut-off jeans, T-shirt, and tennis shoes. I'd let Tan in when I got back since she was too excited at my return to stay in the backyard. She'd been sleeping in the yard and went back to sleep once she got inside. The Black had come out to see that I had returned and then disappeared, he'd reappear when he thought suppertime should occur.

After looking around the house for a while I realized that I'd left the folder in the car. I retrieved it and spread the pages out on the kitchen counter. Since I was working, I really should have gone into my office only I didn't have enough room to spread more than a few sheets out at a time there.

Now that I knew that the combination of letters and numbers represented a particular rifle I was sure I could make some sense out of the pattern. Unfortunately it didn't seem to help at all. Finally I gave up trying to see how the nomenclature that Douglas had used to identify his rifles could be anything other than some fiendish code. I wondered if there had been anything else in the safe that could help break that code. I needed a Rosetta stone or maybe I didn't. Who knows if that had anything to do with his murder? Still, I was going to take the pages into the Press tomorrow and match up page with rifle.

I gave up on trying to figure out how he'd come up with the jumbles and tried looking at the pages just knowing that each one referred to a particular rifle. That's when I remembered the fact that there had been duplicates.

It took a little while but I eventually had reordered the pages from the ledger so that they were in numerical order by rifle. That way seemed to make a little more sense. The flow of the entries now seemed to have a little more consistency even if the reason behind the secrecy was still just as maddening. I kept on trying to make the information important and wasn't able to come up with any rational reason for the whole journal to exist. Now, after every first appearance of a rifle there was a block of notes, abbreviations, and as far as I could tell chicken scratches. Then, on the next line, there was that foolish 1Y, 2Y, 3Y, or 4Y notation. Then started a series of entries that appeared to have occurred over a long period of time. Thank goodness the Press had a color photocopier. I could tell when the inks changed colors and width on the pages. I started following a particularly light and broad entry in blue and found it on some five different rifle records. As a working hypothesis I decided the deceased had had that pen for a period of time and then discarded it.

I looked around at the thirty or so stacks of paper. Time to go back to the database and combine some tables and try some new sorts and combinations. I had a copy of the report on the rifles that Harry had filed with the department. Too bad he hadn't included that string of numbers and letters that was on the bottom right corner of the brass plaques, it would have saved me a trip to the Press. Still, I decided to look on the bright side—any reason to see Bobby again was worthwhile.

. . .

The Black followed me downstairs. Once I'd started spreading the pages out on the counters he'd come to help. He'd been helping by sitting on different pieces of paper so he was disappointed when I put them in one stack and wouldn't let him sit on top. Just to show there weren't any hard feelings, he proceeded to walk across the keyboard. Unfortunately for me, that had a tendency to insert random keystrokes into the database. We finally compromised with him in my lap and my petting him in between my keystrokes. If I took too long between pats, he would carefully extend a claw into my flesh.

Even with all that assistance, it didn't take long to figure out that by far the majority of journal entries were alike in that they contained a sequential series. Every rifle had those entries and all of those entries appeared below that line of Ys. I separated all of those entries out into a separate table. I sorted those in various alphanumeric manners and couldn't come up with a pattern. But what if I cross-referenced the entries with the rifles they were related to? Tying them back to the rifles didn't seem to help. If there was a pattern there I couldn't see it.

TB must have gotten bored about that time and moved to sit at the edge of my desk. He began to methodically lick one paw several times and then draw it across his ear. He'd work on one ear for a while and then switch to the other. I watched for a lick or two then went back to the database.

I dropped the rifle link and tried a link to the Ys and stared at it looking for some pattern. Nope. Broke that link and just sorted the Ys by the first letter and counted how many I had. 4Ys occurred approximately four times as often as 1Ys, and almost twice as often as 2Ys. I checked. Yep, 3Ys occurred about three times as often as 1Ys. So I could translate "Y" as times—maybe. It was a working hypothesis. OK, let's link the Ys with the rifle names.

If there was any pattern, I couldn't see it. Maybe if I knew how to translate what stood for the rifles with the rifles themselves? I'd have to go in to the Press and see how this string of garbage tied in with what I could tell about the rifle. Since I knew squat about rifles, that didn't seem a sure path to success. Maybe I could get Harry to help. I thought a minute about how likely that was going to be. Maybe I could get Captain Ward to see if Harry could help.

I took the Ys table and the rifle name table and linked them to the series table. I wondered if I had too much data to see a pattern. Sometimes you can't see the forest for the trees. I selected the rifles with the most entries associated with their name and from that sort I picked four rifles that were associated with different Ys.

Now this looked promising. The Black jumped on the back of my chair. I waited for him to climb down across my shoulder into my lap, but he stayed put. I was looking at activity that followed a pattern. The 1Y rifle's entry always came between the third and fourth 4Y rifle's entry. The 2Y rifle bracketed the 1Y, and the 3Y had one before and two after. Why hadn't Douglas just used an X? Everybody used it as "times." One time, two times, three—a year. Damn. I slapped the desk and startled TB into a protest. It had been that simple. I was sure of it. The Ys indicated how many times a year Douglas needed to do something to his rifles.

I included all the rifle names and the sequences. I had a relational database. I corrected for the partial years as rifles were added to his collection and the partial current year. It was clear—1Y once a year, 2Y twice a year, 3Y three times a year, and 4Y four times a year. It was a record of when Philip Douglas cleaned his rifles.

What good was that going to do me? I stared at what had to stand for a date and whatever else you'd want to make a note of when you'd cleaned a weapon that was part of a collection. I wondered if Douglas had been left-handed like Da Vinci.

Yep, I was going to need Harry and Jim's help in figuring this out but now I had some knowledge of what we were looking at to bring to the table.

Even before I retired I'd had a high regard for those people whose jobs don't require a daily routine—and yet they get their jobs done. Now that I'm retired my regard has grown.

For years I was able to get up, exercise, shower, shave, dress, eat breakfast, perform chores, and get to work by eight. I no longer seemed capable of doing it. It was closer to nine than it was to eight-thirty before I even got out the door much less to the Press. As I drove along I tried to figure out what was absorbing the extra time. It wasn't that I had more to do than when I was working full time. Nor that I was in a mental fog—not like after Eleanor died when Tan and Mary had to remind me to feed or pay them. Mary got pretty testy about my not washing clothes for her to fold or iron. Tan had made sure I got out and remembered to feed her, if not myself. Oh, I knew what had happened to me. I had started slowing down and smelling the roses. I'd have a cup of coffee while I was still getting dressed instead of gulping it down with whatever was handy for breakfast. The morning newspaper was being read much more thoroughly. I'd slowed down the pace because I could and had learned to enjoy it.

With that thought I pulled into the Press parking lot and discovered that it was nearly full. It looked like the Press was back to business the day after the director's funeral. Life goes on.

I took one of the last available parking spots, grateful for my retiree tag. As a retiree, I was entitled to park for free all over campus. This was after decades of having to pay for the privilege of being able to park legally if I could find a spot in order to go to work. Go figure.

As I got out of my car, I looked around to see if Ward's Crown Victoria was in the lot. Why do police departments always have Crown Victorias as their unmarked cars? The extent of my ignorance regarding police matters is staggering. Anyway, it looked like I'd beat him here, which was a good thing. The more I'd thought about it the more I felt that I'd called him too soon. He'd want some corroboration before he agreed that the entries had to be dates so I called him and postponed the meeting. Then I grabbed my laptop and some folders and headed for the door. There was plenty to do before I called Ward again and the sooner I got to it the better.

. . .

Bobby was interested in how I'd been able to determine—at least to my satisfaction—that Douglas had been keeping a record of when he cleaned the different rifles in his collection. She confirmed that Philip had been left-handed—something, as he had repeatedly pointed out, that he had in common with Alexander the Great, Julius Caesar, Charlemagne, Napoleon Bonaparte, and Leonardo Da Vinci. Now there was another similarity—they were all left-handed and dead.

Bobby remembered the last time Philip had called her in for a consultation and then proceeded to clean a rifle while listening to her arguments for not publishing a manuscript that the Press had already accepted.

"I don't know what made me madder. There was the fact that he'd accepted the manuscript, then committed the Press to publishing it, but had never actually read what turned out to be the most poorly written diatribe I've ever been asked to edit. And there was the fact that he was just sitting there cleaning the damn rifle and muttering 'uh-huh' every minute or so. All the while he's got that 'puppy training pad' covering the rug while he runs that damn rod down the barrel, pulls it out and then peers down the damn thing. And I do not like the smell of whatever he used to clean the rifles."

"OK. Since you remember the date and the rifle, let's go see what the last entry for that rifle looks like."

I'd been a little concerned that Bobby wouldn't be certain as to which of the thirty rifles Philip had cleaned. He had been considerate enough to take the rifle down from the wall in his office and begin to clean it while she was talking to him. She remembered which rifle it had been all right.

We headed into the Press director's office. While, technically it was a crime scene with restricted access, Ward had told me that I could look around but not to remove anything. Bobby pointed out the rifle and I pulled out my phone and took several pictures of it and a close up of the brass plaque. I went ahead and did the same for all the rifles on the office walls, making sure to follow the pictures of the rifle with the picture of the plaque. Wouldn't do to get them confused. I'd wait until I got back home to add the new information into the database.

We went back to Bobby's office where I'd left my laptop. Her phone was ringing so she answered it while I grabbed my computer and headed to the small conference room that wasn't being used.

I fired up the computer and pulled up the record that matched the jumble of letters and numbers that were on the plaque.

I stared at the last entry and tried to transform it, part of it anyway, into the date Bobby had been forced to watch Philip clean the rifle.

Having learned that Philip was left-handed and knowing it's easier for the left-handed to write from right to left, I started trying to interpret Philip's scribble that way. If the jerk had used the English date structure, the first number was the day, then the month, and then the year, unlike the American month, day, year configuration. Whatever, both of them are stupid ways to arrange the numbers. Can't get the dates to sort chronologically with that structure. For me, it was year, month, day—with leading zeros.

OK, if he had written from right to left the last part of the entry could be either the month or the day. After that should come the year. I started at the end and, now that I was looking at it backward, thought I could detect a string of numbers that I could make into dates—provided he was using Roman numerals for the month—I for January, II for February, and so on. So the X in the string stood for October, IX was either September or November, and IIX was August or December depending on which direction he was writing. No wonder I was having such trouble figuring this out.

I looked at the earlier entries for that rifle. It was possible. This was one of the 3Y entities and I had difficulty working with thirds of a year instead of quarters and Philip's handwriting was atrocious.

More data points, that's what I needed. I got up and went in search of Frank Manning. Maybe he could give me a date to go along with a rifle that had been cleaned.

. . .

Frank had been a little fuzzy on the exact date. I refrained from asking if the meeting had been after 4:20. Anyway he was certain about the month and year and positive which rifle was involved. Kent was a great help. Not only did he remember the date and rifle of the last occurrence, he'd also marked on his calendar the other times Philip had taken the opportunity to clean a rifle while meeting with him. It was this year's calendar and he hadn't made notes about which rifle, but I could use it. The other members of the staff weren't quite as helpful, but I had more data points to work with.

That did it. He was using Roman numerals for the months only the direction was from right to left so XII translates to eight or August and IIX is twelve or December. To make it even harder to figure out he had adopted IIII the four from a clock face instead of the classically correct IV to stand for April. Why would you use four characters when two would have done the job? And the cleaning cycle was based on the date he'd purchased the rifle, not the beginning of the year. I had never met the man and still found him irritating.

I had collected pictures of all the remaining rifles and made sure I had clear shots of the plaques. I glanced at my phone. It was a little too early for lunch and Bobby had plans anyway. I made up my mind. Time to take this back to my office and see just what I could do with it.

. . .

On my way home, I stopped at a restaurant to buy a sandwich—a sandwich of which I am particularly fond. I think it's the marinara sauce and melted cheese. It was sort of a consolation prize I was giving myself for not getting to eat with Bobby.

I walked into the house and immediately put the sandwich in the microwave. I had learned that TB liked that sandwich as well. I'm sure Tan would too, but she doesn't get on the kitchen counters. With my lunch safe, I brought in the files and laptop. I'd uploaded the pictures I'd taken with my phone to my cloud account along with a copy of the updated database file before leaving the Press. All I needed to do was download the pictures and overwrite the old database with the updated files. Access to the cloud made all of this so much easier.

The Black was wandering around the kitchen, tail erect and quivering. He smelled the sandwich but couldn't quite figure out where it was. Tan didn't seem to care, she was happy to be back inside and on one of her beds.

I took my files and laptop and went to my office. It still wasn't noon and I wanted to get started.

. . .

The sandwich was cold when I got back to the kitchen. I had gone back to correct my interpretation of the deceased's handwriting. Now that I knew, or thought I knew, what he had been trying to write it was easier to decipher. Once I had those mistakes cleared up I was able to create columns that split the date into year, month, day. I matched up the rifle description with the code from the plaque and now could actually see how he had rotated through his collection in a steady pattern. Fulmer's calendar notes, Frank's fuzzy memory, Bobby's account, they all matched. For no other reason than I could do it, I'd matched a photo with the descriptions and could generate a slide show—one rifle dissolving into another.

Fortunately hunger finally tore me away from the mindless fiddling I was doing with the database. That and the calendar alarm I'd set so I would remember my afternoon appointment. I

microwaved the sandwich back to warm and started on lunch. I
didn't want to be late.

Calvin Beck's office was on the university campus but he wasn't a university employee. Several state agencies had employees who were housed on campus and he happened to be one of them. As a state employee he had none of the perks of working for the university like extended time off between semesters or discounted football tickets but all the inconvenience of having an office on campus—parking, traffic, students. Of course, if he enjoyed looking at attractive coeds maybe there was a plus.

I had parked as soon as I found a space and walked to his office building. The weather was nice, past the heat of summer and not yet into the cold of winter—not that Alabama has cold like Canada does, but you can get pretty miserable on a cold, damp, windy day.

I spotted the front doors nestled between the middle columns that fronted the building and entered. I'd never been in this particular building. Victoria had given me directions to Calvin's office so I knew to take the stairs to the second floor. There were no classrooms in the building so the hallways were narrower, having no need to handle the stampede of students coming or going in intervals. The hall was flanked on either side with closed doors. Numbers were painted on the frosted panes that comprised the top half of the door.

I checked the number on the door with the address I had in my phone and knocked on the door.

"It's open."

I turned the knob and opened the door to see a man get up from his desk and walk around it holding out his hand. The man was short, about five-six or seven, not heavy-set so much as pudgy. Odd, I thought to myself. I'd expected a hook and bullet author to be thin for some reason.

"Come in, come in! You must be James Crawford, right on time. Wish I could be that punctual. I'm always running late. That's why I didn't want to schedule this meeting right after lunch because I might not have been back in time."

He continued to talk as we shook hands. He gestured at a chair in front of his desk and went back around and sat.

"Crawford, that's Scottish, isn't it? Of course Beck is German—at least my line of the family is supposed to be from there. Not that I've really done any genealogical research really."

I was wondering if he would stop to take a breath so I could get a word in edgewise. So far it didn't look like it. I thought you needed to be quiet to be a successful hunter. So maybe he fishes. Don't imagine fish pay much attention to noise.

"Ms. Moore, the provost's assistant, said that you were helping the police with investigating Philip Douglas's murder. Such a sad, sad, thing, I think. Even if he was a widower."

I opened my mouth to reply but he continued to chatter on. This might prove to be the easiest interrogation ever.

"I guess you're checking up on people who might have argued with poor Philip before his death. Certainly I fit that description, but, heaven knows—it's not something I could do." His hands fluttered in the air and I noticed they were larger than I would have suspected—maybe typing tones the fingers.

"Oh, we had argued. There's no doubt about that. I was trying to get the Press to publish a novel I've written—a work of fiction—not really what university presses normally publish, but I thought—and someone had suggested—well what I'd hoped was that Philip would help since he'd published some collections of shorts I'd written—but I wanted to 'graduate,' if you will, to full-length novels."

I sat back and nodded encouragingly—in hindsight as wasted a movement as I've ever made. No wonder his coworkers kept their doors closed. If Calvin dropped in for a "word or two" you'd be trapped for hours.

"Actually he was helpful—I should never have said he wasn't. He was the second person to read the novel and made some very pointed suggestions as to what needed to be changed—tightened up is how he described it—and I already made some changes—so it wasn't like I couldn't take editorial advice, you know? I mean I can learn. Writers do learn, don't you know? They aren't born you know, good writers are made.

"Anyway Philip—I can see what he was doing now—I misunderstood at first—that was what the argument was about—Philip was trying to teach me that I had to believe in myself—to listen to my inner voice—what I should have been doing all along instead of changing things at the slightest suggestion."

The words continued to pour out and I was doing my best to keep abreast of what he was saying. My ears were beginning to hurt.

"When he threw that in my face—all the changes I'd made at his suggestion—saying that he'd never publish a book by an author as spineless as I was—well it was a harsh lesson that I had to learn. I can see that now. He was encouraging me. Oh, I misunderstood you see," he shook his head and kept on talking. "And it did the trick. I put all the parts people had suggested I take out and put them all back in again—mostly—things got moved around and I think I made it better when putting them back in—you learn, you know what I mean?"

The question was purely rhetorical as he never paused, even as he stood up and began to pace back and forth.

"I put it all back, printed it, and mailed it to a real literary agent who loved it! Loved it you understand—even that 'technical' part about chamber adaptors—I'd wondered about putting that back—and now I'm the next John Grisham or Tom Clancy—he believes in the novel just like I should have. He—the agent that is—has gotten some of the major publishing houses to agree to read it. He's already asked for an outline of the next book and I've got some ideas—but here I am thinking of just myself.

"I should have called Philip and thanked him. Alas, I was too full of myself to realize that he had to recognize my talent as well as my weakness. I grieve to think I missed the chance to tell him I'd learned what he was trying to teach me."

I jumped to my feet, taking advantage of the slightest of pauses. "Any chance somebody saw you here that afternoon? That you could have an alibi?"

He rocked back on his heels, eyes wide and blinking. "Why would—an alibi? But I told you how I'd misunderstood what Philip had done. What reason would I have to kill him?"

"No alibi?" I tried to sound tough instead of desperate for escape as I edged toward the door.

"Just the office meeting that afternoon. We always have meetings on Wednesday afternoon."

· · ·

I stood outside on the sidewalk wondering if blood was running out of my ears. I wasn't too sure how I'd escaped. There was a foggy memory of shaking Beck's hand—being surprised at how

firm the grip was—a muttered excuse of another meeting I had
to go to—I shook my head. The relative silence of a university
campus as students rushed to and from classes was a relief. I
walked to my car to wait until the chaos that reigned in those
fifteen minutes between one class period and the next ended.

I headed back to the house.

. . .

I was verbally battered by my experience with Calvin Beck—
maybe I needed to adjust my retirement so that I had more contact with people—a wider range of individuals. I contemplated
that for a moment and then realized that's exactly what I was
doing while trying to solve a murder.

"I need to apply for the investigator license. Get out more." I
muttered to myself, "Design those business cards." My voice
sounded strange in the quiet of the house. I'd headed for my office after I let Tan inside. The Black had been asleep in my chair
and resented being scooped up and dumped on the floor. Who
could blame him?

I called Ward's office instead of his cell phone hoping to get
his voicemail instead of him and was successful. With a feeling
of relief I left him a message about Calvin's regular staff meeting on Wednesday. He had the manpower to check up on whether it really occurred and if Beck had been present. Let Jim's
people handle that while I—while I what?

I tapped the keyboard to wake up my computer and stared at
the database—well, the interface anyway. I couldn't think of a
query I hadn't already tried so I just started the slide show. TB
jumped on the back of my chair and made his way down my

shoulder and chest to my lap. It's not my favorite way for him to get in my lap but life with TB is about give and take.

Once he was comfortable I started looking at the rifles as they one-by-one faded from view and then reappeared. I was using the "Ken Burns effect." Maybe I should try another? Or maybe I should link the images with the floor plan?

I thought for a second. Didn't Victoria send the floor plans over with Rufus that first day? I could scan the plans to get a computer file then. I tried to lean forward to reach the stack of documents I'd collected but I must have startled The Black because he leapt out of my lap onto the stack I was trying to reach. As part of his flight, he dug his claws into the platform he was jumping from—my lap.

It was a combination of TB's leap onto the stack of paper and his subsequent launch off that stack of paper onto the floor and my reaction to razor sharp claws digging into my flesh— very sensitive flesh—that resulted in the transformation of an orderly stack of paper into chaos on the floor. I looked at the mess on the floor and then saw The Black saunter out of the room, tail held straight up with only the tip of it twitching. It was clear who was at fault—me.

I reminded myself of the earlier philosophical thoughts of "give and take" as I sat down on the floor and tried to sort pages into some order. My previously expressed sanguinity had quickly morphed into a few choice expressions, some of which former Boy Scouts knew but weren't supposed to use. Since I'd been in the navy as well as the Boy Scouts I wasn't sure where I'd learned them, but use them I did.

After a few minutes sitting on the floor, I was reminded that a hard floor was not as comfortable as it might have been twenty or thirty years earlier. I picked up all the scattered sheets of paper in my arms and sat back down. I had to push the keyboard out of the way, which woke up the display and the slide show started up again.

As I sorted it all out I came across the police report that Harry Johns had prepared on Philip's rifle collection. I'd just glanced at it after Ward had given me a copy. If I was a gun—excuse me—rifle enthusiast it would have been more interesting. By more interesting I mean interesting at all, of course.

I guess the police don't staple these reports together because they so often have to make copies. On the other hand, maybe Ward hadn't bothered to staple my copy. Whatever. I was going along sorting the pages when I came to the Remington Model 700 30-06 entry. It was one of the few I recognized—I thought of it as the rifle the cat was staring at. Harry had mentioned that it was an extremely common rifle and that made its existence in a collection unusual and that it had been recently cleaned—freshly oiled and dusted.

Cleaned? I stared at the monitor. The slide show had reached its finish and stopped, waiting on me to decide to start over or pick another one. I wasn't sure what rifle I was looking at, but it wasn't the Remington Model 700. The Model 700 wasn't supposed to be cleaned—I held onto that page and put the rest down.

It can be a slow tedious process to build a functional, relational database and you can wonder why you're doing it. But sometimes it comes in handy.

The Remington Model 700 30-06 had been cleaned four months ago and wasn't due to be cleaned for another two months.

If I was right, this was the first and only time Philip had cleaned a rifle out of sequence. So maybe he hadn't cleaned the rifle. Maybe somebody else did—somebody like the killer. I realized I was holding my breath and forced myself to exhale. This, I decided, was definitely worth a phone call.

I'd made arrangements to meet Ward and maybe Harry for lunch at a place called Johnny's. The food was good and you could get in and out pretty quickly. Jim had an afternoon meeting. Harry's presence would depend on the outcome of the ballistics test. If the gun had been used to kill Philip Douglas, I'd see Harry and if it hadn't, I wouldn't. That was fine with me. Ward would have plenty to say about what a stupid idea I'd had if I was wrong—I wouldn't need Harry chiming in.

I picked up the phone and dialed the provost's office. I wanted to see how Victoria was doing on setting up the third interview. Dialed, I thought as my finger punched the buttons in order. Wonder when that word will totally disappear? Nobody dials any more. The phone rang twice and I'd just started wondering if "ring" was just as obsolete as "dial" when Victoria answered the phone.

"Provost's Office, this is Victoria."

"Good morning, Victoria. This is James Crawford, just checking to see if you've heard from Bernard Charles."

"If I had, I would have gotten in touch with you. Just as I would if I'd gotten your invoice." There was a touch of frost in her voice.

"Invoice, right." I'd forgotten that I'd told her that I'd investigate what private detectives charged these days. She'd dismissed Rockford's $200 a day and expenses.

"The provost asked me about your retainer fee just this morning. I didn't like telling him that I was waiting on you."

I bet she didn't. Nobody as organized and resourceful as she was would. "Sorry," I said meekly. "I've been busy."

"Mr. Crawford have you done anything about setting this up as a business?"

Whoops, if I'd thought her tone was frosty before, it was now arctic—and I had been demoted to Mister.

"You were going to talk to your accountant, remember? Check with professional associations of licensed investigators? What about your business cards?"

"Uh," why had I called her I wondered. What had possessed me? "I did check to see if I had a program that could design business cards."

The silence on her end of the line was pretty deafening.

"Are you confusing graphic design with murder investigation?"

I finally got off the phone after promising, cross-my-heart-and-hope-to-die promising that I would do all of that. I tried to remember if I really had called Janet, my accountant, or just thought about it. Did I really want to give up my amateur status? It was time to leave if I wasn't going to be late to lunch. I didn't bother to make a note to remind myself that I had to pay attention to the professional side. I wouldn't be forgetting that conversation.

. . .

I beat Ward and Harry to Johnny's but I didn't have to wait long before I saw Ward's long, thin silhouette outlined in the doorway. He was by himself. Damn. How had I screwed up?

I waved at Ward as he scanned the room. The hostess walked up to him and he pointed at me then headed in my direction. I took a sip of iced tea wondering as I did how Ward was going to bust my chops about being wrong about the rifle.

He pulled his chair out and said, "Good call on the Model whatever—700. Ballistics matched it with the slug that killed Douglas."

"Huh? When Harry wasn't with you I thought—"

"What? You got no more faith in your theory than that?" Ward picked up the menu as if he expected it to have changed from the last time he'd been here. "Harry wanted to check on something about the diameter of the slug or some such and I've got a meeting across town after lunch so we came in separate cars. He's probably looking for a place to park."

"Oh," I said. For some reason I was finding it hard to adjust to being right—not something that was usually a problem for me.

"Diameter of the bullet? It passed the ballistics test then?"

Ward waved his hand dismissively as he flipped the menu over and stared at the dinner menu. "Some technical thing that I know nothing about and don't need to know anything about because I've got him working for me. What's good?"

He did that to me all the time—treating me like I was some dining critic or restaurant reviewer. "I like pretty much everything but on Thursdays you always get the special—the open-faced roast beef sandwich with gravy and mashed potatoes."

"Humph." He put the menu down as the waitress walked up.

"Can I get you something to drink, hon?" Johnny's had been in business for a long time and our waitress had been working there awhile herself. Johnny had retired—sold out to his employees and they continued to run it pretty much the way he had. Daily specials that rarely changed—Friday was fried catfish day, Wednesdays chicken pot pie, and so on. And every day their famous prime rib and biscuits with fries.

Ward looked up at her, nodded, and said, "Brown diet?"

"Diet Pepsi?"

"Sure." He turned back to me. "So what about the first two? You got us the killer?"

"As far as suspects go, these two are pretty lame. Both of them have alibis. She won't allow his name to be used in her presence. He can't stop talking long enough to listen to a question. Neither one feels like a killer to me."

Ward just sat and stared at me. "Christ, Crawford. What do all the neighbors say about the serial killer who lived in their neighborhood? 'He seemed like such a nice young man.' Murderers don't look like murderers. There's not a 'murdering type,' otherwise I'd be out of work and we wouldn't need lawyers. We'll check on the alibis you just pay attention to what they say—and don't say.

"Don't forget that if they won't talk to you, the police will step in. I'll step in and they won't like it. Remind them of that. We're just giving the university an opportunity to help us eliminate some suspects. It's a classic good-cop, bad-cop setup. Use it."

As I listened to Ward, I realized he was right. I wondered if he treated rookie police detectives the same way I was being treated.

"And since I've never in my life heard such a pile of whatever as 'feels like a killer' you're paying and I'm getting the prime rib."

"Prime rib?" The voice came from out of nowhere. I hadn't noticed Harry enter. He pulled a chair out and sat. "I thought Johnny's was more of a meat-and-three kind of place."

Harry turned to me and stuck out his hand, "Congratulations, professor. You nailed the murder weapon."

"I was lucky."

"Hell yes, you were lucky." He turned his attention to the menu.

Having admitted I was right about the weapon, Harry went right back to his original attitude toward me. I was an amateur meddling in business best left to the professionals. He didn't much care for the idea much less the reality of it.

Harry looked up from the menu. "I don't see any prime rib."

"Captain Ward was looking at the dinner menu. At lunch they've got their famous prime rib biscuits with fries. Not quite the same thing."

Ward looked down, flipped the menu over, and stared at it. "Damn."

"I took a closer look at that slug that was the cause of death."

"Yeah," Ward was looking at the lunch menu with a frown on his face. "What of it?"

"It was a .32 ACP."

Ward lifted his face from the menu and stared at Harry.

"ACP?" I looked from Ward to Johns.

"Automatic Colt pistol," said Ward absently. Harry just rolled his eyes.

The waitress reappeared at the table and spoke to Harry. "What can I get you to drink, hon?" Then she looked around the table. "Or are you gentlemen ready to order?"

"Prime rib biscuits and fries sounds pretty good to me." Harry dropped the menu on the table. "And iced tea, please."

Since Ward looked like he was still trying to figure out what to order I spoke up. "I'll have a bowl of the chili. And it's my check."

Harry glanced at me with his eyebrows raised. Maybe he thought I was trying to buy his affection.

Ward shrugged his shoulders. "Open-faced roast beef sandwich, gravy, and mashed potatoes—gravy on both—and the fruit cup."

The waitress smiled at Ward, "Right, your usual." She turned to Harry, "I'll be right back with your tea."

Jim picked up Harry's menu, added it to his, and handed it to the waitress. I held my menu up and she took it out of my hands. I think Ward was still puzzling over what she meant by "the usual."

Harry broke the silence.

"If it had been fired from a .32 ACP caliber handgun it would have had a .311 diameter. This one swaged to a diameter of .308." Harry turned to me. "The rifle's bore diameter." He looked back at Ward. "The rifling marks on the evidence were a slightly different configuration and rate of twist than those inscribed by a pistol's barrel."

I was totally lost. "Does that mean it wasn't the murder weapon?"

Harry turned to face me. Over his shoulder I could see Ward wink at me. I bet he didn't know what Harry was talking about either.

"The rifling signature on the bullet marked as evidence was a perfect match. The victim was murdered by someone using that rifle."

I could tell that he would sound just the same when called to testify in court—a perfect technical witness.

"The pistol round had to have been used in that rifle. In order to do so, the perp—the perpetrator, that is—had to have used a caliber conversion sleeve." Harry looked at my blank expression. "Sometimes referred to as a supplemental chamber?"

Ward spoke up. "Anybody else know about this thing being used?"

Harry shook his head no.

"Keep it out of the press releases then. Let it be our secret."

I had read about the practice in my mystery novels. "This is how you catch false confessions, right? Withhold evidence?"

Ward nodded. "We've got some people around here that confess to every murder, rape, or bank robbery that makes the paper." He grinned. "The bigger the crime the more people come forward."

"And none of them are going to mention the fact that they used a," I paused, "a caliber conversion sleeve. What the hell is 'a caliber conversion sleeve?'"

Harry threw back his head and laughed. I was getting a little tired of Harry and his attitude.

"Caliber conversion sleeves let a gun owner save money by allowing him or her to use cheaper handgun ammo in expensive rifles. Rifle ammunition is expensive. Saturday night special stuff is cheap. If all you want to do is a little target practice, why use the expensive stuff?"

"But Philip had all different types of ammunition in his safe." I was confused. "Was it his caliber thing?"

"Listen," Harry was clearly getting fed up with my ignorance. "Caliber conversion sleeve—a device inserted into the rifle breech to enable the shooter to use a different caliber than the one the rifle was designed to hold. Got it?

"Can't have been the deceased's sleeve. He didn't have any .32 ACP in the safe—just the right loads for each rifle. I guess he was such an enthusiast he would never use the 'wrong' kind. His fingerprints were all over the ammo, but his were the only ones we found in the safe." Harry looked thoughtful for a moment. "Actually, when I think about it, that was pretty shrewd on the murderer's part. All he had to carry with him was some ammo and the sleeve. He could use his ammo but didn't have to use his weapon. This isn't going to make our job any easier."

At which point our waitress arrived with our orders. Ward and Harry started eating while I stared at my bowl of chili.

I'd forgotten to order some sour cream, but the waitress remembered I usually did and had brought a side dish. Either my wanting sour cream with chili had been so unusual that it had stuck in her mind or I had a "usual" too. Caliber conversion, I thought—pretty clever indeed.

Now Ward has always told me that murderers weren't very smart. That it was a sign of stupidity to see no way out except to kill somebody—whether or not the victim deserved killing. I picked up my spoon and took a small taste of the chili. Without asking, the waitress had brought ketchup, hot sauce, and drink refills to the table along with our orders. Harry had covered his fries in ketchup. I reached for the hot sauce. The waitress knew what her customers wanted before they asked for it. The cost of the meal was going up.

Harry wolfed down his biscuits and left. "Back to the salt mines," as he put it. The man could turn a phrase. Couldn't remember to thank me for lunch, but sure could turn a phrase.

"You and Sergeant Johns seem to be getting along famously." Ward had a wide grin stretched across his long face. "Like a house on fire, I'd say."

"You're a funny guy, all right. Does he always go out of his way to bug people?"

"Not everybody, but he's got your number and seems to be enjoying it." Ward shrugged. "He knows his stuff, that's for sure. I can put up with a surly competent easier than a surly buffoon."

"How much did you know about caliber conversion sleeves before today? You were just bluffing, weren't you?"

Ward had saved one of the toothpicks that had held his sandwich together and was chewing on it. The yellow cellophane ribbon that marked one end of the toothpick jiggled in the air. He pulled it out and pointed it at me. "I didn't have to admit my ignorance, yours was more than sufficient.

"So," he put the toothpick back in his mouth, "how does finding the murder weapon help us find the killer?"

It hadn't been that many years ago that the toothpick would have been a cigarette. He'd quit, but some of the habits lingered.

Personally, I was beginning to regret that extra splash of hot sauce. "The murderer had to know about the sleeve-thing, he had to know that there were rifles on display that would fire, and he had to know enough to match the right sleeve to the right rifle—or she did." There was nothing that indicated the sex of the killer. Heck there was nothing that indicated if they were left- or right-handed.

"So we've got a knowledgeable gunman or gun-woman who had been to the Press often enough or long enough to spot a Remington Model 700—one of the most popular rifles ever made." I shook my head. "Not much help."

Jim took the toothpick out of his mouth and looked around the table for a place to put it. In the old days when people smoked in restaurants at least we had ashtrays on the tables that nonsmokers could use for trash. Our efficient and perceptive waitress had cleared our table so there was nothing other than the salt and pepper shakers with a drink menu propped up between them and our drink glasses. I'd given her a good tip—actually she'd earned a good tip and I'd recognized it. Jim leaned forward and stuck a long arm out to the un-bussed table to his right and flipped the toothpick onto a plate.

Freed from the toothpick, he sat back in his chair. "Now we can be pretty sure that the second entrance to the building, the one at 5:07, was meant to confuse us. Philip must have been killed between 4:27 and 5:07."

"How do you figure?"

Jim went on. "Originally I liked the 5:07 time for the murderer's entrance since he'd have been less likely to be seen after hours. And the killer must have wanted not to be seen, right?"

I nodded agreement.

"But the cleaners enter the building at 5:30—some twenty plus minutes later.

"Twenty-two." I was proud of my math skills.

"But now we know that the killer planned on using that rifle." Ward started ticking points off on his fingers. "And he planned on cleaning it and putting it back in place—hiding it from us, if you will. That means he had to count on having enough time to take the rifle from the wall, load the rifle with the sleeve, kill Douglas, get the cleaning equipment, take the sleeve out, clean the rifle, wipe off the fingerprints, put it back on the wall, put up the cleaning supplies, and get out of the building without being seen.

"I can see that happening between 4:27 and 5:07 a whole lot easier than 5:07 and 5:30. What do you think?"

"Think? I think we should have asked Harry how long it takes to get a recently fired rifle as clean as he found it."

"Yeah," Ward nodded his head. "I'll check with him when I get back. But I'm thinking that if the killer knew about the cleaners then he had to have planned the earlier entrance and threw in the second entrance just because he could.

"If he didn't know about the cleaners' schedule—that he'd be discovered if he wasn't out by 5:30—that it was just luck on his part? Then we'll never catch him. He's stupid all right, but too damned lucky to ever get caught."

I thought about how cold-blooded a process the murder had to have been. Shoot Philip, then clean the rifle, hide the evidence, and all the while wanting to get as far away as possible from the scene. I shivered.

"So what's our next step?"

"Our next step is to check out the cocktail party alibi. Fines will be in the clear if we can find a couple of people who got to the party after 4:00 and before 5:00 who saw her while they were there. You need to talk to the last suspect we've got and then we need to decide what to do about this other guy. The one you said was a babbling idiot."

"Calvin Beck. I said he couldn't control his mouth and kept babbling on. I don't think I called him an idiot."

"Well, he's an idiot if he thinks that alibi will hold up. His boss says they do have a regularly scheduled Wednesday meeting that starts at 4:00 and usually lasts an hour. The guy says he schedules it that late to encourage people not to talk so much. Makes sense I guess."

"If any of his coworkers talk like him, it makes a ton of sense. If I have to talk to him again I may try that." I shook my head. "No, you just said he had a solid alibi."

"If they'd had the meeting on Wednesday. They moved it back to Tuesday that week. They had just started having it on Wednesdays two or three weeks ago."

"Really?" I was surprised. Maybe he should be a suspect. "That's interesting, isn't it?"

"Not when you've seen hundreds of alibis that weren't alibis lead to nothing except poor memory." Ward stood up. "His boss said getting the day wrong was pretty typical of the guy. Said he was 'calendar challenged' or some such. Never been good at remembering when things had happened."

With that, Ward stood up. "I've got another meeting to go to and then I've got to go back to the office. Lovely stuff paperwork."

I stood up and shook his hand. "I'll let you know when I get to meet the third suspect." We walked to the door and stepped out into the bright sunshine. Ward's car was parked at the door so he got in. I waved at him and started walking down the street to where I had left my car. I blinked my eyes trying to get them to adjust to the light faster. I really don't know if that does any good but I like the feeling of doing something.

. . .

I got home and did some pet owner chores, then some home-
owner ones. It's easier for me to do a little every day rather than
all at once. While I was going through the routine, I was thinking about what Ward had said.

A killer that was incredibly stupid and even more incredibly
lucky? I didn't like the feel of that. Maybe it was just the thought
of a killer being that stupid and successful. Maybe it was just the
feeling I had about this murder—my second. No, I corrected
myself, the third murder but the second investigation. It could be
all those years dealing with undergraduates. This murder didn't
have the feel of a freshman trying to even up a score. No, this
was more the action of a supremely confident egotist who
couldn't imagine anything he did ever going wrong.

It took a couple of seconds, but then I remembered that if
you wanted arrogant, it was hard to beat a college undergrad—or
high school senior.

We had figured out "how" but this time it didn't tell me
"who." The "how" just made me wonder. Why make it so complex? Why clean the rifle? For that matter, why even put it back
on the wall? Just wipe your fingerprints off or, better yet, wear
gloves. What was the murderer thinking? Surely more than "it
seemed like a good idea at the time."

My phone rang and jerked me out of my musings. It was
Victoria and she'd finally gotten in touch with Bernard Charles.
He'd been in Detroit for the week and hadn't paid any attention
to phone messages until he got back to Atlanta. He had been invited to come to Shelbyville this weekend for the football game
and would be happy to meet with me then. Victoria had gone
ahead and made the appointment for us to meet at the College of
Communication's pregame party.

I got the details, plus his cell phone number, and loaded them into my calendar. That's when I realized that the weekend was nearly here—talk about being calendar challenged—and I hadn't made any arrangements to get together with Bobby. Bad idea, I told myself, she's all too likely to have something to do. If I didn't try to be part of her life, she'd fill it up with other things. She wasn't the kind of woman who needed to have a man around—one of the reasons it made it so pleasant to be around her.

I glanced at the time. She'd still be at work. There was the football game as well as the interview on Saturday. I started dialing her number. Maybe we could find something to do in spite of that.

"This is Bobby Slater, can I help you?"

She had a great voice and I could picture her seated at her desk at the Press.

"Hi Bobby, it's Ford. You busy?" If I'm planning on more that a quick call, I like to make sure the person on the other end of the line has time to chat.

She laughed. "I'm at work, Ford, of course I'm busy—but I can take a phone call—that's why I answered."

"Huh?"

"If I wasn't willing to be interrupted I wouldn't have answered the phone. That's what answering machines are for."

I had to admit what she said made a lot of sense. I just wasn't sure how many other people could ignore a ringing phone. Nevertheless, she had thrown me off my conversational stride and I had to back up and start over. "The reason I called—"

"Was to talk to me, I assume. Unless this is a wrong number?"

I gave up. "Would you like to do something with me this weekend? I know it's a home football game but I was wondering if we couldn't find something else to do."

"I'm going out of town this weekend. Going to see some friends up in Cranbury, Tennessee. Sometimes, I avoid the crowds by getting out of town. Sorry. Thanks for asking."

She sounded like she was sorry and I knew I was. "OK, what about that dinner I owe you? Have you ever been to Trey's?"

"That new little restaurant downtown? I've been meaning to give it a try."

"Let's do it. When should I pick you up?" I had been to Trey's a couple of times. It was pricey but the food was fantastic."

"Tonight? I was planning on packing for my trip."

"You were planning on eating weren't you?"

Her laugh gurgled in her throat. "All right, but I can't stay out late if that's OK?"

"No problem. We'll eat early. Pick you up at six?"

. . .

Which explains why I was driving across the downtown bridge with Bobby in the passenger seat. It was what she called a "school night" since she had to go to work the next day. To my disappointment, but not surprise there was no overnight bag to put in the car. I was glad I'd dressed up a little replacing my usual khakis with dress slacks. Bobby was wearing what I'd call a black cocktail dress—knee length, square yoke with more than a glimpse of cleavage—call it a promise, if you will. A silver necklace and earrings set it off. I hadn't quite howled at the moon when I saw her, but I had pawed the ground.

I found a parking place near the restaurant, parked the car, and went around and opened the door for her. She looked just as good getting out of the car as she had getting in. It was a short walk and I opened the door to the restaurant and followed her in. There was a small sitting area at the door with overstuffed arm-chairs and a sofa, behind that was a short bar, room maybe for six or seven drinkers, behind that a few tables and the entrance to the kitchen. The rest of the seating was through an arch on the left.

A tall man garbed in the almost universal uniform of a waiter, white shirt and black slacks, approached us, smiling warmly. "Two for dinner?"

"I called ahead, just in case. The name's Crawford."

He stopped at a small table, drew a line through what I assumed was my name written on a clipboard, and picked up some menus. "If you'll follow me?" He led us through the archway and into a larger room with tables scattered across the floor and a series of booths across the far wall. I'd guess it could hold sixty people easily enough. There were three people at one table, two couples at another, and nobody else. There hadn't been anybody at the bar either.

I don't pretend to understand the economics of running a restaurant but I didn't see how they stayed in business.

Our waiter led us to a table for four and pulled out the chair for Bobby. I waited until she was seated then sat across from her.

"The chef wants me to encourage you to save room for dessert. We have some specials tonight that are extra special. Would you like to start out with something to drink?"

"Life is uncertain," Bobby met my gaze across the table. "Should we have dessert first?"

"If we were going to have what I want for dessert we should have stayed at your house." I could feel my heart pounding, hear a roaring in my ears as I stared at her green eyes. She held my gaze and began to blush.

The waiter disappeared into the wherever it is that good waiters go when their presence is unwanted.

With her eyes fixed on mine Bobby leaned forward and pulled her shoulders in until the promise of cleavage was fulfilled. I dropped my eyes.

"Made you look."

"That's hardly playing fair."

"Silly boy, if that's what you wanted when you called you should have said so."

I felt my ears turn bright red.

"That would have been the smart thing to have done." My voice was little more than a croak.

She sat back in her chair with a small smile on her lips. "Dessert first sounds good to me. Take me home."

I looked over at the door to the kitchen where the waiter was standing and waved goodbye. I left a twenty on the table for the tip he would have gotten and helped Bobby with her chair.

· · ·

Afterward, Bobby had sent me home since she really did need to get ready for her trip and claimed that I was a distraction. I left after promising to take her back to Trey's for a real meal. Since I hadn't made any arrangements to care for Tan, I had to go home anyway. TB would have been fine.

I had taken the opportunity to meet Bobby's cat, a Mister Whiskers by name. A great fuzzy cat who didn't mind if beauty was only skin deep—how deep did it have to be? Bobby had called him her "no" cat—one that you're always saying "no" to. In fact she thought the cat believed his name to be "No, Mister, no."

Back at the house I was rummaging through the kitchen wondering what I could throw together for supper. I finally decided to sauté some tilapia in olive oil—concoct a lemon and butter sauce—sort of a piccata sauce but without the capers. I would add some angel hair pasta to the sauce. That and a white wine should do it. Hmmm. Maybe a pinot grigio? No, might not be able to stand up to the lemon.

I put some water in a pan and turned on the burner. Cooking the pasta was going to take about as long as the fish, once the water boiled. Time to squeeze the lemon and dust the fillet with flour and then turn the heat on under the frying pan. Since the olive oil was going to be part of the sauce I added more than I needed to just cook the fish. I took a sip of scotch while trying to judge the timing then put the strainer in the sink, preparing for pouring the water off the pasta.

It was a simple enough recipe, you just had to pay attention to the timing.

. . .

After eating I rinsed off my plate, put it, the silverware, and my wine glass in the dishwasher. I went ahead and washed the pot and pan by hand. I could have left them soaking in the sink but it felt better to get it done.

I freshened up my drink and went to see what was on television on a Thursday night. There were a couple of hundred channels available but nothing really appealed to me. I caught the tail end of an old documentary on the Freedom riders. One of the people mentioned in the credits was Adele Morgan Charles, the mother of the man I was going to meet on Saturday. It's a small world. I'm sure I wouldn't have noticed her name if I hadn't recently been reminded of it.

The next show was going to start right after a little break for fund-raising. I'd already sent in my pledge so I shouldn't have to suffer through these drives, but that's not the way it works. I turned the TV off and went searching for a book that I vaguely remembered. It had been Eleanor's but I didn't think I'd gotten rid of it. Couldn't remember if it had been about Adele or written by her. Found the book even though it didn't look like I remembered it. Sure enough, it was published by the Press—we probably bought it at their annual book sale—and it was written by Adele Morgan Charles.

The author's dedication included a reference to M. W. Stefenson and his courage in helping bring the book to publication. Intrigued, I took the book over to my easy chair, turned the reading light on, and started reading. Shortly thereafter, The Black climbed over the back of the chair and stretched out in my lap, purring as he settled down. He was probably tired from playing with his toys all day.

I'd stayed up late reading Mrs. Charles's book—later than I had intended. I meant to flip through it but her chapter on George Wallace's actions as governor and consummate politician during the days leading up to the integration of the university got me hooked. I certainly remembered the event and some of the details, but none of the behind-the-scenes negotiations.

The thought struck me that I'd spent the evening with two very different women in very different manners—and found them both fascinating. I mentioned this to Tan—the other female in my life. She pointed out that I should take her for a walk. So I did.

We started out at a good pace but had to slow it down on our way back to the house. I hadn't put a lead on her, just carried it with me in case something came up, but she didn't wander away from my side like she used to when she was young. I recognized the signs of aging—hell, I sympathized. I tried to figure out how old she was and decided that she couldn't be as old as that. I'd have to check with the vet.

As we walked along, I reviewed my to-do list. I needed to call my accountant back. We'd been playing telephone tag. Fortunately tax season hadn't started so she might be able to meet with me this afternoon. I don't know how she puts up with tax season—from the start of the year through April, OK, the middle of April. Twelve hour days are the short ones.

On another front, I'd started the process of getting licensed as a private investigator in Alabama. Well, state licensing was just a business license. All they wanted was my money—back to my accountant and what she had to say.

Shelbyville actually had licensing requirements. They were basically character related—some references from upright citizens. That and checking for criminal history—making sure I hadn't been convicted of a felony. All-in-all not too rigorous but better than nothing. The city council had to approve my petition. I was thinking about asking Captain Ward to be a reference, if it wasn't a conflict of interest. Rufus had agreed without hesitation as had some others.

What did that leave? I stopped walking and tried to remember what Victoria had scolded me about. Tan immediately sat down and looked up at me, happy for the break. I looked at her. "Business cards?" Tan cocked her head and wagged her tail. "Oh, right, graphic artist for the business cards." I'd mentioned business cards to an artist I'd done some work with and she'd immediately wanted to know if she could use the outline of a gun in the design. I accused her of wanting to do a "gun for hire" kind of thing but she was too young to remember *Have Gun— Will Travel.*

"Richard Boone," I said to Tan. "Paladin. One of the best television shows ever. How can she never even have heard of it?" Tan was as mystified as I was. I could tell from the puzzled look in her eyes. "Youth cannot excuse everything," I exclaimed and we started back to the house.

We came back into the house and Tan went immediately to her water bowl. I could hear the sound of her lapping up water as I picked up the stack of mail that had accumulated on the small table at the door since the last time I'd gone through it. There was a time when I went through the mail on a daily basis, but no longer. I walked over to the kitchen trash can and started sorting—bills on the counter—almost everything else in the trash. There weren't that many bills anymore. I'd gone to online billing when I could. I wasn't as excited about auto-pay as the companies sending the bills were. There was something about giving monopolies and corporations unlimited access to my checking account that made me uneasy. Since my checking account didn't have unlimited resources, I preferred to authorize payment.

"Invoice." The word popped out of my mouth. Tan was standing at the door out to the backyard and looked quizzically at me, once again cocking her head to one side. "Victoria wants me to send the university a bill for services rendered to date—remember?"

I opened the door and let Tan outside so she could sleep in the sun until it got too warm and she moved into the shade. It didn't really matter. I couldn't accuse her of not reminding me since I don't think I'd mentioned it since speaking to Victoria. Maybe I should wait until I had talked to my accountant? Would she buy that? Victoria that is, not my accountant—or Tan.

. . .

After lunch I stopped at the Press while on my way to meet with Janet, my accountant. I didn't have a good reason to be there but it really was on my way—sort of.

Bobby was in a meeting so I wandered over to Frank's office. I hesitated at the open doorway and he looked up from his computer monitor.

"Hey, Crawford, you looking for Bobby?"

"She's in a meeting. I guess I should have called before stopping by."

Frank shrugged his shoulders. "She's real deadline oriented—probably trying to catch up before leaving town. I, on the other hand, am tired of this manuscript. Come in, sit down, and tell me what's up." He turned and pointed at a chair next to the wall.

"Working on a manuscript?" I walked over to the offered chair and sat. "Electronically I see." I nodded at the monitor. "I thought Philip wouldn't let you do that."

"Oh, he didn't like it but here and there we slipped in some exceptions—like this one." He puffed air through his mustache. "My guess is that all of our submissions will be electronic from now on. Most authors don't care—as long as the book gets published."

"What's it about?" Bobby had told me that the Press accepted a wide range of topics.

"It's sort of a hook and bullet book about Robert Clay Allison." Frank waited to see if the name meant anything to me.

"Who he?"

"Western gunslinger only he called himself a 'shootist.' Lived during the mid- to late 1800s. Joined the Confederate Army and got discharged for 'personality problems.'"

"'Personality problems?' You'd think the army would be the place for a gunslinger."

"Had some issues with authority at a guess."

"Hmmm, sounds interesting."

"It will be when I get through editing it. Oh, the manuscript quotes Allison as claiming, 'I never killed a man that didn't need killing.' It's supposed to be on his tombstone. According to what I've read, he killed a sizable number of people."

"Really? And we're supposed to take his word that they all needed killing, I guess?"

"Sure, but that's a clue for you. Lots of people said that Philip 'needed killing.' You just need to find the one who decided to emulate Clay Allison!"

"Thanks, Frank, that's so helpful."

Frank laughed and stroked his mustache. "Hey, you knew the job was dangerous when you took it."

"So, of the suspects, who's the most like Mr. Allison?"

"I don't know that any of the names we gave you has left a string of corpses behind them.

"In general, most of our authors are academics who can be ruthless in the pursuit of truth—or tenure, but the backstabbing is figurative not literal. I mean look at the suspects—one ecologist, one social activist, and one outdoorsman. That's a pretty representative sample of what we deal with."

"How do the outdoorsmen get along with the ecologists? I wouldn't think 'tree huggers' would take to the hunters and fishermen."

"You're mixing up the ecologists with PETA members. More often than not the hunters, fishers, and ecologists are all on the same side—preservation."

"There you are. Hiding in Frank's office again." Bobby appeared in the doorway. I'd never seen her in faded denim before. Evidently the Press observed casual Friday or maybe she was wearing traveling clothes. I couldn't tell by what Frank was wearing, he looked as scruffy as ever.

I stood up and moved forward to hug and kiss her then hesitated, looking for any sign of reluctance—pubic displays of affection in the office place being frowned on and so forth. She wrapped her arms around my neck and lifted up her face so I could kiss her. So much for office protocol.

"Hey, rent a room will ya? Or at least take it out of my office."

I lifted my head. "I think we're bothering Frank."

"Men," replied Bobby, releasing my neck, "are so shy about the silliest things."

I hadn't thought the idea of renting a room was either being shy or silly—initially at least.

Bobby's face lit up with her killer smile. "Are you coming by to tell me what a great time we had last night? Because I already know." She winked at Frank.

"On a work night!" yelped Frank. "Crawford, I'm impressed!"

At first I thought he was kidding me, but he looked like he meant it.

I followed Bobby as we left Frank's office and headed to hers. "Have you changed your mind? Are you coming up to Cranbury with me? I can call Rebecca and tell her there's going to be another guest for supper. I know she won't mind and you'll like her husband, Jack."

"I can't leave until after I meet with Bernard Charles." For a moment I wondered if it was that important. "He doesn't come over to Shelbyville very often; I'm already committed to an appointment with him tomorrow morning." I shrugged my shoulders. "Can I have a rain check?"

"Sure," Bobby seemed a little let down and I appreciated it. "I go up there three or four times a year, you'll have other chances. For that matter they'll be coming down here for The Festival next month. Maybe you can go out to eat with us then?"

The folk art festival had been held on the last weekend of October for the last thirty years, growing more and more popular every year. When the university had a home game on the same weekend as The Festival, the city became gridlocked. Hotels, motels, bed and breakfasts, parking lots, restaurants, fast food joints, they all were filled to capacity. That's what happens when the stadium holds more people than live in the city and The Festival draws people from all across the country.

"How about you planning on coming to my house for supper? It's a football weekend so the restaurants will be packed. I'll grill out steaks."

"Great! Jack would love that, he likes to grill too."

"It's a date then—on one condition."

"And what's that?" Bobby looked puzzled.

"That I don't have to wait until then for our next date."

. . .

I got home later that day with pages of notes from my meeting with my accountant. She'd also given me some self-help articles about being self-employed. It had been an eye-opener for me. I'd seen all the deductions on my paycheck that the university had taken out while I was their employee and hadn't realized it was just the half of it. For all the talk politicians made about helping the small businessman or -woman it didn't seem to me that anybody got hosed more than the self-employed. But what did I know? Janet was self-employed, she could have been biased.

I put my suggested reading down and called Captain Ward of Shelbyville's finest. He was in his office, late on a Friday afternoon and even answered his phone.

"Ward, what you doing there so late? I figured you'd be leaving early what with the game being tomorrow."

"I'm still here trying to finish up some things so that I won't have to be here tomorrow—or the next day. I'm taking the weekend off." His voice was gruff and it didn't seem like a good time to chat.

I'd been wanting to talk to him about how the complexity of the case was beginning to worry me. What was behind the whole plan on using one of the deceased's rifles to murder him with? The murderer had ammunition for a handgun, he probably had a handgun too. Why not use it and take it with him?

"So did you call for a reason? Come on, Crawford, don't waste my time." Gruff had escalated into grumpy.

Yeah, better to keep my worries to myself a little longer.

"I told you I'd let you know when I finally got an appointment with the third suspect."

"Are you going to tell me when it is or just the fact that it is?"

Testy, I decided, not gruff or grumpy, but testy.

"Sorry, it's tomorrow before the game. I'm meeting him at the pregame party at the College of Communications."

Ward snorted. "Pregame party? Really going to grill him aren't you?

"Look, unless he confesses and can't wait to surrender until Monday, I'm taking the weekend off. Got it?"

"Got it," I said and then heard the click. Poor guy sounded stressed. He really should try to take some time off even if it was only a weekend.

Saturday was a beautiful day. It wasn't cool enough for a football game, but that's what happens during September in the South. Still it was clear, sunny, and had a nice breeze to keep things from getting too hot. Once you got in the stadium the breeze would be blocked, the sun directly overhead, and there'd be a few fans that would pass out from heat stroke. Of course, there would be others passing out from too much bourbon as well.

Before the game started, the sidelines would be filled with air conditioners, misting stations, oxygen masks, cold energy drinks, ice, and fans—air-moving fans, not the cheering variety—anything the trainers could concoct to help the players cope with the heat. The visiting team's benches would be directly in the sun, while the home team would sit in the shade.

Some people think that college football is taken too seriously in the South. That it's more like a war or a religion. Some go so far as to say it is linked to the Civil War, or the War between the States as some call it. It is true that the South is the only part of the United States that's been occupied by a hostile army. I can't really say having never lived anywhere else, but there are those who point out that football fields run north and south—as if that orientation meant anything.

At any rate, we take our football seriously but we take our pre- and postgame activities seriously too. Before the game was the time to meet old friends and greet new ones. A time for alumni to reminisce about old times and victories that grow sweeter with time and faded memories. A time for the university to catch those successful alumni in mellow moods, receptive to fund-raising requests that they would ignore at any other time.

All over campus the different colleges were having their own gatherings to celebrate before the game. A chance to reward donors with drink and food while using the same to recruit others. Colleges and departments developed their own lines of donations while trying to avoid the notice of university relations—the official fund-raising branch of the university. Many a college rued the day their donor had caught the attention of the university's professional fund-raisers—the university's gain was the department's loss.

I had parked my car at the edge of campus, being careful to pick a spot that shouldn't get blocked by people parking illegally. The city and the University Police worked together trying to keep emergency routes from being blocked by cars abandoned by drivers desperate to get to the game. The companies that tow those cars away are only concerned about public safety—not the fees they charge. At least that's what they say. Home football games were a boost to the local economy in more ways than one.

My office had been on the other side of campus so I wasn't familiar with the area where I had parked. I wasn't going to get lost since the College of Communications was in a building that stood next to the stadium. It would be more accurate to say that it stood in the shadow of the stadium since the stadium dominated the skyline of Shelbyville. All I had to do was head to the stadium.

Because of its location, Communication's pregame party was second only to the president's in popularity. Location, once again, was of prime importance. The closer you were to the stadium the longer you could stay at the party and the longer you could watch the parade of fans before joining the crowd.

I have no idea why women have decided that going to the game or even just going to the parties requires them to dress in their finest, but they have. Somebody once told me that if you wanted to see what next year's women's fashions were going to be, all you had to do was look at what prostitutes were wearing this year. I found myself believing it.

As I strolled along I realized that all the foot traffic was headed in the same direction. The occasional pedestrian headed in the opposite direction must have felt like a salmon swimming upstream—or maybe not since salmon all swim upstream together. I pondered this as I walked. Maybe we should change the saying? "Felt like a salmon who got halfway up the stream and then changed his mind?" Nope, that needed some work. I shrugged my shoulders and felt the unfamiliar weight of a jacket on my shoulders.

I had bowed to the convention that required me to wear a coat and tie to the pregame party but had drawn the line at the traditional navy-blue wool blazer that most Southern men wore as a fashion uniform. Fashion-wise it was fall, weather-wise it was another story. That dark color would have sucked up the heat from the sun and cooked the wearer. Now that I think about it, I had harkened back to an earlier fashion—the seersucker suit—what every southern gentleman wore before the advent of air conditioning. It had rumpled the moment I put it on, proving its authenticity.

As I got closer to the stadium the foot traffic got thicker and I noticed that I wasn't the only one to have ignored the fashion calendar in favor of comfort. Of course, it was the older and wiser of us that had come to the same fashion decision, but that didn't bother me. I was sorry that I hadn't thought to get a Panama hat to top it off.

And with that thought I saw the classic southern gentleman striding down the sidewalk toward me. White suit, string tie, broad-rimmed Panama hat—he was lacking just the polished cane and black, twisted cheroot—Steven Stefenson. As we came abreast of each other, we stopped and shook hands.

"How goes the investigation, Inspector Crawford?"

I couldn't decide if he was serious or merely making fun of me. "Funny you should ask, I'm on my way to talk to the third suspect now. Hopefully I'll be able to get a word in edgewise with this one."

"I take it you've talked to Mr. Beck then?"

"I wouldn't say that I talked to him, more that I was in the same room as he was while he was talking." I grinned. "I find it hard to consider him a murderer—a talker, yes, but a murderer?"

If I had thought that Stefenson had been condescending before, I was mistaken. "Are you that easily misled, then? I would have thought the provost would have placed his trust in someone more perceptive. I understand the man is quite knowledgeable about rifles, bullets, chamber adaptors, rate of fire—things you should be interested in. Sad," he sniffed. "Still, Calvin does play the buffoon quite well when it suits him, doesn't he? But that's what it is—an act. Trust me on that." With that last remark he walked past me.

I stared after him for a moment or two. He was probably headed for the president's mansion to attend the pregame party there. Nothing but the best for Steven Stefenson. I guess I should have been grateful that he even acknowledged my presence.

I walked up the stairs of the Communications Building. The fact that the building wasn't named after somebody argued well for the integrity of the journalism graduates the college produced. None had gone on to make so much money that they could endow the school and have it named after them. I pulled open the door and entered the rotunda. A staircase leading to the upper floor was directly across; hallways leading to offices and classrooms flanked the stairs. There were a few people here and there, several standing at the bar, while others wandered looking at the plaques and such that adorned the walls.

For the second time in just a matter of minutes I saw a man wearing a white suit. He was reading one of the plaques, so I only saw the back of his head. Funny, Victoria hadn't mentioned to me how I was going to recognize this guy. I hadn't thought about it until this very moment.

The man in the white suit turned around and I wondered—the idea popping into my mind like Minerva springing from Zeus's brow—if he went by the name of Bernard these day.

His signature grin began to stretch across his face, bracketed by dimples as he walked over to me.

"James Crawford or JC, as some called you," he said with obvious delight. "I always thought the allusion to Jesus Christ was overdone."

Back during the undergraduate years of my life I had let my hair and beard grow out until some of my more clean-cut friends felt obliged to tease me about my purported resemblance to biblical figures. As my initials are J. C. the result was inevitable, I suppose.

I gripped him by the shoulders and saw that while the unmistakable grin hadn't changed, the jet-black hair now had flecks of gray in it. "Well, hell, Princeton." I said in the broadest southern accent I could muster. "At least I was using my real name back when we used to close the Polo Grounds down."

I remembered him vividly. He'd come to Shelbyville after having been "asked to withdraw" from Princeton. He'd used the name Charles Bernard Morgan III but we'd all called him Princeton. He'd been pretty evasive about the details of what exactly had happened in New Jersey—other than he'd been asked to leave because of grades—a much more polite way of saying "flunked out" I thought. As I remembered it, he only spent a spring semester and part of the summer here.

At the time I had thought, or had been led to believe, that he'd gotten into a little trouble and was hiding out where no one would think to look for him. Whether it was antiwar protests, drugs, or just what, had never been very clear. Maybe that was because most of us who were antiwar were pro-drugs? I had as smoky a memory of the time as most—certainly as smoky a memory as this guy did.

"When the provost's assistant—Victoria, is that her name? Anyway when she said the provost would appreciate it if I'd agree to talk to one James Crawford, I couldn't resist."

It clicked for me then. I'd met some other Princeton graduates over the years and they all talked about the requirement for seniors to write a thesis as part of their senior year. Had to do it or they couldn't graduate. They talked about it as if it was some rite of passage—maybe it was.

I took a step back and pointed my finger at him. "So what was the title of your senior thesis? That's what you were doing down here, right? Collecting data for your thesis?"

He cocked his head to one side and nodded. "Pretty good, Crawford. Maybe the provost knows what he's doing. Yeah, I compared the civil rights movement to the antiwar movement particularly in the South—Alabama to be exact. Mom suggested it to me and it was a hell of a topic—even if I was too young and ignorant to completely understand it. I used it all the way up to and including my dissertation. But, hey," that wicked grin flashed across his face. "That wasn't the only thing I did while I was here. I made some friends. I came to your wedding, didn't I?"

I laughed and pointed at the bar. "Let's at least get a drink if we're going to start with the reminiscing."

He had come to the wedding at the last moment, calling from the airport for somebody to come pick him up. He'd been wearing a white linen suit then too, jet-black hair and some stubble. Still evasive about where he'd been and what he'd been doing. For a moment I wondered who we'd sent to pick him up. Eleanor would have had the name at the tip of her tongue. It had only been a couple of years after we'd first met. In our wedding pictures I still was pretty shaggy.

"Sorry about Eleanor. I heard, but funerals just aren't my thing."

"It's OK. I don't remember much about that time—who was here and who wasn't." That wasn't entirely true. I didn't have many memories of that time, but the ones I did were sharp, clear—painfully so even now. I took a sip of my screwdriver and Bernard sipped his Bloody Mary. "Charles Bernard Morgan instead of Bernard Morgan Charles? Your mother was Adele?"

He looked at his drink and made a face. "Yeah. She was," he stood up straighter, "she was and I'm proud to say it."

I reached out and took the drink out of his hand." I think the bartender has confused gin with vodka in both our drinks. How about a beer? He should be able to get that right."

"Is that what's wrong with it?"

"Either that or they've developed a vodka that tastes like juniper berries."

After negotiating with the bartender we settled on a Heineken for each of us. We left him staring at two different liquor bottles that held clear liquid. For the department's sake I hoped the bartender kept them straight at least until the game started.

"I thought you told us you were from a suburb of Chicago."

"That was my youthful idea of a cover story. Said I was from outside of Chicago instead of being from outside of Detroit." He took a swallow of beer. "Then I used mom's maiden name as my last name and Dad's last name as my first. Threw my given name in the middle to make it sound like old money and to cover any slips. Worked pretty well, didn't it?"

I wasn't sure why he'd felt it necessary to assume an alias. It's not like Charles is that uncommon a last name. It seemed to me just another example of people making things more complicated than necessary—and that reminded me why I'd wanted to meet Bernard Charles, the son of Adele Morgan Charles in the first place. "You still claim to be a practicing pacifist?"

"Or was that just draft-dodging rhetoric?" Bernard shook his head. "I am my mother's son—and my father's too—he just wasn't as vocal about it. I'm opposed to firearms, pro–passive resistance, admire Gandhi, and am totally opposed to violence in any form—except college football." He threw up his hand—the one without the beer in it. "I confess to that inconsistency, but only to that one. I detest professional football, for instance."

"I suppose you don't believe that a man could need killing, then?"

"Need killing? Are we talking about somebody in particular?" Bernard looked sharply at me. "That woman did mention that you were 'assisting' the provost in 'certain' matters. You trying to solve a murder, Crawford? You always did like to figure things out."

I shrugged my shoulders. As I remembered it, he was the smart one, but we both had our strengths.

"That's it, isn't it? I'm a suspect in the murder of Philip Douglas, aren't I? How delightful."

"Maybe you'd kill for your mother, if not for yourself?"

"Thereby violating one of her principles that was most important to her? What a monument to her memory and her teachings. No," he shook his head. "I was always going to get Mom's books republished. Philip's death might make it easier, but it was going to happen in any case."

"Mr. Charles, I didn't realize that you were already here!" A short heavy-set young man approached us, his right hand held out for a handshake."

I stepped back and watched Bernard turn on his charm.

He reached out and took the proffered hand. "Professor Shuttles, so nice to see you again. Thanks again for inviting me to the game. Let me introduce you to an old acquaintance of mine, James Crawford."

With a puzzled look in his eyes, the young man turned to me and held out his hand. "James Crawford?" As we were shaking hands I could see the wheels turning, after all he was a journalist.

"Professor Shuttles, it's a pleasure. I was just chatting with Bernard about old times." I flashed what I hoped was a disarming smile. "Times before you were born, I'm afraid."

"You with the university, James?"

"Recently retired," I acknowledged.

"And came out of retirement to solve a murder that nobody knew had happened." He grinned at being able to link the name with the story. He snapped his fingers. "No, two murders, right?"

I smiled and glanced over at Bernard. "Let's not let so many years pass before we see each other again. Is there a way I can get in touch with you?"

"Sure, let me give you one of my cards." Bernard reached into a coat pocket and pulled out a card case.

"Mine are at the printer's." I reached out and took the card out of Bernard's hand all the while kicking myself.

"Didn't you want to ask me if I had an alibi?" Bernard was grinning wickedly while his host was glancing back and forth between us.

"Why not?" I sighed. "Everybody else seems to have one."

"Mine might be better than most. When I heard about his death I wondered where I was when it happened, so I checked."

"And?"

"If I can trust the *Shelbyville News* to get the date and general time of day right, I was giving a lecture on the works of Adele Morgan Charles—at Princeton—the university that is."

CHAPTER 20
SATURDAY AFTERNOON

I escaped the throngs of fans on the sidewalks, got to my car, and made somebody's day—once they backed their car up and let me get out of my parking space. It was a prime spot they inherited. I drove carefully away from the campus and stadium. There was a time when I would have tried to use the back streets, side streets, and alleys to slip away from the university. But I gave it up years ago since people were just as likely to be partying there as they were anywhere else, and narrow streets made it harder to miss inebriated pedestrians. I was glad that the broadcast schedule had the game starting at two o'clock. Eleven o'clock is too early, it throws off the rhythm of the partygoers. They have to start drinking really early on a Saturday when the game starts before noon. On the other hand, if it's a night game, then they've been partying for too long—too many of them pass out and miss the point of the party—the game.

Not that you have to be smashed to go to the game, lord no. But gameday is festive, a party atmosphere, nothing else quite like it, people dressed in costumes whether they meant to be or not—excitement and high hopes all dependent on the outcome of a sporting event.

I ignored the ticket scalpers standing on the street corners and headed for the bridge and home.

. . .

When it comes to enjoying football, I usually listen to the radio commentary and watch the game on TV. The money is in the TV broadcast and the announcers seem compelled to hype what really doesn't need hype. If the visitors are down three or four touchdowns going into the fourth quarter—well, it's not likely they will rally and no rabid chattering is going to change that. The radio guys were unabashedly biased—something the TV people seem to overcompensate for to a point that they are rooting for the other team while just trying to keep the viewers watching.

I'd eaten at the pregame party—partly to see what was high fashion in the catering world this year and partly to take the taste of the gin out of my mouth. In all honesty, the bartender had been just as horrified to discover that what he thought was vodka was gin as I had been to taste it.

Anyway, that meant I wasn't really hungry but knew that I was going to be. There was no use thinking I could order a pizza, not on game day. It would take forever for it to get delivered. No, I was going to have to come up with something on my own. Or thaw something out. I usually kept some frozen meals around for times when I didn't feel like cooking. Beef tips, noodles, a salad, bread, and a cabernet. I'd made my decision.

Having resolved the issue of what I was going to eat if not when, I considered having another beer then poured myself a glass of water and began to discuss my day with Tan and The Black.

"Tan, do you remember—no you're not old enough to have met Princeton. What was I thinking?"

Tan had looked up when I spoke her name but as nothing seemed to be happening because of it, she went back to worrying a rawhide bone. Bones came in and out of favor with Tan. Actually that's not strictly true. Rawhide bones she could take or leave depending on some cosmic rule that makes sense to her but not to a human. Real bones, they were always appreciated to the point she ignored everything else.

The Black had his own method of deciding which toy was worth playing with and when. When he lost interest in a toy he'd just leave it—in the food dish, or in the middle of the floor or some other place where a human was bound to step on it. We had worked out a compromise. When I found an abandoned toy I would put it in his toy box—a milk crate in the laundry room. He would leave them there until he decided he was ready to play with them again. We hadn't reached the point where he was willing to put the toys away, but he did have fun getting them back out again. Tonight he was intent on a purple sock kind of thing that Bobby had given him. It crinkled and probably had catnip in it. TB tossed it up in the air and batted it across the kitchen floor.

I took my glass of water with me and went into the den to my recliner. Glanced at the time on the cable box and saw I had plenty of time before the game started. I hated tuning in too early because all announcers feel like they have to tell the audience information that any half-awake fan already knows—not to mention the commercials.

Since I had time, my mind turned back to Philip Douglas's murder—like Tan with his bone, my mind wanted to chew on what we knew, guessed, and suspected. I had to admit that Bernard looked like the least likely of suspects and I was inclined to dismiss him—in part because I had known him years ago and liked him. Obviously I hadn't known him that well back in the day and now I knew even less about him.

I thought about all three of the suspects I'd been given and how unsatisfactory they were. Absentmindedly I lifted up the footrest and leaned back in the recliner. Philip was a jerk—had been a jerk, I mean, but he'd been one for some time, hadn't he? Hmmm. I nodded to myself. Rufus had told me that Philip's behavior had gotten worse after his wife died, so maybe that didn't hold water. I considered that for a little while. Philip had been getting more so for the last two or three years until—until what? Until he got so much worse that he was murdered?

Fines's and Charles's animosity toward Philip was based on books the Press had already published—published under the prior director, at that. Philip was denying their requests for a reason—a reason that didn't seem to make any sense to me. One author had published a book that had been one of the Press's best sellers of all time. All she wanted to do was to re-release it as an anniversary edition. On the surface that looked to make the Press even more money. And Adele Charles? Well, she, her son that is, wanted her books re-released as a set. Thirty years ago, when the Press and the civil rights movement were both young, the books had been published. Their contents were a hell of lot less controversial today—most of the antagonists were dead after all. The Black jumped on the back of the chair and made his way down to my lap. I stroked him as he walked past. So two out of three suspects were connected to the prior director—did that mean anything?

I shook my head. That line of thought didn't seem to be getting me anywhere. I went back to how Philip might have changed. Frank had said that it wasn't unusual to have somebody mad at the director. Somebody was always angry at him. What had been strange or had seemed strange to Frank was that Philip had usually spaced things out—only angering one author or editor at a time. Was this what Rufus meant about how things had gotten worse? Frank had used the expression "actively angry" to describe the situation. Most people had to get on with their lives

and either dealt with Philip as a necessary evil or didn't deal
with him at all—thus dropped out of the "actively angry" cate-
gory into—what? The no-longer-actively-angry group?

But this time he'd gotten into arguments with three people
all within a relatively short period of time—unlike his usual behavior. Frank had said that when he looked back on his years of
working for Philip it seemed to him that Philip would pick his
battles and they were spaced out; well, one would die down before another flared up. What had struck Frank as unusual about
the month leading up to Philip's murder was that Philip had
three arguments going on at the same time—that and the fact
that he'd gotten killed.

TB had stretched out between my legs and I continued to
stroke his back and tail. All three fights had come up at about the
same time. Was Philip losing his ability to pace himself? I
smiled to myself. Clearly the man had liked to fire people up—
probably one of his less-endearing traits. But why would three
people who were heard saying that they'd like to see Philip dead
suddenly pop up right before somebody fulfilled their fantasy
and killed him? Was it just coincidence—or was there more to it
than that? Could the fact that there were others make it easier for
one of them to actually do it? I could feel the small vibration that
was TB's purr.

Yeah, I could see that. If all three of them had known that the
other two were as angry with Philip as they were—or almost as
angry—killing him might appear to be something that needed to
be done. As if the community had agreed that the man "needed
killing." Or if you were—what was the guy's name? right, Robert Clay Allison—you could kill because you never killed a man
who didn't deserve killing. So three suspects could make it more
likely that he'd get killed. You'd think the killer would want

there to be as many suspects as possible. I wondered what Ward would say when I told him of my theory—the murderer would want tons of other suspects. He'd probably tell me that murderers don't care how many suspects there are as long as they aren't numbered among them.

What if this was a case of turn-about? What if the suspects had picked fights with Philip and that's why there were more than usual—when Philip was picking the fights? For a few seconds I liked it as a theory—but what possible reason was there for them to pick fights with him? Talk about grasping at straws—no it had to have come from Philip.

TB sat up and began to lick his paws.

I still needed Ward to check out Bernard's alibi—I stopped myself from calling him. He'd made it pretty clear he was taking the weekend off, the last time we talked. I'm sure that he would think I was just calling him because I didn't know what else to do instead of—that I didn't know what else to do. I got out of the chair carefully leaving The Black as undisturbed as possible and went down to the office.

It didn't take long to find the announcement on the Princeton webpages. The title of the presentation was on the calendar and some undergraduate had written a review of the talk Bernard had given about his mother's work. As New Jersey was a good sixteen-hour drive from Shelbyville it just wasn't possible for him to have killed Philip Douglas.

Of course that alibi was only good for Bernard—what if he'd hired somebody to kill Philip? What if the murderer was a killer for hire?

That was a new wrinkle. I'd never considered that as a possibility before. I sat back in my chair and considered—the suspect with the best alibi, then, would be the most likely one to have paid the killer—right? Or would you know that much about how the killing was done? Or when it was done? Surely a murderer for hire would want some autonomy?

I was contemplating the intricacies involved when one introduces a hired killer into a murder investigation when I tried for the third or fourth time to take a sip of water from an empty glass. I stood up and my house of cards fell down. There was no way a professional would have killed Philip Douglas the way he had been killed. The complications of using a caliber conversion sleeve, cleaning the victim's rifle, using the victim's rifle, all of that struck me as totally unprofessional. And if somebody had tried to hire a killer with those kind of conditions attached they'd never have gotten anyone to agree to take the job.

TB met me at the kitchen door and was disappointed when I just got some crushed ice and water from the fridge door. "I know it seems like I'm wasting my time trying to figure out who the murderer was."

The Black didn't appear to disagree with me. "But it's like how they discovered one of the planets—Neptune I think." For some reason it looked like the cat had stopped to listen—waiting for my explanation. "They were figuring out all the orbits of the solar system—how the orbits of the planets and moons were impacted by gravity, but the model kept predicting the wrong orbits. The only way they could get the model to work was if there was another planet the size of Neptune where Neptune had to be. So they looked and—by damn—there was Neptune. Don't you think that's cool?"

The Black didn't look like he was impressed or thought the discovery of Neptune to be anything close to cool. In fact, he yawned. Tan looked interested but that was probably because she thought it might be a new word for treat.

Could all the complexity surrounding Philip Douglas's murder have been caused by something we don't know about the murder? Was there something out there that was changing the orbits that we couldn't detect except by the strange actions we uncovered? Something out there hidden in the tall grass?

I looked around the kitchen uneasily. There was something "not right" about the afternoon. The game. I had forgotten all about the game! It must be almost halftime by now. It just goes to show you that heavy thinking can ruin your priorities. Shaking my head and laughing at myself, I put my glass in the sink and noticed that the light on the phone was blinking. Not only had I been so lost in thought that I'd forgotten about a game I'd been looking forward to watching, but I hadn't even heard the phone. I told the dog and cat, still chuckling, that one of these days I'd forget to feed them. They didn't seem amused. I'd set the game up to be recorded, so I hadn't missed seeing any of the plays, but I hadn't recorded the radio broadcast. Oh, well. I picked up the phone to see who had called but it was just an out-of-state phone number. Still, it didn't match any numbers I had in my contact list. It was a Tennessee area code. Bobby was visiting friends who lived in Tennessee. I decided to check for messages since I was pretty sure she wasn't calling to ask me about the game. I smiled to myself. Yes, that was Bobby's voice.

It was Sunday morning. It was early Sunday morning. Actually it was so early that it didn't matter what day of the week it was—that's how early it was. I had given up lying in bed staring at the ceiling and not falling back asleep. The kitty litter had been cleaned out. The newspaper brought in. Coffee drunk. I'd checked the sports section and all of yesterday's games had turned out just like I had seen them end the day before. There were a few West Coast scores that were news to me but that was because I hadn't cared enough to stay up past midnight to watch them.

The day was starting out dark and wet. The clouds were low and it looked like the weather couldn't decide between a drizzle, light rain, or mist. A perfectly good day to spend in bed.

I'd read the sports section, local news, regional news, editorials, and comics. Hell, I'd even looked at the classifieds. And it was still early Sunday morning—too early to call anybody, much less an old friend from college who had just found out he was a murder suspect. Nope, when I had known him, Bernard Charles hadn't been an early riser and I didn't much think that would have changed. And I wanted to ask a favor of him, so I sure didn't want to irritate him by calling too early.

I changed the water bowl and put the three toys that TB had scattered around his food bowl back in his toy box.

Something was making me jittery and it wasn't the coffee. A walk would help. So why was I resisting it?

"Well, a little water never hurt us before, did it, Tan?"

I'd opened the door to the backyard earlier and Tan had looked at the dampness and looked back up at me like, "Are you kidding?" She'd gone back to her bed and curled up. She wasn't having any problems with sleeping on a rainy day.

I got a light jacket with a hood off of the coatrack and slipped it on. Water wouldn't hurt my sneakers or anything else. The cell phone was in an Otter Box so it should be safe. With a shrug I threw my wallet on the counter and just slipped the case with my driver's license and insurance card into my pocket. If anything did happen, they'd be able to tell who I was and that I had health insurance. Just being careful.

As I picked up her lead, Tan was galvanized into action. She bounded to the door and began to leap up and down. I grinned and made no pretense of trying to actually connect the lead to her collar. I opened the door and we stepped out into the elements. It was misting and the tiny drops seemed to hang in the air, clinging to us as we walked through them.

Within a few minutes I could feel the familiar relaxation I got from walking the neighborhood ease some of my nervousness. Tan seemed to find the smells heightened by the dampness. Or maybe there were critters out in the early fall rain that she could sense that a mere human would never have noticed—with his mere human nose, that is.

I made sure to keep her close since the road was slick and visibility limited. She didn't need much encouragement—most of the smells seemed to be on the shoulders of the road instead of the middle. The mist was beginning to soak my hair, so I flipped the hood up and found that I'd wiped out much of my peripheral vision. Now I remembered why I didn't much care for hoods.

When we got to the end of our subdivision where our street dead-ended into a main street the mist had changed to drizzle.

Tan and I conferred and decided to head back to the house. It wasn't going to be one of our long walks, but it should serve.

It had switched to a steady rain before we got to the house so when we did get there both of us were soaked to the skin. I'm not sure who looked more bedraggled but at least Tan's feet weren't squishing as she walked. I hated the feel of soaking wet shoes on my feet, heavy and clumsy. But Tan appreciated being toweled dry, her long brown hair looking tousled and almost fluffy after I was through. Getting her dry had made sure that I was even wetter than when I'd started so it made sense to go ahead and shower.

. . .

Out of the shower, dressed in dry clothes, hair dry in most places, I felt better about the day. It was still too early to call Bernard, but we'd killed a nice chunk of time with our walk and subsequent cleanup.

I was back at the kitchen counter with a fresh cup of coffee and a couple of powdered donuts feeling pretty good. The Black had given up on finding any patches of sunlight and had settled down on the towel I left on top of the refrigerator. It's not that TB is spoiled or anything. He'd been sleeping up there for weeks before I first put a towel up there.

While Bobby and I were talking last night, she'd told me that the way she remembered it, the three arguments between Philip and the different suspects had all originated in about a week's time. If she had access to her calendar she'd have been able to confirm that for me, but she wouldn't be able to get to the calendar until she was back at work. She'd claimed that even Philip was pretty good about making sure that all outside contacts were noted on the calendar.

It struck me then that she was talking about the online calendar the Press used—the one everybody at the Press had access to—the one I'd already hacked. For some reason when I was talking to her last night I had envisioned her standing at a wall calendar covered with multicolored sticky notes. Maybe that was what had clouded my mind, envisioning her. I indulged myself for a few minutes then turned my mind back to the calendar.

Having finished the donuts, I rinsed the plate off, stuck it in the dishwasher, picked up the coffee mug, and headed for my office. I had proved to myself that it was easy enough to get to the website and that Philip's haircut appointment had been posted for all to see, but I hadn't really noted what other information was up there. What if somebody else had? Somebody we knew nothing about could easily get access to the site and find out who knew what. It would be just like they were hidden in the tall grass.

· · ·

After about thirty minutes, I stopped and stared at the screen. I'd gotten the twenty-seven-inch iMac the last time I'd upgraded my system. I'd told myself my eyes weren't getting any younger and I'd need the larger screen. Of course, I'd cluttered up the big screen just like I had the smaller. It hadn't taken a handful of seconds before I gave up trying to use the calendar like it was a database. I did figure out how to export some of the content as text files, comma delimited. I'd had to get the details of recurring events off the screen, but once I had them it was easy enough to populate the database with them.

As I figured out abbreviations and variations on how the author's name was spelled I started trying to plot them against a timeline to see if there was a pattern. It looked like activity spiked the week of what appeared to be quarterly board meetings. Philip was the only Press member who attended those. Monthly staff meetings were surrounded by spikes in contacts, meetings, interviews, packages getting received and shipped. And every once in a while there'd be a staff member's birthday noted. I'd gotten interested and tried to find Bobby's but hadn't come across it as yet. Maybe she was trying to keep that a secret? I loved a mystery.

Working with the calendar entries hadn't done me much good as far as I could tell. I mean Frank's sick days did tend to fall on Fridays and Mondays, but that didn't really help much. I was able to confirm Bobby's memory. While Beck had been meeting with Philip on a pretty regular basis, Fines and Charles had presented their proposals during a ten-day period that encompassed Beck's last meeting with Philip. Some wit had noted "shouts heard" on the calendar.

I stood up and stretched my back. I try not to sit for long periods of time glued to the computer screen. There've been too many studies proving that breaks help reduce stress and repetitive injuries.

Besides I'd spent enough time at the computer that it was now a perfectly reasonable time to call somebody on a Sunday morning. Time to do a little investigating. I smiled to myself. And why not start with somebody who might be enticed into helping the investigation by turning his considerable intellect onto the puzzle that was unfolding. Who killed Philip Douglas and more important—to me at the moment—why had it been done the way it had?

I picked up my cell phone and called the number I'd been given. I was reminded again to do something about getting business cards.

The voice on the other end of the line was guarded and only uttered a single word. "Yes?"

I thought to myself "the voice on the other end of the line"—what line? It was a cell phone connecting to a cell phone. "A voice on the other end of the ether?"

"It's just me, Princeton—or Bernard if you prefer—James Crawford. I'm calling from my cell phone so you can capture the number. It was real good to see you yesterday."

There was a pause. "James Crawford, you didn't call to tell me that." Bernard's voice was quick and to the point. "We did all that small talk yesterday. You didn't call me up so we could do it again. Why are you calling me?"

I considered the question for a moment but I'd known what I was going to have to do when I decided to call. He was too damn smart and observant to handle in any other way so I had to tell him the truth—mostly.

I checked an app. "I see you haven't left town yet. Looks like you're staying at the hotel on campus."

"How the—oh. I've got my phone location service on and you've got an app that shows you where my phone thinks it is."

"Can you make your phone lie about where it is?" The idea for a new app popped into existence. "How cool would that be!"

"Crawford."

"Oh, right; it just sounded intriguing." I made a mental note to see if one already existed. "I need your help. How about we talk about it over brunch? There's a pretty good one there at your hotel or we could go to that restaurant that's on the river."

"Let me get this straight. Yesterday you had a meeting with a man who's a suspect in a murder investigation and now you want to take him to brunch?"

"That was before I knew that the suspect was you. Now I want to know how you got to be a suspect."

"You think there's more to it than that this guy was a total jerk?" I could tell he was working that over in his mind.

"There are lots of people who need killing who die of natural causes."

"Do I have to eat grits?"

I laughed. "No, you don't have to eat grits. We even serve hash browns down here now." If I had ever known he hadn't taken to grits I'd forgotten.

We agreed on the brunch at the hotel since he wanted to get on the road after eating. Actually there was a great place that served breakfast year round that he might have remembered if I'd brought it up. It was too famous and too popular to try to get into the Sunday after a home game—not unless you were willing to wait and wait and wait.

. . .

We talked about his mother's books over our eggs Benedict and mimosas. I admitted to having just read part of one and he took that conversational topic and ran with it. It was true that the books had aged gracefully. His mother had been able to report the events that happened with the historian's eye and voice. The good and evil, anger, duplicity, and political backing-and-forthing wasn't just on one side. There were men of principal who worked to make life better for everybody and men so short-sighted they couldn't tie their shoes.

I'd finished eating before he did and had abandoned the mimosa in favor of an excellent cup of coffee. Bernard was finishing the last of his hollandaise sauce with a bit of Portuguese muffin—a new addition to my eating experience and one that I recommend. They are larger than English muffins and hold up well under all the ingredients of a truly superb eggs Benedict.

"So it was your idea to reissue your mother's books?" I took another sip of coffee.

"Well, it was and it wasn't, now that I think about it." Bernard paused with a piece of muffin on his fork. "I had first thought about it a couple of years ago, but hadn't followed up on it.

"Then a few months ago I was on campus for a dinner honoring Dan Shuttles's father. You remember, the young man who was my host at the College of Communications? His father was one of my mother's contemporaries—they marched together—and they held each other in high regard. The only reason I'd been invited was Daniel Senior had suggested it and I was so flattered I came.

"During his speech that night he mentioned Adele Morgan Charles and pointed out that her son was in attendance. Afterward, a number of people came up to meet me and tell me stories about Mom.

"The way I remember it is that somebody asked if I'd ever thought to have her books that had been published by the University Press re-released. I said I'd thought about it but never had done anything about it. The upshot was that I got in touch with Philip Douglas shortly thereafter—and had a rather heated argument with him soon after that initial contact."

Bernard leaned back in his chair and grinned. "I'm guessing that wasn't much help."

"Maybe it was and maybe it wasn't; at this point I think it's too early to tell. You don't remember the names of the people you talked to do you? Any of them?"

"You know what those things are like, Crawford. Most people walk up saying they had known my mother and never even introduce themselves, and those that do, just give a first name. I'd ask Dan if he remembered but he was standing next to his father."

I hated to let it go that easily. "University function—was there a photographer?"

"I don't—yeah, there was. I remember now." He nodded his head. "There were some posed pictures for sure. I don't remember if there were any casuals."

"If they thought to have a photographer, there's a chance of some pictures of you and whoever you were talking to. I'll check it out. Thanks."

"And I'll try to see if I can remember any names" Bernard stood and put out his hand. "Thanks for brunch, Crawford. I need to get on the road."

. . .

I watched him pull out of the hotel's parking lot and head toward the interstate. I'd warned him that apparently most visitors only knew of one entrance so there'd be a long line of traffic waiting to turn left and get on the interstate and given him a shortcut. Interesting guy, Bernard—with a very interesting mother.

It was Sunday so there wasn't any point in trying to find out which of the university's photographers had covered a dinner where the Honorable Daniel Shuttles Sr. was the guest of honor until tomorrow, but I had hopes. The university always looked at

events like that as providing them with access to potential donors. Well, maybe the university didn't but Advancement did.
And the photographers worked for Advancement.

Whenever the event had been it had to have been since
school started. The university wouldn't have been able to pull
off a dinner like that between semesters. I smiled to myself. I
had an ace in the hole.

While candid shots would be much better, all of the rooms
regularly used by the university proper to hold functions had
been wired to automatically videotape functions—sort of like
what stores do to detect criminals, but nowhere near as obvious.
We weren't trying to deter crime—or spook donors.

On the other hand, I'm not sure if the vice president in
charge of advancement (read fund-raising) thought she might be
able to capture something on tape that could be used as black-
mail or what. She claimed it was backup. She had a recurring
nightmare that somebody would come up to her at one of these
functions and want to pledge a couple of million dollars anony-
mously and the next day she couldn't remember who had said
it—or even who had been there.

While I was still working at the university, Stan and I had
written the specs and had overseen the installations. We hadn't
used videotape, of course. That was just how the VP had described what she wanted. The digital cameras fed hard drives
that were networked. Everything that was captured got forward-
ed to file servers located at the university's computer center.
That data was held on high-speed disks for about a week before
it was moved to slower speed storage devices and finally to tape.
Even then, the data had to eventually be erased. You'd be
stunned at how much storage video eats up—and how much it
costs. It was a cost-benefit kind of thing.

We'd done a really sweet job. We used the VP's clout to computerize function room reservations, putting them online. That way the recordings could be tied to specific information about the function. She'd used her clout to get it funded—the golden goose could stifle any resistance. As long as she continued to successfully shake the money tree no one was going to seriously question her actions.

The pictures might be fuzzy, out-of-focus, and inconclusive but I was going to be a fly-on-the-wall. You can't ask for more than that.

This happens to me all the time. I get fired up working on some-thing and then—poof—I'm at a dead end, spinning my wheels. It drives me crazy. So I started pacing around the house. Within minutes Tan had begged to go outside and The Black had disap-peared. They recognized the outward and visible signs, if you will, of an inner turmoil.

I wanted to see if I could find any pictures of Bernard at the Shuttles dinner. For some reason I wanted to know if it had been Bernard's idea or not. I felt like he'd have less of a motive if it had been somebody else's idea. I wanted to get Ward to confirm my validation of Bernard's alibi. I wanted to know if we had any leads on the caliber conversion sleeve. I wanted to discuss the case with Ward. I wanted my business cards.

And I wanted to talk to Bobby.

At that point, I had the honesty to laugh at myself. Wanting to talk to Bobby had nothing to do with my feeling of not want-ing to stand still, of wanting to get on with the case. But, on se-cond thought, maybe her absence was part of the problem. If she were here I doubt the only thing I'd want to talk to her about was the publishing process.

Oh, I wanted to talk to somebody who knew something about how presses work—particularly this university press. There was no doubt about that. All three of the suspects I'd talked to had been upset that the Press had decided not to publish their works—in Bernard's case his mother's. What I wondered was if that was the exception, not the rule. I thought that writers were rejected more often than accepted. Isn't that how it works?

So why were these people so upset? Or is it that once you get something published, then you can get everything published?

Bernard was not a stupid man. How could he have been so mistaken about the chances of the Press re-releasing his mother's books? The same with Joyce Fines. She'd published a number of popular books after the success of her first. If the Press had come to her with the idea, then I could see being angry. But to ask the Press to accept an anniversary edition reprinting—wasn't there at least the chance of it being turned down?

And what of Calvin Beck—the novelist-to-be? He must have been aware that there was no guarantee that letting Philip edit his manuscript would result in its being published.

I stopped pacing. No, his motive differed from the other two. Not that they themselves had the same motive between them. No, Calvin must have felt that Philip had teased him with his suggested revisions only then to jerk the rug out from under him. I nodded to myself. My guess was that behavior such as that wasn't so common in publishing. But that's all it was—a guess.

I realized that I was standing at a window looking out onto my front yard. It wasn't that I was looking at anything in particular, I was just staring out the window. I wandered back across the house and out onto the screen porch.

Philip was a jerk. As a child he probably pulled the wings off flies. Having no fondness for flies, I'm not sure that was as appalling to me as it would be to others. Still, maybe he liked to make people think he was going to publish their books and then turn them down. That wouldn't be common in the publishing world, would it? Not everybody in publishing is a jerk, right?

I sat down at the table. Maybe he did that all the time? Maybe he usually just did it to one person at a time and only now had done it to three?

Now I really wanted to talk to Bobby but she wouldn't be back in town until late this evening. I thought about calling Ward but I didn't really have anything to say to him that couldn't wait until tomorrow. Heck, he'd probably say it could wait until Tuesday—and I can imagine what he'd say if I called him today.

I decided to call Frank Manning as the next best thing to talking to Bobby—at least about publishing and Philip Douglas. I called the number I'd been given but he didn't answer. In the old days it would have meant he wasn't home, but nowadays it might be caller ID and he didn't want to talk to me—after all it was Sunday.

The Black had reappeared after I had sat down and was curled up on one of the other chair cushions. The cushion was dark green and he looked good curled up on it. Of course, he looked good curled up on just about anything.

With a shrug, I picked up the phone and called Steven Stefenson. He was on the board of the Press and seemed to know something about publishing and Philip Douglas. I was desperate enough to even put up with his condescending sarcasm. At least I thought I was until the phone began to ring and then I had an almost overwhelming desire to hang up—instead I hoped he wouldn't answer.

"Yes?" His voice was as cold and aloof as before.

Drat. My heart sank. "Dr. Stefenson? This is James Crawford."

"Yes."

This was going to be as easy as I remembered it. Wishing I had remembered how much fun the last phone conversation had been before I'd dialed the number, I pushed on.

"If you've got the time, I'd like to ask you a few questions about publishing in general and Philip Douglas in particular."

"I have a few minutes. It is, after all, Sunday afternoon, late afternoon at that."

"I am aware of that, Dr. Stefenson and I apologize if I'm disturbing you."

"Humph. This is all about the investigation into Philip's death, is it not? The questions you have that is. How is the investigation going, by the way?"

I was conversationally knocked off stride by the last question. He actually sounded interested. I thought for a second about what I should or shouldn't say. Ward wouldn't want too much to be public knowledge.

"We've identified the murder weapon. Now we've got to figure out who the murderer is."

"Have you?"

"Yes, ballistics got a match with one of the rifles in Philip's collection—a 30-06."

There was a pause, then Steven spoke. "That sounds fairly significant."

"Not so much," I replied. "It had been wiped clean of fingerprints. In many ways finding it has confused things more than cleared them up. I can't figure why the murderer went to such lengths. He could have just wiped the rifle clean of fingerprints and dropped it on the floor, but he didn't. He went to some trouble to hide the weapon."

"And the police? What do they think about your concerns?"

"They tell me that murderers are usually stupid people or, at least, act stupidly. Captain Ward thinks the murderer might have read some murder mystery and gotten the idea from it."

"Really." There was ice in Steven's voice. "So murderers are stupid? What an interesting observation from a man who doesn't appear to be making any progress in solving this murder."

"True." Ward didn't want to be bothered by the case this weekend, so why should I defend him? "We now know how, but we just don't know who. If the rifle had belonged to somebody else it might have told us who."

"I think you're being too dismissive of how significant this discovery is. For instance, there's the fact that you've found it. The killer might have thought he'd picked the perfect place to hide it. Who would look for the murder weapon in the victim's own collection? He might have thought the idea of hiding it there was inspired."

"It bothered me that the rifles were fully functional. It seemed like hubris for Philip to have surrounded himself with functioning weapons while he went around treating people with such contempt."

"So it's thanks to you that the police found the murder weapon?"

I hesitated to say just how much I hadn't known and wouldn't have without the police. "It's nice of you to think so but—"

"You had questions for me?"

I will say this about Steven Stefenson. He could keep me off balance better than anybody I'd ever met. "Oh, right." Now what the heck had I wanted to ask him? Oh yeah.

"I was a little surprised at how angry the suspects had gotten over what was—essentially—a rejection from a publisher. Shouldn't writers be used to that?"

"Except that our Philip loved rejecting authors. He liked to build them up so that his rejection would come as a complete surprise. The way he did it was cruel. It would be some solace to the writers' community if that turned out to be what got him killed."

"I had wondered if he'd been like that to other authors. I know what he did to Calvin Beck. Philip made Calvin rewrite his novel and then refused to publish it because Calvin had listened to his advice."

"Really!" Steven sounded surprised. "How incredibly angry that must have made him."

"Right," I nodded my head even though he couldn't see me. "I was thinking his motive might have been stronger than the others; then I wondered if Philip did that to all his authors. Thanks for clearing that up."

"Well, I don't think Philip usually went that far. He might make some small suggestions."

"No, it's just the fact that he led them on—using his position to make them think they were going to be successful and then jerking the promise of publication away from them. Calvin wasn't treated that differently."

For a heartbeat I thought Stefenson was going to argue with me but the moment passed. "Was there anything else you wanted to ask me?"

If there had been, for the life of me I couldn't remember what it would have been. I should have written my questions down. "No. You've been very helpful. Thank you very much."

"Mr. Crawford, I think you are underestimating the evidence you've collected and, at the same time, overanalyzing what it means. Recalling your comments the other day about Calvin Beck, I fear that you are in danger of being artfully deceived by the suspects you've interviewed so that you underestimate them—underestimate their ability to kill. Surely you must realize that murderers are people too?

"Pardon me if I've spoken out of turn. Good night."

And with that he was gone. He'd hung up on me. I put my phone down, stood up, and headed for the kitchen. I needed a drink. And I needed to let the puzzle go for the rest of the evening.

It was a murder mystery, pure and simple. And if I was going to solve a murder mystery I had to let it be a mystery.

And it could be a mystery until it was time to solve it.

I turned on the radio and tuned it to the public radio station. As I'd hoped, fund-raising was over and it was the beginning of a two-hour show featuring big band music. I was too young to have grown up with that music, but I found it relaxing and enjoyed the weekly show. I had to adjust the sound level since I don't listen to Glenn Miller at the same volume as football.

I went back into the kitchen and pulled a small porterhouse steak out of the freezer and put it in the microwave. I gave it a short zap to get it started defrosting. It'd be close to two hours before I was going to put it on the grill so it didn't need much. Baked potato and a salad would fill out the menu. There was half a bottle of zinfandel in the fridge that I took out to let warm up. I was set. I took a sip of the scotch and felt the tension of the day drop away. Now it was time to feed Tan and TB so they could relax as well.

Monday morning I got up with the alarm, started the coffee that I'd prepared the night before, and headed out for a walk with Tan. Apparently The Black was sleeping in.

Years ago I read an article on a study about pets and pet owners. According to the article something like 97 percent of pet owners said they talked to their pets. It didn't matter if it was a goldfish, they talked to it. The author had then asked the researcher about the 3 percent who didn't? His reply: "They lied."

So I didn't mind having lengthy conversations with Tan and The Black. As we set out I began to explain to Tan how I had come to the realization that this murder case was very much like the murder mysteries that I like to read. I rarely figure out who the murderer is until the author cleverly reveals how, who, and why. So why was I stressing about not being able to figure this case out? It was a mystery! I had to accept that before going on to solve the case.

Tan was perfectly willing to accept my logic as being unarguable while she concentrated on the various odors that were making the walk so pleasant to her. I had the feeling that TB might have been more skeptical, but that's a cat for you. I also had the feeling that Ward would be more than skeptical, dismissive if you will. But I needed to take a step back. I wasn't going to be able to figure out every little detail, so I should be satisfied with trying to get a handle on the bigger picture.

We take different routes on our walks. I stopped talking as we came into the part of this route that was uphill. When I got to the top I had to stop and wait for Tan. Even at her own pace she was panting heavily as she caught up. I cut the pace back until we just strolled on home. It hadn't been that long ago when that hill hadn't bothered her. I was going to have to start splitting my walks into ones with Tan and ones without. I was having trouble coming to grips with that.

Once we got in the door I went over to the phone to see if anybody had called. Nope. Looked like I was getting as early a start as anybody.

I'd emailed Stan about the Shuttles dinner last night. He'd find out who the photographer was that had been assigned to the event, have whoever it was forward the pics to him, and make sure the streaming video data files for the event were marked "do not delete." It was a little galling not to be able to do that part of it myself, but I couldn't argue with their changing the passwords after I retired. I really shouldn't have access. I smiled to myself. Besides, Sean—excuse me Dr. Thomas—would have insisted. Once he'd gotten rid of me he wanted shut of me as well. Wonder if they told him in hell that I was the one who had solved his murder? Probably, since it was bound to add to his suffering.

The coffee was done so I poured myself a cup into an insulated plastic mug. I took a sip and then headed for the shower. There was something almost sinful about being able to shower and drink the morning's first cup of coffee at the same time.

· · ·

I was out of the shower, dressed, and starting on my third cup of coffee when the phone rang. Caller ID said B. Slater—Bobby. I snatched the phone up and said, "Hey!" I have a way with words.

"Did you miss me?" asked Bobby teasingly.

"Yeah, tons," I replied without thinking.

She responded with her throaty chuckle. "Good answer, Ford. That means I can admit that I missed you too."

"Praise the lord!" I blurted.

That drew an outright laugh. "An even better answer! So, big boy, what's been going on? Want to tell me about your weekend?"

"Yeah, I wanted—" I caught myself. She was the one who had done something unusual over the weekend, not me. "But first, what about your weekend? How was the trip? How's your cousin Rachel? What's Cranbury like?"

"She's fine," responded Bobby drily. "Her name happens to be Rebecca, but she'll recover from your not remembering her name. Especially," amusement was in her voice, "since I won't tell her."

"Well, it will be easier for me to remember her name once I meet her and her husband—Jack, isn't it? Jack Clarke and Rebecca Ralston." I had put the information in my contacts list, I just hadn't thought to check it.

Bobby laughed and said there had been an article in the Cranbury newspaper that referred to "historic, crime-free downtown Cranbury." They'd all had a good laugh about it saying that it was crime-free only while it was deserted much like historic downtown Shelbyville. Every town it seemed had a historic downtown. Cranbury's downtown, at least, had a brewpub that served great pizza and sandwiches.

Shelbyville had a brewpub for about two years, but we couldn't make a go of it. How can you have a brewpub in a college town and not make a go of it? You have to be really bad businessmen, in my opinion.

As I was listening to Bobby I kept hearing a noise on her end of the line that seemed to be getting louder and louder until I finally asked. "What's that noise?"

"Yikes! It's the alarm telling me it's time to go to work. So are you going to take me to lunch so that you can ask the questions you really wanted to ask me before you remembered to be polite?"

Without hesitation I agreed to lunch and hung up. I stared at the phone for a few heartbeats. Was I that transparent or was she that perceptive? I decided to go with perceptive—and intelligent—and sexy. I shook myself and reached for the phone. A conversation with Captain Ward would be the splash of cold water I needed to get my mind back on murder.

Ward picked up the phone and didn't even say hello. "What you got for me? Find the killer? Of course you didn't because if you had you would have called me even though I'd told you not to."

"How could I have found the killer?" He did seem rejuvenated. The weekend off must have done him some good.

"I take it that the guy you met on Saturday didn't do us the favor of confessing? Or did he confess and you decided he didn't really mean it? Come on, tell Uncle Jim what happened."

I explained that Bernard Charles had turned out to be someone I'd known back in our college days, he had an alibi, and he wasn't the murdering type. That as far as I could see none of the suspects were the murdering type. I threw in my opinion of a murderer who cleaned and put up the murder weapon for good measure.

Having vented my frustrations I was greeted with Ward's full-throated horselaugh. I could see him throwing his head back and letting loose.

"You got the why-did-I-ever-agree-to-do-this blues, huh? Looked pretty easy after your first case, didn't it? And now you're wondering if you're cut out for it? And you called me looking for sympathy?" For a second I thought he was going to go off again—consumed with laughter. "Hell, welcome to the club my friend. This isn't easy; that's what makes it rewarding. Get off your butt you sorry excuse for a private detective! Stop feeling sorry for your sorry self and get back in the game!"

There was a pause and then Ward said, in his normal tones, "I'll get that alibi checked out and get back to you."

I hung up the phone and reminded myself that Ward had played high school football and at some point in his life had wanted to be a football coach.

"Rah, rah, go team," I murmured to The Black. The cat was staring at his wand as if he could will it to fly through the air. I called it the wand for want of a better name. It had started out as a plastic rod with a clump of feathers on a string at one end and a handle on the other. Time had not been kind to it.

I needed to call Stan and see what, if anything, he'd been able to track down about the dinner for Mr. Shuttles. I wondered if the other suspects had been to university functions this semester. I could ask them, couldn't I? I had time to start calling before picking Bobby up for lunch.

Maybe Coach Ward's pep talk had worked. I reminded myself that I should get to the Press early enough to talk to Frank.

Carefully I picked up one end of TB's wand and began to wave it through the air. The cat sat back on his haunches and swiped at the wand, one paw and then the other, all the while uttering a deep chattering cry in his throat.

So maybe he can work magic. What do I know?

. . .

I pulled open the door to the M. W. Stefenson Building and walked past the bookcase into the small open area where Rufus and I had met Hazel Murphy. There wasn't a stocky, gray-haired female there today. But there was a beautiful Russian blue stretched out in a patch of sunlight. He had his paw draped across his eyes like he was trying to block the sunlight while he slept.

I was early for lunch so I stopped and squatted down to properly say hello. "Hello, Peter the Gray." The cat yawned and stared up at me.

I stuck out my finger and the cat sniffed it gingerly, then rubbed his face against it. Taking that as tentative approval, I scratched behind his ears and stroked his wonderfully smooth coat. He'd been in the sun so long that his fur was hot.

"So," I muttered as I stroked him, "do you know who killed Philip? It's like what's-his-name says, 'Cats see things people don't.' What did you see? You showed me the murder weapon."

Peter stood up, arched his back, and then sat and began to lick his paws and wash his ears. I watched him for a moment or two and then stood up. I could almost hear my joints creaking. "That's right. You didn't like Philip, did you? It was nice enough of you to show me the murder weapon, even if I didn't understand at first. So the rest is up to me, huh?"

The cat continued with its personal hygiene, and I, honored to have been allowed to admire and praise him, went on with my life. I was pretty sure that was the way he saw it.

. . .

I poked my head into Frank's office and saw that he was grimacing at his computer monitor.

"Bad news?"

Frank shook his head, still staring at the screen. "Nope. It's worse. Bad writing." He turned away from the screen and waved me in.

"Come in, come in. Save me from having to deal with an author whose work consists of a frustrating combination of bad grammar and incoherent writing. Too much to take on a Monday morning."

I took the proffered chair. "One of the things I was looking forward to in retirement was the elimination of Mondays."

"How's that working out for you?" Frank exhaled heavily puffing out his mustache hairs.

"Not so much difference, so far." I laughed. "It's Monday and here I am. So how was your weekend?"

"Good. Caught a nice gig Sunday evening—a rock and bluegrass pick-up band jamming way out in the country somewhere. Friend of mine thought I'd be interested and dragged me out to hell-and-gone. She was right."

"Oh, that must have been where you were—"

"When you called. Yeah, I saw that you'd called, but since you hadn't left a message . . ." He shrugged his shoulders.

"No problem. I was trying to puzzle something out and instead of letting it go until today I starting calling people who shouldn't have been disturbed. How'd you like the game?"

In Shelbyville, during football season, there was no reason to say which game. The same, I'm sure, is true in college towns all over America.

"They did well. I had expected the defense to score, so I was a little disappointed, but we won. Beat the spread. Actually, all of my picks did pretty well. I'm in pretty good shape this early in the season."

I shook my head sadly. "I can't bet on these games, at least not seriously. It's bad enough they break your heart, I couldn't take it if my wallet hurt too."

Frank laughed. "I don't make enough working at the Press to do any serious betting! Besides it would be my luck to get busted. Nope, my friends and I have a different way of trying to prove we know what's going on in college football."

"Something like fantasy football? How does that work? I thought that was for professional ball?"

"No, no," said Frank. "This is more about picking winners. Every week we put together a list of college football games from every conference in the country—big and little—semipro to real students—the whole gamut. The only restriction we've got is that the score has to be reported somewhere reputable. You pick the game you want everybody to bet on and put it in the pot. There are ten of us, so you list your first choice, second, and so on. We pull them out of the hat, no duplicates, and then everybody tries to pick the winner of each game on the list—and what a list it is. I've had to pick a winner between two schools that I would have sworn were women's colleges."

"Sounds fun."

"Say, do you know anything about the Ivy League? I can't get a handle on how to handicap those guys. Whenever one of their games gets on the list I know I'm starting down one."

I laughed. Handicapping schools where the athletes were interested in academics? "If you want to handicap the Ivy League I'd suggest getting each school's academic calendar. Bet against the team that just had midterms."

Frank looked shocked then thoughtful. "Would that information be available?"

"I've never done a study on it, it just came to me." I grinned. "I wouldn't think it would be a factor at the football factories, but with real scholar-athletes, who knows?"

We both sat there for a moment or two, lost in thought. I was wondering what would happen if I ran some linear regressions factoring in academic calendars plus scheduled testing dates for grad school, law school, and the like—college football had always been more unpredictable than the pros.

"That's something to think about." Frank shook himself. I guessed he was wondering if we'd just found the edge in betting on college football. I know I was.

"If you're here to see Bobby, why are you visiting me?"

"Did I say I was here to see Bobby?" I held my hand up. "OK. In addition to picking Bobby up, I've got some concerns about the suspect list you gave me."

"Really? How so?"

"Oh, they don't seem like people who could have killed Philip or anybody else."

Frank laughed. "Oh yeah? Well somebody did it. It's just like Steven said, 'Who knows what a real suspect looks like? It's up to Mr. Crawford and the police to sort it out.'"

"Remember, I didn't want to come up with names."

I nodded my head. "I told you that Captain Ward was satisfied that neither you nor Kent were likely to have committed murder?"

"Right. Thanks for your help on that."

I went back to what was bothering me. "The list you gave me just had authors on it. Who else might have had reasons to kill Philip?"

"Other than the people who had the misfortune to work for him?"

"Frank, we've already investigated the Press employees. Neither the police nor I can figure out how you all can be in two places at once. You and Kent had the weakest alibis for 'where were you when.' I figure that maybe—just maybe—all of you working together with split-second timing and lots of lying might have been able to pull it off. Captain Ward just snorts."

"OK." Frank leaned back in his chair, put his feet on his desk, crossed his fingers behind his head, and looked at the ceiling. If this had been a Rex Stout mystery I would have expected to see him purse his lips. He started to speak.

"Other people besides the ones in this building had to work with him—deal with him—graphic artists, printers, designers, people on the board, HR and purchasing at the university—why the guy who cut his hair might have followed him back here and shot him because Philip never tipped him."

"Point of fact—the police did look into the hairdresser. The guy says that Philip demanded complete silence while cutting his hair and he never tipped."

I shook my head. "The guy who cuts my hair couldn't be quiet that long. Anyway, he says he upped his price to compensate and would remind himself of the fact every time he was tempted to cut off an ear. He's got an alibi. He claims to have had another appointment after Philip and it checks out."

"So this is where you're hiding! I should have known. Everybody likes to shoot the breeze with Frank." Bobby was standing in the doorway her arms akimbo.

I stood up while Frank threw his arms in the air and, rocking backward, almost fell out of his chair. "God, woman, don't scare me like that!"

"How would you like me to scare you?"

"My fault," I said, raising my hand to confess. "I just wanted better suspects." Instead of black, today Bobby was dressed in a deep, emerald green blouse and tan slacks. "Now I'm focused on lunch." I smiled as I glanced up and down. "What sounds good to you?"

"Lunch sounds good to me. I'm hungry." A smile flitted across her lips. "What about Indian?"

The memory of a missed meal made me step closer to Bobby and smile as well.

In Shelbyville there are not an unlimited number of restaurants. We've got some variety—more than we would have without the university—but when you specify Indian— "The Taj Mahal it is then!" I turned back to Frank. "Want to join us? There's plenty of room in the car."

For a second Frank looked liked I'd tapped him between the eyes with a two-by-four. "I love that food."

Bobby turned to me and said, "I should have remembered. Frank was just recently introduced to Indian food and he's hooked—addicted, I'd say."

Frank looked at us, swallowed, and said, "How about bringing me back some take-out?"

I realized that I was standing closer to Bobby than I would have a week or so ago. We were comfortable with where we were but Frank was trying to figure out how to handle this change in our relationship.

"Frank," I said as dryly as I could, "lunch is a buffet. You want take-out from a buffet? Get in the car."

He claimed to have an errand and said he would meet us there, so I promised to save him a seat.

On our way out of the building, Bobby and I passed the spot where Peter the Gray had been sunning. "Who said 'cats see things people don't'?'"

"B. Kliban," responded Bobby immediately. "What brought that up?"

"Peter the Gray was sunning himself here and I stopped to say hello. He let me pet him. I think he could tell me who killed Philip if he could talk."

"And cared enough to tell you. I'm surprised he let you touch him, he's usually pretty stand-offish. He's scratched most of the visitors who had the audacity to touch him."

I pushed open the door to the outside and let Bobby walk through before me. "I asked before I touched him—and The Black probably vouched for me."

Bobby laughed. "Yes, that would have done it. The Black is one special cat."

As we walked to my car, I explained that I'd been having some difficulty with the suspects that Frank had given me. "I mean, they're just not suspicious enough."

"And that's what you wanted to talk to me about this morning?"

"Yep, that's it." I backed the car out of the space and then headed off campus. It was faster to drive around the university than to drive through it to get to the other side.

"Well, let me see." Out of the corner of my eye I caught a quick glimpse of Bobby frowning. "Frank canvassed everybody in the office—seeing who had heard Philip arguing or comments he might have made over the last month or two. He talked to me about it, Hazel, Kent, the retired librarian who was acting as Philip's assistant—what is her name? Anyway, anybody who came by the Press those days after Philip's murder pretty much had a chance to add a name to the list. Once he had three names, he came back around to see if we agreed. The list is sort of a consensus of opinion as to whom Philip had made the angriest."

"So, if by chance, Philip had been killed by somebody with no connection to the Press—other than choosing it as a murder site—they wouldn't have made the list?"

"Well, of course not. How could we suspect people we don't even know exist?"

I wondered if Ward realized that our investigation was ignoring anybody not connected to the Press in some manner. Maybe he had another track going?

"So the suspects you did know, did they come to the Press very often?"

"The Press doesn't have that many regular visitors, really. Calvin Beck came by to see Philip pretty regularly for the last couple of months while they were working on his novel. But the other two didn't do much but have a phone conversation or some such with Philip and then come in to see him so he could watch their faces as he refused to do what they asked for."

Something about that description struck me as strange. "How's that again?"

"Oh, they both made presentations—pitches for their books, but they really hadn't been in negotiations for very long. Philip usually dragged things out more than he did with Fines and Charles.

"Beck's dealings with Philip were more typical. The author thinking he was getting closer and closer to publication with every meeting until Philip dropped the bomb on him."

I kept on hitting green traffic lights—just when I'd like to look at my passenger.

"I've known Dr. Fines for years, but can't think of that many times she's come to the Press. Now the Charles guy, I'm sure the day he came to the Press was the only time I'd ever seen him. I'd have remembered him."

"Really, how's that?"

"Oh I wouldn't have forgotten that grin—something about it."

"The grin or the dimples?"

"That's right, I forgot, you've met him. What's your first impression?"

"My first impression of him was twenty—no thirty—years ago, and I'd guess you'd have to say it was favorable."

"Really?"

I glanced her way and looked back at the road. "Must have been. I invited him to my wedding—or maybe Eleanor did. He's always had a way with the ladies."

"And how did that happen?"

I pulled into the parking lot of the Indian restaurant and parked the car. I turned and smiled at her. "I'll tell you about it some time. Meanwhile, let's see about some lunch."

· · ·

We stepped inside the restaurant and I took a deep breath. I love that smell. This is not to say that I don't like the smell of most restaurants. This one served a buffet for lunch so the smells of the different spices filled the air, and the spices and scents were not the ones one normally encountered wafting from Alabama steam tables. But I didn't come here for traditional southern cuisine.

It wasn't strictly true that you couldn't order from the menu at lunch. It's just that no one did. The buffet gave you a chance to experiment—to try new things while enjoying the dishes you already knew.

The clientele was nicely mixed—town and gown. And both town and gown seemed a little less traditional then the usual mix—less traditional or more casual—what was I trying to say? Nicely enough for those of us who wondered how close the food was to being authentic, Indians ate here too. Their gustatory enthusiasm reinforced the impression that the food was really good here.

We followed the waiter to the table but as he appeared to have no concept of seating guests, I pulled out a chair and held it for Bobby. She graciously allowed me to show off with this display of chivalry. I looked around and, feeling comfortable, both with the restaurant and with being with Bobby, said, "You know, this is just not Rufus's kind of place."

"You mean Provost George?"

I nodded my head and sat down across from her.

"I think," she said, "that he feels like he needs to do business at the University Club. I think he's been on their board forever—ever since it nearly went bankrupt and the university refused to bail them out. But I don't think he'd be that uncomfortable here—after all the traveling he's done in India and Pakistan trying to set up joint programs. The university has some great international relationships because of him."

I threw up my hands. "I'd forgotten the money problems the club used to have. And I hereby retract my comment about this not being Rufus's kind of place. I for one should know not to

underestimate Rufus George. He sees beyond the surface. I
should have picked on somebody like Steven Stefenson."

"What about good ol' Steve?" Frank walked up to the table
sniffing the air. "Is that tandoori chicken I smell? Joyous day!"
He stopped at the table and looked down at both of us. "Can we
just head to the buffet line? Can't we talk and eat at the same
time?"

Bobby and I stood and followed Frank to get in line.

. . .

After we'd gotten back with our loaded plates, a couple of small
bowls of raita, and another bowl of a spicy something I'd never
gotten the name of, and had ordered our drinks, conversation
stopped for a few moments as we all sampled the different tastes
we'd selected. I picked back up on what Frank had said.

"Good ol' Steve? Are you calling Dr. Steven Stefenson good
ol' Steve or are we talking about somebody else?" I looked at
the slightly scruffy individual with raita caught in his mustache
and compared him to the vision I had of the impeccable Steven
Stefenson.

Frank laughed and wiped his mustache with his napkin. "If
you really want to get him mad, call him Stevie. I think Philip
used to do that just to watch Steven turn red and bite his
tongue."

I had some difficulty with the picture of the man I knew as
Steven Stefenson being rattled. "Did Philip actually bait Steven
like that?"

"You're underestimating Philip's talent for making people
hate him! Philip went out of his way to irritate people. Once he
knew it bothered Steven he wouldn't let up."

Bobby laughed. "The way he picked on Steven was awful. It made all of us realize just how much worse life with Philip could be. Of course, with Philip concentrating on Steven, some members of the staff," she looked pointedly at Frank, "actually appreciated Steven's ability to turn Philip's attention from abusing them to abusing Steven."

Frank showed no remorse, not even looking up from his plate as he wiped up some of the chicken afghani sauce with a bit of naan. "Better him than me."

"That's not exactly how I'd imagined life with Philip Douglas—but maybe it's just a failure of imagination on my part. I mean I knew it was bad, but—"

Bobby reached over and patted my hand. "Don't worry—nobody believed it until they saw it in action. Just the same as it was with you and Sean Thomas."

"Lately I'd wondered if Steven had figured out some way to know when Philip was going to be out of the office the way he'd slip in and out without the usual fuss." Frank popped another piece of garlic naan in his mouth. "I dunno, maybe he learned to check and see if Philip's parking spot was empty."

Bobby shook her head. "He wouldn't have known that until he got to the Press. By then he was already there."

"What about the Press's online calendar? Could he have checked it to see if Philip was there?" I'd eaten too much, but I always did. I was just wondering if I'd eaten way too much. I could feel the need for a nap.

"He knows about it. He's probably seen us check it, but what good would it have done him," asked Bobby. "You can only access it from the university's network."

I had thought that's what the network security guys must have told the staff when they'd installed it—even though it wasn't strictly true. Philip must have demanded so many security "holes" that the people setting up the site had taken the easy route. Once you give up on requiring users to log on with userIDs and strong passwords that have to be changed regularly, it's a slippery slope—security-wise that is.

"Well, it just goes to show you how little I know about Steven Stefenson—judging a book by its cover. First time I met him was at the University Club, I was dining with the provost." I took a sip of tea. "Must have been the day Rufus introduced me to the Press."

"I can believe that." Frank chuckled. "Steven would have wanted to meet you as soon as he heard you were going to be investigating Philip's murder."

I opened my mouth and then shut it. I was trying to remember the sequence. "How could he have found that out? We didn't announce it to anyone before we talked to you."

Frank and Bobby laughed at my naïveté.

Bobby shook her head, "No, you don't know our Steven very well do you? I know him well enough to know that he's got sources all over town. The stuff he knows and how quickly he learns it is utterly amazing. Tell him, Frank. You've known Steven forever."

"Yeah, I've known him so long that I can even guess at his methods." He wiped his mustache with another napkin. We all knew to pick up extras when we went through the buffet line. "Let's see how it could have happened. Hazel gets a call from the provost's secretary—"

"Administrative assistant," I interrupted.

"Assistant, then." Frank shrugged his shoulders. "Whatever her title is she tells Hazel that the provost is going to show up at the Press after lunch—maybe she even says lunch at the Univer-

sity Club—and he plans on making an announcement and intro-
duction to the Press staff. Hazel, in turn, goes from one staff
member to the next telling us to be back from lunch in plenty of
time to be here when the provost shows up. Somebody here has
to break a lunch date and when they do they explain that the
provost is coming to the Press with somebody. You can be sure
that the whole university pays attention to what the provost does.
Boom, the word is out."

Bobby joined in. "The only reason the provost would be
coming to the Press would be about the murder. The whole campus knows that you solved the mystery of who killed those two
people at the computer center and that you'd been working for
the provost when you did."

"So," Frank picked up the narrative again, "your name and
the provost's have already been linked together over a murder
investigation. There's been a murder at the Press. The provost
has announced that he's going to make an announcement at the
Press—the announcement is that you're going to be assisting the
police in their investigation of the murder of Philip Douglas. Not
that hard to figure out.

"Everybody knows that the provost regularly eats at the University Club—bingo Steven goes to the club and meets you and
the provost. Maybe it was a fishing expedition on Steven's part,
but not that farfetched, was it?"

"You're telling me it wasn't a coincidence that Steven was at
the University Club that day?" I'm not sure why that made me
uncomfortable but it did. I'm sure people do go to the club with
the intent of seeing Rufus, but I—it wasn't something I would
have thought to do. "I remember he said something to Rufus
about being happy to help if he could. He was even willing to
stay on the board if it would help."

Frank snorted. "Offered to stay on the board? I bet that went over big. The provost was the one who decided there ought to be limits on how long people served on the board and that he was starting with Steven. Steven tried everything he could think of to change his mind, but Provost Rufus George is not known for going back on his decisions." He cocked his head at me. "Interesting that you're on a first-name basis."

I ignored that comment and went back to my original puzzlement. "But how is it you know Steven Stefenson so well?"

"Didn't you know? They were frat brothers." Bobby's grin was almost wicked.

I looked from Bobby to Frank. "You were in a fraternity? With Steven?"

"I was a legacy," mumbled Frank. "They had to take me."

Bobby chuckled. "Everybody was young once, Frank. You've made up for it, trust me. No one would suspect that you'd been in any fraternity, much less one of the most prestigious ones on campus—in their minds anyway." She flashed her grin again. "In fact, you may have even overcompensated."

"So you've known Steven since you were in college?"

Frank shifted in his chair as if it was suddenly uncomfortable. "Yeah. He was a couple of years ahead of me." He shook his head and grinned. "Well, a couple ahead when I pledged, a couple more years ahead before I graduated. I enjoyed my college experience."

"So did I, only I did my enjoying a couple of decades earlier. Was Steven involved with the Press even then?"

"He's the reason I'm at the Press."

I think even Bobby was surprised at that revelation. I know I was.

"How so?"

Frank leaned back in his chair. "Oh, he told me that there was an opening at the Press—something he thought I'd be good at, a good fit for me and the Press. He told me that I'd better not mention that I'd heard about it from him or that he thought I'd be good at it to Philip. Philip never followed Steven's suggestions. Claimed it made it easy to make decisions—just do the opposite of what Steven suggested."

He looked at Bobby and then at me. "Steven was right, that time at least. I'm good at what I do and the Press is better for it."

Mentally I took a step back and realized I needed to rethink the situation—look at things in another way.

Our waiter walked by and casually dropped our checks on the table. He'd assumed separate checks so there were three of them. I reached out and scooped them up. "This one is on me. I know I've got my money's worth."

Frank had held his palm out so that I could give him his check. "Yeah?" he said dropping his hand. "There was a time I didn't feel like I got my money's worth if I hadn't paid for it."

Bobby and I both laughed but afterward I wondered if he'd really been kidding.

. . .

I dropped Bobby back at the Press and then drove over to the computer building. I lucked out and found a legal parking spot nearby that my retiree tag entitled me to use. My luck held. Stan was in his office and with some help from the provost's office was able to set me up with an online account to remotely access the Department of Advancement's photo library—and related databases. The big problem was security. Advancement had demanded tight security and whoever designed the site had done their best. There were the usual security features—individual userIDs, passwords, and being on the university's network, either physically or via a VPN. But that hadn't been enough. Beyond that, you had to be accessing the site from a machine with a registered MAC address.

Now, I'm a geek, but I didn't happen to know the MAC address of my iMac. I confess that I used to think MAC was short for machine address not media access control address. Anyway it's a string of six pairs of hexadecimal digits—not something that comes easily to mind. It turns out that the university recorded the MAC address along with a bunch of other stuff when you logged onto the network from home via the VPN. So the network guy who was helping us just looked up the addresses associated with my last connection and added it to the list of authorized addresses. I'd have to test it when I got home, but we were pretty sure that it would work. Meanwhile we used Stan's account to look at the site.

I was impressed. The website was pretty well designed. Once I logged in and authenticated, I could search the database by photographer, room, date, function title, and, to a certain extent, attendees. If I wanted to see all the photos of the president or head football coach taken in the last six months, there was no problem. The head of the physics department was a different matter, as was Daniel Shuttles Sr.—and junior for that matter.

Still, I was going to be able to track down the function, find the photographer, find the photos, and scan the official photographs and all the candid shots taken as well. And if I didn't see what I wanted in those shots there was a link to the "automatic function recordings"—recordings from the monitoring cameras we'd installed in the rooms.

I wasn't sure how I felt about the Big Brother aspects of all the monitoring in the abstract, but I was delighted to have access to it.

Stan had to leave to cover some event that in the eyes of the university needed his attention. I promised that the drinks were on me the next time we were at the Polo Grounds and headed back home.

I walked into the house and went to drop my keys in the brass bowl that sits on a table near the door only to find that The Black had left his toy orange mouse sitting there. TB was nowhere to be seen, but Tan was wagging her tail outside the door, beating on the siding. I went over to the door and let her inside. Instead of rushing to her food or water bowl she sat down at my feet, panting slightly, tail sweeping the floor, her liquid brown eyes looking up at me.

Stop to smell the roses? I needed to stop and pet the dog. Nothing could be more important. I knelt down and scratched her behind her ears and then at the base of her tail—that spot that made her quiver with delight. That close to her it was clear that there was a lot of gray in her muzzle and her eyes were starting to turn cloudy. I sighed to myself and stood up. Life goes on.

Bobby had plans for the evening. She'd said I was more than welcome to come along, but I'd declined. I had to start thinking further ahead—and I would, but right now I was thinking about a murder and how to solve it.

I glanced around the kitchen and saw that there was a blinking light on the home phone, meaning that somebody had called and left a message. I shrugged my shoulders. Actually with this phone the caller could have hung up and it might still think there was a message. I checked caller ID and it admitted that the call had come from the Shelbyville police station. Ward had probably told somebody to get in touch with me and they'd called the home phone instead of my cell.

As soon as I thought of it my cell barked at me. It was Ward. "I was just getting around to checking my messages."

"Well, don't bother—all it says is to call me."

"So should I hang up?" Hang up, I thought to myself, how archaic is that? "I mean disconnect and call you back?"

"Just how stupid do you want to be? Just listen and I'll tell you. I'm trying to wrap some things up and go home."

It was getting close to five o'clock. I wandered over to the liquor cabinet. "I'm listening." I decided a drink could wait and walked out on the screen porch.

"Bernard Charles isn't our killer. His alibi checks out better than Professor Fines's and Beck's. Like you thought, Charles was in New Jersey in front of an audience from 5:00 to 7:00 Eastern Time on the day Douglas was murdered. He can't be in two places at the same time."

"So he's in the clear." I sat down and scratched my head.

"Yeah, great set of suspects you've got there Crawford. One who was out of state, another who may have been in Birmingham, and one who thinks he was in a meeting that didn't happen."

"Hey, I'm only working with what I was given! What's happening on your end?"

"My end?"

From Ward's tone I could tell that it had been a rough Monday and he was close to losing it.

"My end? If I had anything would I be bothering to call you? Let's see. I've got the murder weapon. Thanks for that, by the way. I've got the scene of the crime and I've got the body. There are no fingerprints on the murder weapon, no clues at the scene, and no confession to the crime. For that matter the only thing the coroner tells me is that the victim died from being shot in the head from behind—and I'd already noticed that on my own."

I decided he needed to blow off a little steam. "Have you checked his finances? Was he going bankrupt?"

"What?" exploded Ward. "Like it was suicide? Do you think suicides shoot themselves in the back of the head and then clean the murder weapon? Damn it, Crawford, this was no suicide!"

Good. Sounded like he'd gotten some stuff off his chest. "Finances means money, Ward, and money is a powerful force. Lots of people have been killed either trying to keep it or trying to get it. Besides, it's something that the police should investigate, not me. What do you think would happen if I walked into his bank and asked to see all the large deposits and withdrawals he'd made in the last year?"

"Besides asking for your credentials and then laughing at you? They'd let us know since we'd already gotten that information."

"Oh." I didn't know the police had already looked into that. Ward had failed to mention it to me. Just what else had the police done that he hadn't bothered to mention? "And what did you find?"

"Not one suspicious withdrawal or deposit. If I had found something I'd have listed it with finding the murder weapon."

"Then I guess we'll have to pin our hopes on finding out who purchased the whatchamacallit." I tried to nonchalantly gloss over the fact that I'd, once again, forgotten the name of the thing."

"Just which 'whatchamacallit' would that be?" Ward sounded like he was trying to keep his temper in check. I appreciated the effort.

"I can't remember the name of the thing the killer used so he could shoot a pistol bullet in a rifle—remember? It's one of the things we're keeping from the public."

"And we're doing such a good job of keeping it a secret we can't even remember what to call a caliber conversion sleeve?"

Now it sounded like Ward was trying to keep from laughing out loud. Well, it's a fine line between anger and laughter.

"Right! That's what Harry called it. Caliber conversion sleeve or supplemental chamber. Right?"

"Do you really think that the government has stricter controls on caliber conversion sleeves than it does on guns or ammunition?"

"Oh." I'd just assumed that it was a clue worth pursuing. "No way to trace it?"

"Trace it?" It was easier to tell that Ward was trying not to laugh. "We don't have it, do we? The killer took it away with him—or her, I guess we should keep an open mind on that—so it's kind of hard to find out much about it. All we know is what it did."

"So it's sort of like looking for a needle in a haystack?"

"Not so much. I know what a needle looks like. However I did do a little research on the subject. Got any idea how popular caliber conversion sleeves are with a certain fringe group?"

It sounded like Ward had gone through the stages of anger and amusement and was now settling into a conversational mood. I decided to throw out a verbal tidbit to keep the conversation going. "Hunters?"

"Fringe group, I said." Ward chuckled. "Don't go calling hunters a fringe group around here."

"Right, hunters aren't a fringe group." I was at a loss—at least hunters use guns. "Assassins?"

Ward broke down and laughed at that. "No, idiot—survivalists. With caliber conversion sleeves you can use all sorts of 'scavenged' ammunition. Much, much cheaper to stock

the sleeves than a bunch of different guns. Fits in with their phi-
losophy: It's the end of the world, got to make do with what
we've got."

"I get it—the TEOTWAWKI people. Sure they'd want to
have a bunch of them—makes a lot of sense."

"I don't know about 'tea-wack' people, but the survivalists
don't see letting everybody know what their plans for survival
include—certainly not the police."

I pronounced it again. "TEOTWAWKI. It stands for 'the end
of the world as we know it.' It's a common enough concept in
speculative fiction. Do you think there's a group of them near
here?"

"Do you have any idea where you're living? Do you read the
letters to the editor? Take a ride out into the country some day.
It's filled with people who vote against any kind of zoning every
time the issue comes up because 'nobody's telling me what I can
or can't do with my land.'"

"So as far as being evidence the sleeve thing is a dead end,
huh?" I hated to give that up.

"No, not at all." Ward laughed. "Give me the name of the
person who killed Philip Douglas and enough evidence to convince a judge to issue it, and I'll get a search warrant. If he was
stupid enough to keep it and I'm lucky enough to find it, that
will be the icing on the cake. The prosecutor will love it and the
jury will surely be convinced. Until then, find me a suspect that
was in town the day of the murder."

I could hear Ward slam the receiver down in the cradle to
end the call. It was such a satisfying way to end a frustrating
phone conversation—too bad it was going the way of the buggy
whip. How could you slam your cell phone down? I guess you
could throw it against the wall, but that missed the point. The

phone company had worked hard to make those old phones stur-
dy enough to take a pounding. I looked at my cell phone and
wondered for the umpteenth time if I should get rid of my land-
line and go strictly wireless.

I headed back into the house. I'd passed on getting a drink
earlier but now it seemed like a good idea. I took a step toward
the door and stepped on one of The Black's toys—the one I
called the wand. I still hadn't seen the cat—that was unusual.
Maybe I should look for The Black? A moment's consideration
reminded me that he could hide better than I could seek. He'd
come out for supper.

Still I had cat toys all over the place and no sign of a cat—
what did that make me think of? Oh, right. Suspects all over the
place but no real candidate for the murderer. I poured myself a
short scotch and headed for my office. It was time to see what
the cameras had caught.

. . .

Seated in front of the computer, I started the process of opening
a browser, accessing the site, logging in, and so on. The network
guy must have gotten the right MAC address; I had no trouble
connecting.

As I sat waiting for the images to download, I was bothered
by the complexity of the murder case—was it really necessary?

All the extra effort the killer had exercised to hide the rifle
from the police—to even use the rifle in the first place—how did
that fit in? All of that meant he'd be on the premises longer than
absolutely necessary—and that made it more dangerous.

If I just looked at the facts, I'd eliminated two of the three
suspects on alibis alone. That left Calvin Beck as the only sus-

pect who could not prove he hadn't been there. And you could argue that he was a likely candidate. He knew rifles, he'd been physically present in the Press a number of times—enough times to have known which rifles were on display—and to see that they were fully functional. Heck, I sipped a little scotch and felt the warmth in my throat, Philip might have told him they were functional. Caliber conversion sleeves—yeah, he was the most likely of the suspects to know about them. Something I'd heard said by somebody—I couldn't quite bring it into focus—anyway Calvin would know about those sleeves. His office computer is on the university's network. He could access the online calendar. He could clean a rifle. So why didn't I think he did those things?

Weekly Wednesday meetings that used to be on Tuesday? Where did that come from? Right, Jim had told me that Calvin's boss had moved the Tuesday meetings to Wednesday. I went back to the Press calendar and looked at the appointments Calvin had scheduled with Philip. They were on Wednesday. So why didn't that seem suspicious to me?

I didn't know why. So I decided to look at pictures. Looking at pictures had helped me solve the first mystery, maybe it would help solve this one too.

The Black jumped into my lap instead of using that over-the-shoulder approach he usually took and started to purr. Absently I patted him as I started looking at images on the screen.

CHAPTER 26
TUESDAY MORNING

The next morning after coffee and breakfast, I went back over the notes I'd made the night before. There were a few loose strings to tidy up, but it held together in the cold light of day. I picked up the phone and called the provost's office. Victoria answered and I told her I needed to meet with the provost. She didn't ask what the meeting was about, she just asked how long I thought I needed.

I answered honestly. "I don't know, Victoria. In these circumstances I don't think anybody knows. How long do you think it's going to take for me to explain why I'm sure I know who the murderer is and then for us to decide how to handle the situation?"

There was a little noise on the other end of the connection—she might have stifled a gasp—I don't know. But when she spoke her voice was calm and steady. "I think we'd best let him decide how much time he's going to want, but it needs to be soon, yes?"

"Yes," I sighed. I wasn't liking this part of solving crimes particularly. "A thing best done quickly."

"Then hold for one moment, please."

It was more than a moment but the next voice I heard was Rufus's. "Ms. Moore tells me we have a hard decision in store for us, James."

"Yes, sir." I was glad to hear that my voice too sounded pretty steady.

"Not something to discuss over lunch, I think."

"I agree." I nodded my head even though he couldn't see me. "And it's probably best that we keep it as low key as possible. We don't want to tip our hand."

"Is that a possibility? Hmmm." Rufus paused. "Canceling this afternoon's meeting with the trustees would cause comment and we don't want that. Why don't you come to my office this afternoon after five? Come the back way and Ms. Moore will let you in. You'll have to wait for me for a little, but at least we can have a drink afterward."

I put the phone down and stared at it. I'm not sure how I thought he'd react but I was sure that Rufus George continued to impress me.

Frank and I were standing at the back entrance to the Press building looking out onto the almost empty parking lot waiting for Steven Stefenson. It was after working hours, but we weren't meeting about business—not Press business anyway.

I wasn't sure if Frank had taken his 4:20 walk today or not. I hoped so. I had tried to make this meeting as innocuous as possible—just a poor computer geek who needed to talk to two of the people who knew the Press and Philip Douglas as well as anyone else. Men of intelligence and wisdom who could look at the situation with their insights—cool, logical, and precise. People love to be asked for advice—it reinforces their good opinion of themselves. So far it seemed to have worked.

A car pulled into a parking space. Steven got out and headed toward the building.

Peter the Gray walked out in front of us—appearing, as cats do, out of nowhere. He sat down and stared wide-eyed at me as I stepped forward to push the door open. "Dr. Stefenson, thanks so much for coming."

The man was dressed in another of his tailor-made suits with matching tie, gleaming shoes, crisp shirt—he was impeccable. He nodded at Frank and then said to me with a slight sniff. "I'm glad you have the good sense to ask for advice when you need it."

I don't think Steven stepped on the cat on purpose, he just wasn't watching his step. The cat didn't care if it was on purpose or not, he screamed, arching his back and hissing.

Steven looked down at the cat and then over at Frank. "I appreciate the fact that the Press staff kept this beast around since

Philip had even less tolerance for cats than I do, but that small act of rebellion is no longer necessary."

Frank raised his eyebrows. "I never realized how much PTG dislikes you, Steven." He turned around and started into the building. "I thought we'd meet in the director's lobby. The chairs are comfortable and it's hardly getting used lately. Unless," Frank glanced back at me, "you've got a PowerPoint presentation?"

I confessed that I hadn't prepared a formal presentation and we followed Frank down the hallway that led to the murder scene. It didn't seem polite to mention that I'd suggested that location earlier—let it be his idea.

. . .

We sat down in the overstuffed leather chairs that faced one another across a coffee table. Frank sank back and rested his head on the back of the chair. Steven, after twitching his pants legs to eliminate any wrinkles, crossed his legs and looked inquiringly at me.

I was sitting on the edge of my chair, leaning forward, with my hands clasped in front of me.

"I want to start by saying how much I appreciate both of you being willing to talk about Philip's murder with me. I've learned that there are times when I need to talk things out with wiser heads—I call it a sanity check—to see if my conjectures make sense to somebody other than myself."

Steven nodded and Frank blew through his mustache making the hairs fluff. I took the reactions as signs for me to continue.

"Two weeks ago today, Philip Douglas returned to the Press after getting a haircut. He and his killer entered the building through his private entrance at 4:27 p.m., Philip in front, the murderer following. Philip opened the door into his office—the pocket door from the hallway—and entered the room. The killer walked past the doorway to the Remington Model 700 .30-06 rifle that was mounted on the wall. He took the rifle down, loaded it, stepped into the doorway, and shot Philip in the back of the head. Philip fell to the carpet dead.

"The murderer then got the cleaning equipment out of Philip's desk, cleaned the rifle, put it back where he'd found it—having wiped it clean of fingerprints, stored the cleaning equipment, wrapped up the disposable cleaning supplies, rags and such—picked up Philip's door pass, exited the building, dumped the soiled cleaning supplies into the picnic area trash can, used the door pass to return to the scene of the crime at 5:07, returned the pass to the desk as if Philip had dropped it there—as he might have done—and having checked the scene one last time, left. Leaving the tableau just as he wanted us to find it."

Steven stirred in his chair. "Quite an intriguing account, even if it is entirely imaginary. But do go on. How does this lead us to the murderer's identity?"

"This is the point where the police investigation—or line of reasoning—and mine diverge."

"Oh?" Steven smiled. "And how do you interpret the evidence? I take it that the police think it means one thing and you another."

"Exactly! How perceptive of you." I leaned toward Steven nodding my head enthusiastically. "The police recognize the evidence but don't realize everything it tells them. They don't see how intricate and complex this masterful plan to murder Philip Douglas was. They think of it as a crime of passion—the killer seizing an opportunity. I see it as an elaborate, meticulously planned, clearly premeditated murder precisely executed in cold blood."

Steven nodded slowly. "Interesting. Masterful, you say?"

"One of the first things that struck me was that the murder occurred while there weren't any witnesses or potential witnesses. The police think the murderer took advantage of an opportunity—that he happened to be in the right place at the right time. I think the murderer chose the place and selected the time to minimize any danger to himself while maximizing his chances of success."

Frank shifted in his seat but I kept my eyes on Steven.

"First, I don't believe in luck. I believe our murderer had the ability to check the schedules of the entire Press staff without anybody being aware and leaving no traces."

"You're talking about the online calendar the Press uses for scheduling." Frank sat up. "But access to the calendar is restricted."

"Right, but I was able to access it once you told me it existed." I sat back and smiled. "All I had to do was connect to the Internet via the university's domain. I used a VPN connection and, once I found the site, it was easy to see why the murderer picked late Wednesday afternoon.

Frank looked puzzled.

"You have to be logged onto the university's network to access the calendar," I said, "but you can do that remotely via a VPN—virtual private network."

He nodded, comforted by the jargon.

"Second, there's the choice of the murder weapon or more accurately the source of the murder weapon. The murderer didn't have to conceal the fact that he was carrying a weapon or use a weapon that might get traced back to him. Once he and the victim were in the Press building, the weapon was right at hand. But he had to know that the weapon he selected actually worked—was functional. That he could use it to kill Philip. The police originally assumed, and I did too, that the guns had had their firing pins removed or had in some way been made harmless. This argues that our murderer had more than a general knowledge of rifles. He had to know a lot about guns to have used the ammunition he used.

"In addition, he also knew or deduced that the rifles were routinely cleaned, wiped of fingerprints, and returned to display in some seemingly random pattern. So he could and did clean the gun after killing Philip—cleaned it with the same equipment Philip used and then returned the gun to its place on the wall. That was truly inspired. If Philip hadn't left behind a ledger of how often and when he cleaned his rifles we would never have run ballistic tests on a rifle that had just been cleaned—months ahead of when it was due to be cleaned."

"Surely the police would have tested all the rifles eventually."

I shook my head at Steven. "I made the same mistake and got slapped down: 'the public wants the best possible police force at the lowest possible cost.' The police don't have an unlimited budget and running ballistic tests on every rifle because one of them might have been used as the murder weapon—it just wasn't going to happen. Another sign of how clever the murderer is.

"But as clever as he is, he did make one mistake. He took the dirtied swabs, pads, and such that he used to clean the rifle with him so the police wouldn't know that a rifle had been cleaned. That was clever, but in his understandable haste to get away from the murder scene he chose to dump the rags in the trash can outside."

Frank snapped his fingers. "The trash can that caught on fire when Kent dropped his cigarette in it! I wondered why you were so interested in it."

It had been unusual. That was the only reason I had been interested in it. Once I knew that the murder weapon had been cleaned on the premises, it wasn't hard to guess why the trash had caught on fire. The murderer must have rolled up all the solvent-soaked swabs and such in the disposable pad he'd used to protect the carpet. Once the cigarette melted through the pad—poof, evidence up in flames.

"But let's get back to the murder weapon—the Remington Model 700 .30-06—the all-time best-selling line of bolt-action sporting rifles. There's a good possibility that he owned one just like it and knew how to load it.

"You see," I glanced from Steven to Frank, "the guns were useless without ammunition. Philip didn't believe in gun control; he believed in ammo control. The killer had to bring the ammunition with him."

Steven stirred as if to say something. I hurried on. "And the killer needed to be able to shoot a rifle."

"At that distance?" scoffed Frank. "From the doorway to Philip's desk? All the killer had to do was aim and fire."

"Let's just say that the killer had to have access to ammunition that could fit the weapon and know how to shoot it. Agreed?"

They both nodded their heads.

. . .

"Finally we get to our suspects. While lots of people have indicated that they didn't particularly care for the deceased, no one had killed him—or even tried to, to the best of my knowledge, to date. The location and timing of the murder first seemed to implicate people that worked at the Press, but the staff all had alibis. Once we eliminated coworkers, the field was wide open. Whom do we investigate next?

"As it turns out—thanks to Frank here—we were able to determine that there were three people who had recently had arguments with the dead man, arguments so loud and rancorous that they were generally known throughout the Press community."

Frank shrugged his shoulders. "Lots of people helped with that, Steven not the least of them."

"At first, three suspects seemed to me like a lot of people who might want Philip dead."

"Proving," chuckled Frank, "that you never met the man."

Steven smiled and nodded in agreement.

"Good point. Still, Fines, Beck, and Charles were the people who had most recently met Philip and were heard—I'm sorry, overheard—to suggest that the world would be a better place if he was no longer in it. So I started my investigation with them.

"Bernard Charles was the last person I investigated, but the easiest to eliminate. He was in New Jersey the day Philip was murdered.

"Professor Fines also claimed to be elsewhere—in Birmingham, actually, at a retirement party. She went to the party but the police haven't been able to prove to their satisfaction that her alibi is totally airtight.

"Then there is Calvin Beck. He claimed to have been in a weekly staff meeting, but the staff meeting took place on Tuesday that week and nobody that he works with remembers if he was in his office on Wednesday afternoon or not."

Steven stirred in his seat. "Oh?" He sounded mildly interested.

"Calvin?" Frank leaned forward. "The hook and bullet author? He works here on campus."

"Right," I nodded my head. "His office computer is on the university network; he could access the online calendar from there if he knew it existed."

"As many appointments as he had with Philip, it must have come up. Heck, Philip might have told him about it or even showed it to him. No," Frank shook his head. "I'm forgetting how anticomputer Philip was. But Calvin certainly could have found out about it.

"Hey," Frank snapped his fingers. "I think his appointments with Philip were usually on Wednesday afternoons!"

"Really?" Steven looked thoughtful. "I've forgotten, if I ever knew, what he wrote. Was he more 'hook' than 'bullet' or vice versa?"

"Oh he's a 'bullet' author for sure. How could you have forgotten? His work has some hunting stuff in it, but mostly it's about guns." Frank's eyes grew bigger. "He knows tons about guns. He'd have been able to tell that the guns were fully functional. As interested in guns as he is, he must have talked to Philip about them. Heck, he could have picked one up to look at it— even though Philip had forbidden anyone to touch them."

"That's right," Steven joined in. "Now that you mention it, I do remember some of his work. It was filled with stuff about guns, ammunition, chamber adaptors, and the like."

Frank snapped his fingers. "And I bet Philip cleaned one of the rifles in front of him during all those meetings. He certainly did that with the staff. So he'd know about the cleaning supplies too!"

He settled back in the leather chair. "Looks like he's the guy. I know he did a lot of work rewriting that novel, making all the changes Philip wanted. Then when Philip refused to publish it— something must have snapped."

"It appears that congratulations are in order, Mr. Crawford." Steven favored me with a thin smile. "I'm sure the provost will be glad you've solved the mystery."

Frank started to work his way out of the depths of the chair. "That's what you wanted, right? For us to agree with your logic?"

"Oh, I could tell the evidence pointed to Calvin Beck. I saw that right away. That's what made me nervous."

"Nervous?" Steven frowned. "It seems clear the young man had motive enough and the knowledge he needed to kill Philip."

"Exactly. That's what made him the prime suspect. All the evidence we've discovered points directly at him. That's what bothers me—or, more accurately, bothered me."

"Bothers you?" Frank tugged at his mustache. "But you're the one who found the evidence. You identified the murder weapon by deciphering that ledger. The police were never going to find it unless they ran ballistic tests on all the rifles in the collection."

"Yeah, and then I wondered why—why was there so much evidence? Why was it so complicated?" I glanced at Frank and then turned back to Steven. "Why did the killer bother? Why didn't he just put on gloves so he could shoot Philip and then walk away? Why bother with all the rest? It made one suspicious.

"I told you it was an incredibly complex and intricate plan and I meant it. Right now the only evidence against Calvin is his lack of an alibi. He claims to have found an agent for his novel—in its original format—including that section on chamber adaptors—sometimes called caliber conversion sleeves—you encouraged him to leave out." I gestured in Steven's direction. "He's so excited that he can barely remember being mad at Philip."

"He heard from this agent before Philip was murdered?"

"Yep," I nodded my head. "I checked with the agent, who is quite reputable and very excited about the book as well. He thinks he's found the next Tom Clancy or John Grisham."

"Really?" Steven flicked an invisible speck off the sleeve of his jacket. "I wasn't that impressed with it."

Frank looked puzzled. "He showed you his novel? I didn't think you knew him."

"Oh, he wanted my opinion on whether it was worth submitting to Philip. Having been on the board for so long and Philip having the reputation that he had, it happens all the time."

"But Bernard Charles didn't come to you—you went to him. You're the one who suggested that the Press would be interested in reprinting his mother's books, aren't you?"

Steven raised his eyebrows. "Have I met the man? I don't remember. Surely he has me confused with somebody else."

"I don't think so. Professor Fines remembers it much the same way. She had given a talk and, in the crowd afterward, someone encouraged her to re-release her first book. Said the Press would be excited at the idea. That was you, wasn't it, Steven? Even though you knew Philip would ultimately reject the idea and do it as cruelly as possible."

Steven laughed. "Surely you jest. Anyone could have suggested reprinting the books. I'm sure someone mentions it at
every party they go to. You know well enough what those functions are like. Who can remember whom they meet or what was
said?"

Interesting, I thought to myself, Steven was getting practically loquacious. "I think you had Calvin all set up to be framed for
the murder and you threw the other two in to make it just that
much more complex."

. . .

Steven stood up. "I don't like the tone this meeting has taken.
It's almost as if you suspect me of murdering Philip. Quite out-
rageous." He turned to Frank who was leaning back in the chair
with his legs outstretched. "If you'll excuse me?"

I pulled a stiff piece of paper out of my shirt pocket and held
it between my thumb and forefinger. "Bernard still had your
card. He'd kept it with the program and hadn't gotten around to
throwing either away.

"So did Professor Fines. Hers was in a stack of paper she
was recycling."

Steven stared at my hand.

"You hand them out without even thinking don't you?

"I need to get some myself. So I've been thinking about
them—and I wondered if you'd forgotten."

"How dare you insinuate that I killed Philip!"

"It was a masterful plan, Steven." I looked up at him. "But
just a little bit too complicated for your own good. Take the
online calendar for instance, Apache—the web server software—captures the IP address and MAC address of every ma-

chine that connects to the site and writes it to a log file." I pursed my lips and frowned. "Calvin's computer? It doesn't show up in the logs. He didn't know the Press's schedule."

Steven just stood there staring at me.

"But you knew how to access the university's network. You had to in order to use the library's databases—access is restricted to users on the network." I stared back. "What you probably didn't know is that every time you connect—you're using a VPN, by the way—your userID, MAC address, and IP address are written to another log file."

I stood. "I know you accessed that site and can prove it."

I glanced at Frank who was staring at Steven like he had sprouted horns. I looked back at Steven. "And you know about chamber adaptors, or conversion sleeves as they're sometimes called."

"Many people know about chamber adaptors. That is not a crime."

"But you keep mentioning them. You did it today and when we met on campus before the game. I told you I didn't think much of Calvin as a suspect—after you'd gone to so much trouble to set him up. You must have been exasperated at how stupid I was being. You told me then that Calvin was familiar with chamber adaptors, only I knew them as caliber conversion sleeves." I shook my head. "I'd never heard of chamber adaptors before so I didn't understand how important it was that Calvin Beck knew about them."

"I still do not see—"

I interrupted him. "The police kept that part of the murder secret—that the killer had used a caliber conversion sleeve, aka chamber adaptor, so that he could kill Philip Douglas with hand-gun ammunition."

The blood drained from Steven's face and he sank back down into his chair, holding on to the overstuffed arms. He opened his mouth and closed it several times but no sound came out.

"Nobody knew about the chamber adaptor but the people investigating the murder—and the murderer."

Steven opened his mouth as if to speak then closed it.

"What was it? What made you pull the trigger? He'd ridiculed you for years. Ignoring your advice or doing exactly the opposite of whatever you suggested—except for the times the idea was so good that he stole it and refused to give you credit. What finally made you decide to kill him?"

He gave the smallest of nods. "I went to him about being rotated off the board. I asked him to speak to Rufus about it—to ask if I could stay." He was looking down at his hands as he spoke.

"He laughed at me. He laughed and said why should he? That it was the best idea Rufus George had ever had." Steven lifted his head and met my eyes. "So he had to die. He needed to die."

He stared off into space and spoke, his voice barely above a whisper. "When should I expect the police? Are they outside?"

I took a deep breath. "I've got an appointment with Captain Ward tomorrow morning."

Steven's eyes focused on me for a moment, then he dropped them. "You knew before I mentioned the adaptor."

"Yes. There was too much evidence. It didn't make sense unless somebody was trying to frame Calvin Beck but I wasn't sure about who was doing the framing until I saw a picture of you talking to Bernard Charles. Then I knew. Once I knew that, it was easy to find the evidence."

Steven nodded his head. "And then you went to Rufus." He looked up at me. "Telling me before going to the police was Rufus George's idea, wasn't it?"

I'd argued against it but Rufus wouldn't hear of it. In the end, I did it his way. "That's right."

"Always the southern gentleman, Rufus George." Steven stood up, twitched his pant leg so that it broke properly on his shoe, buttoned his jacket, and headed toward the exit. "You'll excuse me if I don't shake your hand. Tell Rufus I appreciate his sensitivity. He won't regret it."

I stood there watching as he walked away.

Frank stood up and stroked his mustache. "I wondered what that was about a chamber adaptor. Nothing to do with chamber music, I take it."

It was a little after eight o'clock when I was ushered into Captain Ward's office. I'd brought a thermos of coffee with me since I'd had the misfortune of tasting what they claimed was "fresh brewed." I wasn't sure how long this was going to take but I wasn't going to try and get through it drinking that mud.

Ward finished signing a form, put it on top of a stack of forms, and handed the stack to the policewoman who'd led me in. "Paperwork," Ward growled. "Off of my desk and back to yours. Thanks, Donna."

He looked at me. "I was hoping you'd bring your own coffee."

I held up the thermos.

"Take a seat," he nodded at a chair centered across from where he sat and pushed his coffee mug forward.

I put the thermos on his desk and took a seat. Ward reached into a desk drawer and pulled out another mug. "Here," he said, pushing it across the desk. "You don't want to use the cup that comes with the thermos. Have a real mug." He pulled out a jar of powdered creamer.

I unscrewed the cup he was talking about and set it aside. "I've already added half-and-half."

"Excellent." The jar disappeared.

I poured the coffee into the mugs and watched the steam rise.

"I've got the tape recorder like you wanted." Ward pointed at the corner of his desk. "Before we start do you mind telling me what's going on?"

I shrugged. "The provost wanted me to wait until today to tell you what I've come up with. Since I'm doing this because he asked me to—and he's paying me—I figured I'd do what he said. I'm not really comfortable with this but—"

Ward's phone rang and he glanced at the caller ID then back at me. "It's John Forte, head of the University Police."

"You'd better take it."

Ward cocked his head at me but picked up the phone. "Howdy, John, what's up?"

I picked up my coffee and took a sip. From where I sat I could barely make out the sound of someone talking. I was pretty sure I knew what he was saying. Ward opened his mouth to speak then stopped. The one-sided conversation went on for another moment.

"OK, John, I'll have a squad car out there as soon as possible and I'll be out a little later." He hung up the phone and stared at me.

"Are you going to tell me why Steven Stefenson was found dead in his car this morning? The University Police found the car parked in the Press director's reserved space with a rubber hose running from the exhaust pipe to the driver's window. The car was still running—he must have made sure he had plenty of gasoline. His business card was in the passenger seat and there was something written on it.

"Ask Mr. Crawford."

KEEP READING FOR A PREVIEW OF
SHE NEEDED KILLING
BOOK 3 IN THE NEEDED KILLING SERIES

"Yo, Crawford!" Stan had turned around and caught sight of me.

"Hey, Stan, Paul." I put TB's carrier down on the table and then proceeded to clench and unclench my hand trying to work the blood back into it. The so-called handle had made a dent in my palm. Why hadn't I used both hands to carry TB? Macho idiot.

Stan had been over to the house countless times and had been on good terms with The Black. He walked over and looked through the top of TB's carrier. "Hey, TB. Thanks for coming." It was easy to see that there was an angry cat in the carrier so Stan wisely didn't stick his finger through the wires. The Black was glaring and radiating rage. Paul followed him over.

Paul had been one of Stan's student assistants before I retired. Stan referred to his students as "minions" realizing that it made him sound like a B-movie villain. Since my retirement, Paul had been hired as a full-time employee.

"Wow! What a handsome cat. Is he solid black?"

"Pretty much," I agreed.

"Aren't you the handsome beast?" Paul continued to talk to TB in the way any cat lover speaks to a cat. "Now I know why Mr. Stan wanted to take your picture—what a great cat. What's his name? TeeBee?"

"His real name is The Black but I call him TB for short." As I watched I could tell that Paul was having a calming effect on the cat. Of course, he loved being talked to and told how wonderful he was—he the cat, that is. Although I guess Paul wouldn't have minded some praise himself.

"Congratulations on getting on the university's payroll. Glad they made you full time. I know Stan's glad to have your help."

Paul looked up from TB's cage and grinned. "He told me that after you retired the department discovered there was a little extra money available for payroll—so thanks for retiring."

I laughed and grinned back at him. "Then it was a win-win situation."

Stan coughed into his hand. "Do you suppose you could let The Black out of the carrier? I really wasn't thinking of pictures of him in a carrier when I came up with this promotional shot."

"I think Paul may have soothed him down—nothing like compliments to turn a cat's head." I unhooked the top of the carrier and lifted The Black up out of the container. He stiff-armed me when I tried to drape him over my shoulder, so I knew I hadn't been forgiven. I moved the carrier to the side and set the cat down on the table. Paul grabbed the carrier and moved it out of sight of the cameras and I started to stroke The Black's ears. We seemed to have reached something of an understanding.

Stan waved me to one side and I stepped back as he and Paul started shooting. At first The Black just sat on the table, tail wrapped around his feet, then he began to stretch. Maybe he'd felt cramped in the carrier. It wasn't a big table, but it was big enough for a Ouija board or a tarot tableau.

I'd forgotten just how long TB can be when he stretches out.

"That is one big cat," whispered Paul. He stepped back to the video camera and started filming.

Just then the flap of the front entrance to the tent swung open and Dot Fields came stumbling out of her tent and almost ran into the table.

"Damn that door lip! One of these days I'm going to fall flat on my face." I glanced at the entrance and saw where the floor of the tent was curved up by three or four inches. The tent was built to keep rain and snow from seeping into it. Dot had turned around to glare at the offending tent then turned back to face us.

Tall, heavyset, with her long black hair in a single braid draped over her shoulder, she was wearing a pair of faded bib overalls and work boots. "Howdee, folks! Sorry about that entrance," she bellowed. She must have been in the tent putting on her gypsy costume, at least that was the only excuse I could come up with for her tying a couple of scarves around her head, putting on some garish earrings, and covering her fingers in costume jewelry.

That's right, I reminded myself, Stan was doing promotional pieces for The Festival and Dot had demanded he include a piece on her fortune-telling tent. The university was going to run the spots on its TV station as a part of its ongoing support of The Festival. Stan was trying to give the pieces a Halloween flair to justify highlighting Dot's booth over the others. It was easier to do it that way than to fight with Dot.

We humans had all seen Dot before, I guess, since none of us reacted to her appearance the way The Black did—or maybe it was just because we'd been taught to try and be polite. Not so the cat.

TB arched his back, every hair standing on end, opened his mouth wide, and hissed at the creature that had appeared before him. I could see the claws extend and contract as he continued to wail at her. I'd seen The Black express his displeasure at other cats and dogs, but nothing like this. Stan and Paul were falling all over themselves trying to get as many shots as possible. Dot, for her part, stood there looking surprised and, for once, not saying anything.

I'd say that Stan got the shot he was looking for.

. . .

Dot took a half step back. "My," she said. "Animals always love me." For a brief moment Dot appeared to be uncertain, then her usual annoying bluster returned. "Oh, she must smell the snake. That's what it is. Dogs and cats always love me!"

The human's step back had broken the confrontation as far as The Black was concerned and he had won. He sat on the table and began to vigorously wash himself. The human had flinched and he was willing to leave it at that. I stepped back up to the table and scratched him behind the ears. I didn't want TB to bolt or to attack Dot. I'm not sure what I thought I could have done about it. "He's a he. The cat that is."

"What's that about a snake?" Stan, having captured The Black in full fury, was trying to smooth things over as usual. I bet that was just the shot he was hoping to get—not with Dot in it—mind you, just the classic Halloween black cat live and on film.

"All cats are female."

Dot had returned to her normal full bluster. I've had other people tell me the same thing—or that all dogs are male—and it never bothered me. In fact, some of them are dear friends. In this case, all I can say is that Dot had a way with her.

"Well, this one isn't." I picked up The Black and draped him over my right shoulder and then turned so that he could keep an eye on Dot as I talked to Stan.

"You got all you need?"

Stan hesitated and Dot broke in. "You must get a picture of the cat with our snake! It will be like one of those animal pictures on the Internet that everybody loves! It won't take long. Coba should be here any minute."

I had my own idea of how The Black was going to react to a snake and I wasn't sure we'd want to post it.

"Coba?" I looked at Stan.

"Coba Boucher—the assistant director of The Festival." He was quick to reply.

"My current assistant," added Dot. "Who won't be my assistant for long if she keeps me waiting. You must be that Craw-*ferd* fella, the one with the cat Stan told me about."

"Crawford." Stan corrected Dot and then pointed down the path at a figure walking our way carrying a box in both hands. At least she had sense enough to use both hands.

As I watched the person approach I realized how little I knew about The Festival and how it worked. I knew who Dot was but we'd never really met before, and at this point I was inclined to keep it that way. The Black began to purr quietly as I continued to scratch his ears. Maybe he was ready to forgive me for this misadventure.

ACKNOWLEDGMENTS

For me, writing books is a collaborative effort. So, again, I extend my thanks to everyone who encouraged me along the way (you know who you are); to Hawk, who is muse and model; to Amos, who says he would be less of a nuisance if he could just live on the screen porch; and to Tucker, who believes that being beautiful is enough.

Thanks to Rusty, who kept me from shooting myself in the foot, so to speak; to Whit for the extra suspect and other excellent suggestions; to Tom, who read the book in two sittings while we were in Orange Beach; to Donna in Clarksville, who let me know she had pulled an "all-nighter" to finish the book; to Jill for advice about police procedures and how to piss Harry off; to Anita and Wayne for their careful reading of the manuscript; to Ann for her helpful list of "huhs?"; to Van for his continued support; to Ruth, who says the book helped make her commute easier. And to Eva (pronounced, so she said, Evah, "as in whatevah"), a waitress in the Florida Keys who wanted to be in my book sight unseen, here you are again.

Thanks also to my former coworkers for the headset and Pandora for the music.

ABOUT THE AUTHOR

Writers do not create their works in a vacuum. Or so I believe. They are influenced, sometimes consciously, often unconsciously, by the world around them—by the people they know, the movies and TV shows they watch, the plays and concerts they attend, and, of course, by the books they read.

From the Hardy Boys and Nancy Drew to Perry Mason and Nero Wolfe, I was raised on a steady diet of detective stories. Later, I added to my reading list such authors as Dorothy Sayers, Dick Francis, and Robert B. Parker. They and other writers helped shape my understanding of how to construct a mystery and fueled my love of a good whodunit. Authors outside the genre, notably Robert A. Heinlein, kindled my imagination as a young reader and engendered in me a love of reading that continues to this day. I thank them all for the many wonderful hours I have spent in cloud-cuckoo-land, from the English countryside to the streets of Boston to the far reaches of outer space.

I also owe an odd kind of thank you to the tornado that swept across parts of the South, including Tuscaloosa, Ala., on April 27, 2011. My wife and I came through the tornado physically unharmed, but our lives were changed forever. Like others who have survived an event of such enormity, we began to assess our needs and wants, our hopes and dreams from the perspective of survivors—with the visceral understanding that life is short and the future uncertain.

As a result, I retired from the University of Alabama in September 2011 and took up writing mysteries. I am having a wonderful time, and I hope you enjoy reading my books as much as I enjoy writing them. It's too late for me to keep the day job.

VISIT BILL'S WEBSITE AT BILLFITTSAUTHOR.COM
FOR RECIPES, TESTIMONIALS, AND INFORMATION
ABOUT HOW TO ORDER PAPERBACKS AND EBOOKS
IN THE NEEDED KILLING SERIES.

CPSIA information can be obtained
at www.ICGtesting.com
Printed in the USA
EDOW021510180213
682ED

9 780988 389335